BEATS
AND
BLOW

SHAUN SINCLAIR

BEATS
AND
BLOW

DAFINA

www.kensingtonbooks.com

BEATS
AND
BLOW

Prologue

The man dropped to the shiny tiled floor and banged out a set of pushups. His sinewy arms flexed, and beads of sweat dripped from his torso. The brand new Airpods stuffed into his ears blasted a thumping hip-hop beat with a Middle Eastern melody. As his body slowly rose and fell to the floor, he closed his eyes and hissed lyrics to accompany the beat invading his eardrums. He pushed the floor until his arms became spaghetti. Then he collapsed with his chest heaving. Once he reined his breath in, he rolled over, sat up, and picked the phone up from the floor.

He exhaled his angst as he checked the news feed once again. The wire was ablaze with rumors of his status:

"Imprisoned Rap Mogul Due in Court Today for Bond Hearing."
"Founder of the Deadly Crescent Crew to Face the Music in Rico Allegations."
"It Was All Good Just a Week Ago: Rap Mogul Faces Bankruptcy."

He rolled over to bang out another set of pushups. As he pressed the floor, he addressed each headline in his head.

He had a lot riding on the bond hearing today. When he was initially extradited back home to Carolina, they had denied his bond. Because he owned multiple homes on several continents, they deemed him a flight risk. For months they had him on ice, refusing to hear any motion his high-powered attorney filed, denying him access to the courts. Now, they finally allowed him a crack at the system, and by all accounts his nightmare was coming to an end. This wasn't his first foray into incarceration, of course. Years ago, when he was still a youth finding his way, he was sent upstate to do a bid. However, bidding as a *thousandaire* was different than bidding as a multimillionaire. Pulling time as a "nobody" was different than pulling time as a somebody. Before, he was a squirrel trying to get a nut; now, he owned the forest!

Still, no matter how high he climbed, there were certain factions that wanted to see him chopped down to size.

Founder of the Deadly Crescent Crew to Face the Music in Rico Allegations.

He read the headline again and chuckled. Someone had a sick sense of humor. His whole career, he had to fight to escape the stench of the streets. It was well known that he had founded his record label with dirty money. However, the gift and the curse of street cred was that to the streets, you would forever be a hero; to the world, you would forever be a suspect. He had beat the odds before and now he was eager to battle them again.

His phone buzzed to life in his palm with a familiar number. This was the only number that could snatch him from his military mindset. He smiled and answered the phone.

"Hey, my love, are you okay?" Lisa Ivory sang into the phone. Her voice was just as vibrant through the receiver as it was when she serenaded millions on stage. "Today's the big day. You coming home to me, baby!"

He allowed himself a slight smile, although he wasn't as optimistic. He was in bid mode and the quickest way to depression was to set your expectations outside of anyone's hand besides your own. Still, he had to save face for his wife.

"Yes baby, talk that talk!" He joked. "This shit is almost over, and I will be there soon enough."

"Ahhh, I can't wait." He could picture her beautiful smile through the phone.

"Me either."

Lisa took a heavy sigh. "Baby, I have some news that can't wait until after court. It's about business . . ."

The word business switched his mental gears immediately. At the time he was arrested, he was negotiating a billion-dollar deal. In his absence, his wife had stepped up to the plate to keep the show on the road. But his wife wasn't the shrewd businessman he had become, and in his absence, some of the plans had derailed. It seemed his new business partner in his new venture, Liam Cohen, was clashing with his old business partner and comrade, Doe. His wife, speaking on his behalf, was struggling to keep it all together.

"I need for you to have a word with Doe about Liam. Liam is trying to push through with Wave, but Doe is fighting him," Lisa explained.

"What's the problem?"

"Money, mo' money . . . mo' money," she said, exasperated. "It's always about money."

Lisa was beyond frustrated. She wasn't cut out for this life. She was an R&B starlet, not a business titan. She was in *waaay* over her head trying to wear her husband's crown.

"I mean, what's the problem? We're straight on the money, right?"

"Nah, not really."

"What you mean?"

"I mean, things came up, baby. Taxes on the homes, the cars, maintaining the other businesses . . . it cost to live this life. And with no real revenue coming in, things got tight really fast."

Qwess nodded. He understood more than she ever knew. "So, what exactly is Doe doing to help?"

"Doe has his own family to think about. And to be honest, I think he is second guessing the decision to invest in Wave. Nearly six months ago, we dropped all that money and nothing yet, baby. Can you blame him?"

"Look, Doe know what it is. We just have to ride this out and trust the process," he assured her. "But what do you think though?"

This was the billion-dollar question. Was she still all in or was she looking at the front door? Was she his ride or die or was she plotting to fly?

"I trust your word. Always have and always will," she assured him.

Just before he could respond, he heard keys jangling. He tucked the phone away right before the guard opened the door.

The guard peeked in. "You ready to go, Qwess?" He called him by the name the world knew him by. Even inside, he still commanded respect.

"Yep. Let's roll!"

Qwess had seen it all, been through it all. Now he was ready to face his music.

Chapter 1

Wilmington, North Carolina

Maleek Money pushed the button and the cream top peeled back on his brand-new Porsche 911. The sun poured into the coupe and the cream leather interior seemed to glow, contrasting magically with the matte emerald-green paint coating the car. He revved the engine and peeked in his rearview mirror, adjusting the heavy chain around his neck. He pulled up beneath the awning of the Hilton and watched as the crown jewel of his heart strutted out of the plush hotel looking like a ghetto goddess. Keisha was wearing short jean shorts that clenched her thick thighs and cupped her camel toe in a vice grip. The tall Dior heels she wore made her thigh muscles flex every time she walked, and Maleek Money loved the view as he admired the way her 38DDs bounced around inside her tank top.

Keisha opened the door and sank into the leather seat in a huff. "Them mothafuckas in there giving me a hard time," she complained. "Knocking on the door while I was in the shower and shit. I told them I was coming!"

Maleek Money smiled and caressed her smooth brown cheek. "Calm down, beautiful. Don't worry about them motherfuckers. They not on our level. Shit, I might buy this motherfucker for you," he quipped. Although he was semi-joking, he was nearly in position to do just that if he chose to.

After executing his former comrade Twin, Maleek Money had stepped into his shoes to run the drug traffic for Wilmington. Little Maleek had turned all the way up and got to the money—and his new name reminded everyone of his status. He was controlling the Crescent Crew's operation in the Port City and had been well rewarded for it. In less than six months, he had imported a few of his soldiers from Fayettenam and built a new line of young hustlers from Wilmington. Although they weren't as thorough as the old crew—yet— things were turning out nicely.

Maleek Money pulled out of the hotel and cruised the city with the top down. As he drove, he caught the stares of passersby. In a predominately white town like Wilmington, North Carolina, seeing a young Black man pushing a droptop Porsche was an anomaly. Rides like this were reserved for the people in the higher echelons of the city. Unknown to the uninitiated, there was another industry tickling the current of the city, and Maleek Money was at the top of that food chain.

Maleek Money piloted the Porsche into an upscale neighborhood off 17th Street, just past New Hanover Regional Medical Center. He hung a right, then a left, then pulled in front of a huge brown colonial-style house with white pillars. The house was pushed back from the street, and a huge green lawn sprawled from the street to the home. Maleek Money parked on the lawn and surfed through his phone calmly while lighting a blunt.

As Maleek Money searched his phone, Keisha peered

around nervously. "Uhh . . . babe, what are you doing?" She asked. She knew the neighborhood well, a place where doctors and attorneys lived. They even had their own private police patrolling the neighborhood. "You can't do that out here in this neighborhood," Keisha reminded him. "And why are you on these people lawn like this?"

Maleek Money smiled. "Baby, you rolling with Double M, we can do whatever the fuck we want to do." He pushed a button the behind rearview mirror and the garage door to the house glided open. He turned to Keisha and beamed his brightest smile. "Welcome home, Keisha. This *our* shit!"

Keisha was speechless for a moment. "Ohmigod! Are you serious?"

"Hell yeah! Come on, check it out." Maleek Money and Keisha walked across the gorgeous lawn toward the garage. "I got another surprise for you too," he claimed.

Maleek Money flicked the light on, and there in the garage sat a shiny new white 650 BMW convertible with a red bow wrapped around the hood. Maleek Money held a button on the key fob and the car roared to life, much to Keisha's delight.

"Is this mine?" Keisha asked.

"Hell yeah! Your man is a boss; we can't have you riding around in no bullshit. You represent me out here in these streets, and everybody needs to know it."

Maleek Money was new to real money. He had seen some money before but not on this level, and he wasn't going to miss a chance to show everyone how much he had come up.

Unfortunately, he hadn't learned that all attention wasn't good attention.

He also didn't know that someone was watching him, and they were about to make themselves known.

Atlanta, Georgia

While Maleek Money spoiled himself with his ill-gotten riches, Bone strolled into Two Urban Licks looking like a Middle Eastern sheikh. His long green thobe and pointy-toed ostrich boots blended well with the cream *shemagh* wrapped around his head. Only the huge necklace dangling from his neck added the sauce that signified him as an American boss. The popular Atlanta eatery was tucked off in the cut, yet still upscale, which was perfect for a meeting of this sort.

Bone spotted his guest at the table in the back and quickly joined him.

"*Hola, El Señor,*" Bone greeted with a bow.

"*Hola, El Señor,*" the man returned with a smile.

Their greetings were a mutual sign of respect, the names actual titles.

"*¿Jefe, cómo estás? ¿Todo bien?*" Bone asked in perfect Spanish.

"English, please," Jefe returned in perfect English.

While Bone cut a spectacle everywhere he stepped, in either designer threads or the finest in Islamic gear, Jefe was more lowkey in slacks and Polo shirts. Jefe even went to great pains to downplay his Mexican heritage when he moved around in the States, dying his dark hair dirty blond, and donning blue contacts. His disguise served its purpose, and it also made him a hit with the ladies. Being one of the biggest drug distributors in the Western Hemisphere gifted him numerous perks.

"So, what is this all about?" Bone queried. He wasn't due to see Jefe for another two months. "We're early, Jefe."

"Ja, ja, things are well on the business side," Jefe assured him.

"Word," Bone uttered with a strong nod.

"But sometimes business is about more than just business."

Bone's ears perked up. "Oh yeah?"

"Yesss, my friend! Real business is about relationships."

Bone was confused as to where the conversation was going. His business was intact as far as all the money being on point. His relationships were also good, as far as the palms he greased to keep things running smoothly. Yet his connect was in town early discussing relationships.

"Ah, I'm confused, Jefe—which is rare these days. I pride myself on keeping the confusion down in my life."

"As do I, which is why I am confused as well."

Bone glanced at the Richard Millie on his wrist and frowned. "All due respect, Jefe, I'm a little short on time; I have an empire to maintain," he reminded him. "What's this all about?"

"This is about that thing from a few months ago."

Bone was still confused. Then, like an anvil, it hit him. "You talking about the King Rats?"

Jefe nodded.

"Oh, we haven't found one of them yet, and we haven't been able to get our hands on the other one, but we will get them."

Bone was referring to Samson and his twin brother, Hulk. They were founding members of the Crescent Crew—big dog OGs in the organization—who had defected. Samson turned State while in the Feds, according to Qwess's paperwork. Months ago, Bone had issued an on-site order. A ticket was placed on Samson's head inside the penitentiary, but he was proving to be very elusive. As for his brother, Hulk, he had disappeared months ago, shortly before Qwess's paperwork was revealed.

Jefe shook his head slowly. "Well, it's a good thing you haven't been able to complete your mission."

"What do you mean?"

Jefe raised his hands and pumped his palms. "You must hold off on that mission," he whispered.

The waiter arrived and filled their glasses with expensive water. He took their orders and disappeared as silently as he had come.

When the waiter skated off, Jefe continued, "Some new information has come to my attention that runs contrary to the kind you provided me about our friend."

"He ain't my motherfucking friend; he's my enemy. You'll see!"

Jefe frowned and shook his head slightly. "You're not understanding me, my friend. I'm saying that we cannot 'take care of' a man of his stature unless we have concrete proof that he did those things."

Bone spread his palms in exasperation. He couldn't believe what he was hearing. "What more proof do you need? There's paperwork showing he signed statements. Paperwork proving he is a rat."

"Ah, the American justice system cannot be trusted! I have three attorneys here, and one of them is so good with paperwork, he has me believing I am a saint—and we both know that isn't true." Jefe chuckled. "So I cannot feel comfortable with your decision until I am sure with my decision. Right now, I cannot do that."

Bone leaned away from the table and eyed his supplier. He may have been the man in his faction, but Bone ran the Crescent Crew. He oversaw his family, and he had issued an edict that Crew Business would be enacted on the two defectors. Now his supplier was attempting to impede his business. Bone wasn't going for it.

Bone steepled his hands on the table. "Jefe, with all due respect, I run my organization, and I have determined that these guys are rats. Therefore, I have issued an order." He paused to let his words sink in before he softened his blow. "Now I also respect your contribution to my organization. We cannot do what we do without your resources. So . . . it appears we have a stalemate."

Jefe smiled and looked away from the table. A beautiful woman walking by briefly captured his attention. He could've sworn he'd seen her on one of the American television shows.

He returned his attention to the table, "Chess is my favorite game in the world—"

"Mine too," Bone interjected.

Jefe raised his eyebrows. "Well, it seems you are confused with your position on the board," he said. "In this particular game, you are not in the center of the back row. Rather, you are on the end—pick a side, the left or the right. Now those are important pieces for sure, but if they get captured, the game still goes on. ¿Entiendes? Now, if the piece in the center of the back row gets removed, then the game is over. I am that piece."

Bone picked up what he was putting down, and he didn't appreciate being checked. "So what are you saying, Jefe?"

"I am saying that this situation is above your pay grade, Lil Jefe. I decide whether these individuals live or die. Until I give that order, stand down."

Now Bone understood why he referenced relationships. He was essentially telling Bone that if he murdered Samson, then he would cut off his supply. He knew he possessed the upper hand, because Bone couldn't lead a drug organization without drugs. For all his grinding to reach the top, he was still being sonned by someone. This didn't sit well with Bone at all, but he was in "check."

"Okay Jefe, I got you. I'll stand down on this one. But my Big Homie is going to court real soon, so some more info may be coming out. I'll be sure to keep you informed."

Jefe waved his hand dismissively. "No need; I'll know what is going on before you. I appreciate the gesture though."

The waiter placed their meals on the table, and Jefe smiled triumphantly. "Now let's eat!"

Bone smiled and dug into his food, but in the back of his mind, he began strategizing how to truly put himself in the center of the back row on the board.

Chapter 2

The courtroom was packed with spectators as everyone awaited the defendant's arrival. All the leading news crews were present, as this was sure to be the top story of the day. The federal prosecutor repeatedly checked his watch while glancing cutting looks at the judge. He was ready to tear into his prey and make his mark on the legal stage. He knew the entire world was tuned into the ongoing saga of a mogul's fall from grace.

All eyes were on Qwess's bond hearing. After all, it wasn't every day that an entertainment mogul faced the death penalty, especially a mogul as rich, famous, and beloved by his community as Qwess. See, while other rap artists either clout-chased or clung to minimal past street exploits to solidify their credibility, Qwess was the antithesis to this type of foolery. Although he had co-founded what went on to become one of the biggest crime conglomerates in the nation, he had shunned that life and chased his destiny. Instead, he opted to uplift his community by giving to charity and preaching independence. When he rapped on wax, he spoke of obtaining knowledge of self, and made practicing the tenets of Islam cool again.

Now, despite all his growth and accomplishments and his constant elevation, he was still being dragged into court by U.S. Marshals like a common criminal to fight for his life. Well, not exactly a common criminal. Common criminals weren't represented by million-dollar legal teams.

Malik Shabazz greeted Qwess as the Marshals guided him to the table. "As-salamu alaykum, brother. How are you?"

Qwess rubbed his wrists to ease the pain of where the cuffs were clasped just moments ago. "Shit, I'm here, but they making it hard on a Black man," he complained.

Qwess made a show of looking around the room to see who was there to support him among the gallery. This was his first time out in public in six months, and even under these dire circumstances, it still felt good to see real people instead of guards all day. Hell, it felt good just to see different colors and smell something different than the stale stench of jail. He had grown accustomed to a very lavish lifestyle over the years, and this visit reminded him of just how much he was missing.

"I'm ready to get out of here. This shit here is draining," Qwess groused.

"Well, that all should be coming to an end today, brother," Malik Shabazz assured him with a strong pat on the back.

Qwess continued to scan the courtroom. He spotted his wife in the front row along with his parents and instantly felt a sense of peace. He continued to scan the room, and before he could recognize anyone else, his attention was garnered by another face in the crowd. The lead civil attorney for AMG Records sat in the front row, all smug and debonair in a three-thousand-dollar suit and a two-dollar grin.

Qwess returned his smirk and gave him a head nod to let him know he saw him. Qwess caught the implication; AMG wanted him to know that they were on his ass too. AMG had a seventy-five-million-dollar lawsuit pending against Qwess personally as well as a lien on royalties from his company. So they essentially had a stake in Qwess's freedom too. Their presence was to apply pressure on Qwess to settle out of court. They had offered to settle out of court for just under fifty million a month ago, but Qwess was undaunted in his quest to take them to court. He didn't plan on giving them shit!

Qwess sat at the table in his county issue uniform, and the judge called court into session. The judge went through his spiel, then got down to business.

"So, we're here today to see if Mr. Salim here should be granted a bond pending the outcome of his trial. Is that correct?" the judge asked.

"Yes, Your Honor," Malik Shabazz piped up with confidence. "We're ready to send this great man home to his family and the community he serves."

Malik Shabazz knew the eyes of the world were on him. He was a celebrity attorney; he was what the late great Johnny Cochran would've been had he practiced law in the social media era. Malik Shabazz was usually more popular than the clients he represented, due to his high presence on social media, where he regularly flaunted his lavish lifestyle, piloting speedboats, frolicking on mega-yachts, and cruising the world in his exotic sports cars. When he came to court, it was a spectacle. The world recognized once-in-a-lifetime greatness, and he was one of the sharpest legal minds in the world today at the height of his power. The public dubbed him the "LeBron James of Law," except where the NBA star held court in arenas around the country, Malik Shabazz held court in the legal halls of America.

Unimpressed with Malik Shabazz's theatrics, Judge Thomas looked down at the papers before him and scoffed.

"Looks like your client has been serving his community all right, Mr. Shabazz," he quipped. "According to this paperwork, he's been serving his community death and dope."

Judge Thomas was aware of the enormity of this proceeding as well. He recognized he was also on stage, and he was looking to make a statement and thrust his name into the mouths of America as well.

Malik Shabazz scoffed. "That's nonsense. My client is an international superstar, philanthropist, and businessman. He's no criminal."

"Ah, from my understanding, we're not deciding guilt or innocence today, are we?" the federal prosecutor piped up. He saw that Malik Shabazz was already attempting to wield his legendary charm around the courtroom. "In that case, can we get on with it?"

Malik Shabazz shot his adversary for the day a cruel look. He was trying to soften the judge up, bend him to his side. "Very well, let's get to it," Malik Shabazz said, and addressed the court. "Your Honor, for the reasons I just stated, we request that my client be released on his own recognizance."

"Yeah, right! Your Honor, these are some very serious charges, charges that we can prove. We have witnesses here today ready to testify as to the veracity of these charges," the prosecutor alleged. He expelled a deep sigh and stated his case. "Sir, for years, this common criminal here has been hiding behind the music industry to appear to be a legit businessman. He is very rich, very dangerous, and very capable of fleeing justice. We cannot play with this matter and give him a bail. He is facing the death penalty, for God's sake! He has *every* reason to flee."

Malik Shabazz bellowed in laughter, as if he were front row at a Kevin Hart comedy special. "You Honor, Mr. Salim would never flee and desecrate the stellar reputation he has built. We look forward to embarrassing the government and making them pay dearly for besmirching the character of such a great man."

"A great criminal."

"A GREAT man!" Malik Shabazz repeated with a scowl.

"Your Honor, I reiterate that this is a capital case—"

"He's innocent."

"If this was Joe Blow from off the street, we wouldn't even be entertaining this conversation."

"But he isn't Joe Blow; he's an international music mogul."

"A murdering music mogul."

"Enough!" Judge Thomas had heard enough. "Now, I have heard you both bicker, cackling like old hens. Both of you are this close to being in contempt. Let's hash this out before my bailiffs cart you two off to jail."

Malik Shabazz settled down and prepared to present his case. But Judge Thomas had other plans.

"You know, I've been following your career, Mr. Salim," Judge Thomas said to Qwess. "My son is a huge fan of yours, and he was shocked the way this all went down."

Qwess inwardly breathed a sigh of relief. This is the part of his stardom he loved—the privilege. The judge's son was a fan. This could only bode well for Qwess. Or so he thought.

"I can't say I share his sentiment, sir. My son is a lot more naïve than I am," Judge Thomas pointed out. "For the past decade I have watched guys like you come in my courtroom and hide your crimes under the auspices of legitimate business, and nothing is worse than you misleading children like mine with your dirty music. Frankly, I'm sick of it. Especially guys like you—you have it all, but you can't leave your past behind."

Malik Shabazz was on his feet. "Uh, Your Honor, I don't think this is proper . . . sir. You are declaring my client guilty from the bench," he said, shrugging his shoulders. "How can he even remotely be expected to receive a fair trial under these circumstances?"

Judge Thomas beamed his beady eyes on Johnny Cochran 2.0. "I'm not here to ascertain your client's guilt or innocence—"

"You're doing a mighty fine job to me."

"That's for a jury to decide. My only job today is to make sure he gets there," Judge Thomas clarified. "So on that note . . . your request for bail is *denied*. Bailiffs, take him back into custody!"

The courtroom erupted. Judge Thomas had shocked the world with his abrupt decision. He was batting for the media fences and hit a home run on his first time at bat. The courtroom was in a frenzy as reporters and photographers rushed to be the first to get that important shot or soundbite.

Malik Shabazz was livid! The abrupt decision had thieved his cool visage. "Your Honor, this isn't right!" He roared as he was forced to watch the bailiffs take Qwess into custody.

Judge Thomas offered him a cruel smirk and winked at Qwess before he stood to retire to his chambers. His decision had been made; his work here was done.

The judge's antics only emboldened Qwess. He realized they were trying to break his spirit—something he would never allow. He forced a smile onto his face and turned to face his supporters. He pumped his hands to quiet them.

"I'm fine," Qwess assured them. He looked to his parents, then to his wife, and his business partners. "You know I got this. You know me, I will NOT lose," he reminded them. They had seen him escape danger plenty of times, but how could he be so cool with a death penalty hanging over his head?

Qwess looked to the rep from AMG's legal team as the bailiffs wrenched his arms behind his back. They locked eyes while Qwess continued to address his family. "No one has ever broken me, and I'm not going to let them now."

He was talking to no one in particular and everyone simultaneously. His voice was as vibrant and strong as his resolve appeared to be. Inwardly he was beginning to question a few things, but again, he could never let them see him sweat.

Someone in the back of the courtroom caught Qwess's attention, someone he hadn't noticed until the bailiffs were escorting him out of the room. He hadn't seen him in six months; he'd only heard of his progress. Now seeing him—even from a distance—was refreshing. That small glimpse at his lil homie was all the encouragement Qwess needed.

If he could overcome his odds, then so could Qwess.

Chapter 3

Flame exited the courthouse and anxiety gripped his stomach. It took everything in him to make an appearance this day, but he had to. It was important that he support Qwess and let him know that he had his back. Flame hadn't seen Qwess since he was released from the hospital, and just seeing him elicited so many memories—good and bad.

In a weird way, Flame felt Qwess was responsible for his misfortune. In his mind, if Qwess hadn't ghosted Sasha and left an indelible impression of revenge on her soul, then chances are she wouldn't have leaked the tape of their sexual tryst to the public. At least, that's what Flame rationalized on his bad days.

On his good days, he admitted that it was his fault. Truth was, neither Qwess nor anyone else told him to stick his dick in Sasha Beaufont. In fact, it was Qwess who had warned him against the move, and Flame didn't listen. So yeah, on a good day, Flame was honest with himself, and he was forced to admit that his problems began with the man in the mirror.

Today, Flame was having a bad day. As his right-hand

man and best friend, 8-Ball, pushed him in his wheelchair through the crowd of spectators snapping photos, he caught flashbacks of what his life used to be like. With each camera that was thrust into his face, he reminisced on how things were when he was the man, back when he was showering his energy on tens of thousands of concertgoers hanging on his every word, shouting his lyrics back at him at the top of their lungs. He was a GOD then—if only for the hour or so, he baptized the crowd with his freaky sermon. Now he was a shell of that man, outwardly anyway. Now he was a mere mortal being rolled through the crowd, and he could've sworn he saw the frowns of disappointment on their faces.

For many, this was their first time seeing the elusive former chart-topper out in public since his ordeal, and they couldn't wait to plaster him on the blogs. Flame had fallen from grace on the biggest stage and now he was forced to wear the consequences of his transgressions on his sleeve. Well, in this case, his legs. He still had not regained use of his legs. It had been nearly a year since Diamond had power bombed the mobility out of his body, and each day things got worse in the public for him. Every day there was new speculation about his condition. Flame just took things in stride. There was no quitting in him. He was committed to walking again, regardless of the doctors' prognosis.

"Amen, praise God! Look at all these people; they still love you, Joey," Flame heard to his right.

It was Kim Rawls, bending his ear with a burst of positivity, the same thing she had been doing since she barged in his hospital room that fateful day and snatched him from his pity party.

Flame looked up and scoffed. "Yeah right," he sniped.

"They do! Look at them. They've never seen a star in the flesh," Kim insisted, but Flame wasn't convinced. He shook his head and looked at the ground.

Flame managed to make it to the Mercedes Sprinter van. While the other members of the security team set up a perimeter, 8-Ball loaded him into the side of the van. This was the lowest part of Flame's new life—having to be loaded into a van. Even *riding* in a van was disrespectful to Flame. He was a man that had driven the finest of automobiles, and he still owned an exotic fleet of Italian stallions, spread throughout his numerous properties. Of course, some of them were on the verge of being sold because he was practicing financial triage. Since his handicap prevented him from performing, he lost millions of dollars in performance money and was forced to cut back on his spending. Not to mention, his therapy was costing him a gang of money as well. Flame was definitely at a low point, and the only bright spot in his life was the lady who had just sat beside him in the Sprinter.

"Joey, you got to snap out of it!" Kim urged, cupping his sad face inside her palms. "God still gave you your life; that's all you need to get back. You'll see. We gonna get you back up and walking in no time," she promised.

"Yeah, you keep saying that, but I don't feel no different. I mean, I know you say God got this, but I don't know sometimes," Flame admitted.

Kim smiled, "That's perfectly normal to have doubts. It's not easy to trust in Jesus, especially with the life you lived. But I've seen him do miracles, and he still in the Miracle business."

Flame looked down at his shirt. The words *#Im4God* were stenciled across his chest in big gold and white letters. Every time he wore the shirt he felt as if God's Grace was descending upon him. Kim had found the apparel line and blessed Flame with all types of clothing from the line. She swore the clothing was anointed, and Flame could attest that every time he wore the clothing, great things occurred.

"I mean, I'm not being ungrateful," Flame claimed. "It's just that I'm tired of feeling helpless."

"Helpless is facing the death penalty and all the money you amassed not being able to help you," Kim pointed out, referring to Qwess.

Flame shook his head, "I know . . . for so long I blamed him for all this, ya know? Like, after everything Sasha told me, I felt like it was his fault that Diamond did this to me. So I was hoping something happened to him." Flame shook off the evil thoughts. "Now, seeing him in there like that, fighting for his life, I feel a little guilty. Bruh ain't do nothing to me but change my life, and turned me all the way up. He helped my dreams come true."

"God made your dreams come true!" Kim corrected him.

"Yeah, but Qwess was the conduit to do that, and now everyone he helped has turned their back on him. I don't want to be one of those people."

Kim shrugged. "Then don't," she simply said. She paused for a second, pondering her next thought. "I have an idea, Joey. This could be a way for you to give your glory to God for all that he has done, and also a way for you to atone for everything you put Qwess through."

Flame perked up. "Oh really?"

Kim nodded vigorously. "Yes!"

Flame wasn't as confident in this new idea as Kim was, but she hadn't steered him wrong yet, so he was willing to take a listen.

When Kim walked into his hospital room, she had vowed to not leave his side until he was back to normal. Thus far, she had been with him every step of the way. She had changed his perception of the role of a woman in a man's life. Before her, he was overtly misogynistic and toxic, a regular savage. In his life, women were only for pleasure and sport. He never knew that a woman could uplift a man, speak life into him, and aid him by healing his soul. But that's exactly what Kim had done for him—healed him from the inside out, and it felt good. His unfortunate incident was a gift and a curse. It allowed him to sit back and analyze his life and reshuffle the deck.

Now if he could only regain use of his legs.

Chapter 4

A week after Qwess was denied bail, a gift fell in the Crescent Crew's lap.

Qwess's case hinged upon the statements given by his former bodyguard, Hulk, and his twin brother, Samson. Hulk had been with Qwess every day for the past ten years. He was a founding member of the Crescent Crew along with his twin brother. They both put in vicious work in the early days of the gang's inception, up until the Crew split when Qwess delved into the music industry. While Samson opted to ride the streets out with King Reece and help him build his empire, Hulk chose to ride shotgun with Qwess up the ladder to legit success. He became Qwess's shadow, following him around the world and protecting him at all costs. Then Qwess's loyal thoroughbred had turned into a viper.

To secure his brother's freedom, Hulk told the Feds everything he knew about Qwess's illegal activities, including his part in the murders of Dee and Scar. Where the pieces didn't fit, he embellished the truth a bit. He knew Qwess wasn't personally involved in the murders, but he had issued the order by proxy, and the way Hulk painted the picture for the federal government, Qwess might as well have pulled the triggers. Hulk drew a masterpiece with his poisonous pen, then vanished into thin air.

Until now.

With Qwess in jail, Hulk thought the smoke had cleared enough for him to ease back into Fayetteville and visit his daughter he thought no one knew about off Cliffdale Road.

He was wrong.

It was Hulk's five-year-old daughter's first day of school, and he vowed that he wouldn't miss it for the world. What he didn't know was the neighbor of his daughter's mother was creeping with a member of the Crescent Crew. Because Hulk's Escalade was too big to pull into the garage, he was forced to park outside and expose himself to the world.

That's how he was spotted by Khalil.

As soon as Khalil saw Hulk duck from the Escalade, he immediately got on the phone with Maleek Money, Bone's second-in-command.

"As-salamu alaykum, Brother Maleek. You not gonna believe who I just saw," Khalil hissed into the phone.

"Wa alaykum as-salam," Maleek Money returned, groggily. He rolled over and glanced at his Rolex. The hashes on the watch glowed in the dark. *6:45.* "Brother, you better be about to tell me you saw the Mahdi, calling me this early in the morning," Maleek Money grunted.

"Even better," Khalil assured him. "I got eyes on that rat bastard right now."

Maleek Money sat straight up in the bed. "Say word?"

"Word!"

"And the nigga still breathing?"

"Say no more."

Khalil ended the call and proceeded to his mission. He crept through the side door of his girl's house and tiptoed behind the Escalade to see if Hulk was rolling alone, but the tint was too dark to see through. He figured he would just have to take his chances.

He crept around the home and peered through the kitchen window. There he saw Hulk bending down adjusting his daughter's uniform.

Khalil's breath caught in his throat. This was the first time seeing the giant in the flesh. He'd heard so much about him since joining the crew that in his mind Hulk was like a unicorn, a myth. Seeing him in the flesh was like discovering Bigfoot. Hulk was huge! At 6'7" he was already big, but he had gained a massive amount of weight that was mostly muscle. Even tucked beneath the large trench coat he wore, his shoulders resembled mountains from behind, and his massive hands were like baseball mitts. His bald head looked like a shiny boulder, and the funny spectacles he wore made him look even more dangerous.

"Fuck . . ." Khalil whispered aloud. He was beginning to have second thoughts about his mission. *What if he missed? What if he wasn't quick enough to execute the giant and he got ahold of him and put those big mittens on him?* For a second, Khalil visualized Hulk's massive hands around his neck and started wheezing as if it were happening. Khalil had to slap himself upside the head to snap out of it.

Khalil pulled the slide back on his Sig Sauer and eased around the corner to approach the back door. As soon as he turned the corner, he saw a flash. A split second later, a burst of pain exploded in the center of his chest. Khalil never saw the double-aught buckshot that opened his chest. All he felt was the pain, excruciating pain. He rolled around on the ground writhing in agony, clutching his chest where blood poured from the open wound like a faucet. He blinked rapidly, attempting to stifle the pain, but there was no relief.

Each blink only brought more pain and confusion. His vision was blurred, and his head pounded from the sensation of pain rushing to his brain. He sensed someone walking to him slowly. The footsteps felt so heavy from his spot on the ground that it felt like a dinosaur was approaching him. Finally, the footsteps stopped, and he felt a large presence standing above him.

"Yeahhh nigga," Hulk taunted, pointing the sawed-off shotgun at Khalil. "You thought you was gonna catch me slipping huh? I saw you from the time you dipped behind my truck," he explained.

It was true. The moment Khalil made his move, Hulk was on him. He had scoped his every move. Even when he was playing with his daughter with his back turned to the window, he had seen Khalil peeking at him through the mirror on the wall. When Khalil disappeared, Hulk was coming out the back door to catch him from the other side. Unfortunately, Khalil ran right into him. Now he was paying the price for his underestimation. The predator had turned into prey.

"I wonder who convinced you to go on a dummy mission?" Hulk asked. He kicked Khalil in the ass with his heavy size fourteen boot. "I'm gonna hunt all you mothafuckas down, one by one. Me and my brother started this shit. We put in work to build this Crescent Crew! Y'all think you can deny us or rights, you fake ass Muslim!"

"Y-you . . . s-sn-snitch ass nigga!" Khalil mustered up the gumption to get his words out. "F-fuck y'all!"

Hulk chuckled. "See, you still going by the old rules. You don't understand the game. The name of the game is survival and right now, your time has expired."

Hulk pushed the barrel of the shotgun into Khalil's head to deliver the kill shot when suddenly something caught his eye. Khalil's phone illuminated on the ground from an incoming call. The phone had fallen from his pocket when he tumbled to the ground. Hulk scooped the phone up and looked at the caller. On the screen was a photo of the Crescent Crew logo with the letters *M&M* for the name of the caller. Hulk figured that it was whoever had sent this flunkie calling to check on the progress. Hulk smiled and answered the call.

"As-salamu alaykum! You good?" Hulk heard Maleek Money ask on the other end. "Yo, Akhi, you good?"

Hulk pushed the icon to turn on the camera for Face-Time. While Maleek Money answered, he turned the camera around so Maleek Money could see Khalil's face with the barrel pressed against his temple. As soon as Maleek Money's face appeared, Hulk pulled the trigger.

Boom!

From his comfy bed in his new home in the Port City, Maleek Money watched a chunk of Khalil's head disintegrate from the blast, leaving a gaping hole in his skull. The sound of the blast made him drop the phone. When he picked the phone back up, he was face-to-face with Hulk.

Hulk breathed into the phone heavily. Mist blew from his nose as if he was a bull. He pointed his finger at the screen. "You are next!"

Maleek Money was speechless. He expected to see his man showing him that he had handled business. Instead, he had witnessed his death.

"I'm going to hunt each and every one of you niggas down," Hulk vowed. "You coming after me? Me? I'll show you new niggas what made us legends."

Maleek Money found his courage (and his voice). "Nah, nigga. You food—you and your bitch ass brother. It's Crew Business on site for y'all."

"Oh yeah?"

"Yep! You'll see."

"Well, the score is one-zip. Catch up!" Hulk ended the call.

Maleek Money was furious! Khalil had botched the hit and now their hand was exposed. Not only did he have to bury a brother, but now heat had also been brought to their door in vain. It would be one thing if he had executed the hit; then things could have made sense. Now, because the hit was unsuccessful, they had to contend with an enemy who knew no bounds. Hulk was a confirmed snitch, so there was no telling what kind of resources he had at his disposal. Would he tell the Feds that a hit had been attempted on his life? If so, would the Feds protect him by initiating a campaign against the Crescent Crew? Did he have immunity to operate with impunity? Were his murders now sanctioned? Would he come for them in a police car with the police driving and point them out?

There were too many questions to Maleek Money's conundrum. It was one thing to handle things on the street level where street rules applied. In a weird sense, there was honor among thieves on the street. For example, you hit one of mine, I hit one of yours . . . or two, or ten. It didn't matter the amount, as long as it was understood that the matter was to be handled in the streets. However, with the way the game was being played now, that wasn't the case. If I hit one of yours, would you go to the police and have me arrested? An outlaw informing on an outlaw?

There was no telling who was "one of his." Would Hulk come for him himself? Would he send the authorities? Was he aligned with his brother's crew of Mexicans? Did he have a crew of country gangsters imported from his native Alabama? There were too many questions to answer.

Maleek Money eased out of bed and padded to the bathroom. He washed his face off and collected his thoughts. He exhaled a ball of stress into the mirror. He was really starting to see some money and enjoy his position as a boss. He was living the good life in a new home with his new ghetto queen whom he had upgraded to a goddess. He was finally the man he always knew he could be.

Now, all of that was being threatened because he had just started a war.

Chapter 5

FCI Butner Medium II
Butner, North Carolina

The man lounged on his bunk, surfing *Pornhub* on his smuggled cellphone. His large foot was propped up on the mountain of canteen items littering his solo cell. On a yard with a population of nearly 1,400 inmates, having his own cell was a testament to his power. But a solo cell was just a small testament to his power. The fact was, he held sway on a huge portion of the federal prison system. He was a man connected to two worlds—three if you counted the federal government silently backing him—and he rejoiced in his power. He never missed an opportunity to put his dick on the table and flex his power.

A tap on the door interrupted his personal freak session. He put the phone away and welcomed his uninvited guest.

"Come in!" he barked.

The cell door creaked open, and a diminutive Mexican man walked in with his head bowed. "*Perdóname, El Patrón,*" the man said. "*Pero tengo mucho hambre. ¿Puedes ayúdarme?*"

The man smiled. He lived for moments like this, a moment to share the wealth with his comrades, and remind them he was the boss. Of course, this man already knew who was boss, evidenced by him calling him *El Patrón*—Godfather.

"*Si, hermanito, venga aqui,*" he said, beckoning him inside. "*¿Qué quieres?*"

He welcomed him to the pile of canteen items littering the floor and encouraged him to have whatever his heart desired.

"*Gracias, Monstruoso. Eres hombre generoso,*" the small Mexican uttered as he picked up items.

"*Ah no es nada,*" Samson returned in perfect Spanish. He retrieved his phone and scrolled through social media while his little comrade gathered a meal. The man scooped up an armful of food and exited the cell. No sooner than he left, there was another knock at the door.

"Come in!" Samson barked.

A tall Black man walked in with his chest poked out. He wore a tank top that bared his long sleeve of tattoos. Down one side of his arm in gothic script was the word *Crescent*. Down the other arm in the exact same script was the word *Crew*.

"Peace, O.G.," the man greeted.

"Gangsta Black, what's good, lil homie," Samson returned. He stood to embrace the brother.

Gangsta Black was a Crescent Crew member Samson had personally recruited. He was from Los Angeles, California, and had ties to Houston, Texas. He was a high-ranking Blood member who defected on his gang to join the Crescent Crew. The infighting and destitution of his Blood ranks prompted him to seek greener pastures in the form of another gang. He had heard of the Crescent Crew, of course. They were legendary for their exploits in the streets, and even more legendary for the way they managed to go legit. They had finagled their street reputation into a wealthy entertainment empire, and it was common knowledge that Samson was a big part of that success. A few months back, Gangsta Black had come to Butner on an administrative transfer after some of his ex-homies had DPed him and made him food. As soon as he hit the yard, he had learned that the notorious Samson was on the yard and running things. Gangsta Black had sought Samson out, and after a long powwow, sworn his allegiance to Samson's flag. Now Gangsta Black was second-in-command in Samson's Crescent Crew. He used the skills he acquired to grow the ranks of his Blood gang in order to bolster the ranks of the new and improved Crescent Crew. In under six short months, the ranks inside the prison swelled to double their original size.

"Everything is peace, bro," Gangsta Black assured him. He leaned over the pile of food on the floor and scooped up a bag of chips and a soda. "What's the word with you? You heard from your people?"

"Yeah, he in the Ville right now scoping things out. His kid start school today so he there with her. When he done, he going to do some scouting for us."

Gangsta Black slapped his hands and rubbed his palms together. "Man, I cannot WAIT to get out there and touch the turf again, bro. These niggas gonna feel it! I'm straight going *brazy* on that ass!" He promised, using Blood lingo. He had been a Blood so long, their slick vocabulary was a part of his being.

Samson chuckled. "I can imagine, lil homie. It won't be long now."

Gangsta Black picked up a *Don Diva* magazine with Qwess on the cover. He flipped to the article, read a few lines, and sighed in disbelief. "Man, can you believe the Big Homie facing the death penalty?" Gangsta Black said. "All that he done in the music industry, left the game alone and showed niggas like us a way to legitimize, and now *he* the one in the clink."

Samson perked up. "Yeah, that's crazy, but you know how the shit go—the game is the game. Lowkey, I'm hearing some things about the Big Homie that suggest he may not be as solid as we think though."

"Huh? What you mean?"

Samson waved his hand dismissively. "It's nothing right now, but when I find out if it's true or not, I'll pull you up to speed on things."

Samson was planting the seed of doubt, sprinkling salt on Qwess's name before the pendulum swung his way. Thus far, him being a confidential informant hadn't spread to the penitentiary yet. Only members of the Crew and Qwess's legal team were aware of Samson's betrayal, and even then, some had their doubts. Samson had become a man of respect, so it was unfathomable to even think of him turning snitch. But sure enough, he was going full Sammy Gravano, and just like Sammy, he wasn't done with the game. In fact, he was more ready than ever to make his own mark in the underworld with his new team.

"But yo, how much you got left?" Samson asked. He knew exactly how much time Gangsta Black had remaining; he just wanted to change the subject to allow the seed he planted to grow in Gangsta Black's head. The mind is funny like that—plant a seed and it will find its own water to make it grow.

"I'm down to four weeks now," Gangsta Black answered.

"Yeah, by the time you get out, I'll be right behind you."

"Oh yeah?" This was a shock to Gangsta Black. As far as he knew, Samson hadn't even put a dent in the fifteen years he had been sentenced to.

"Yeah, I got the best attorney in the country," Samson claimed. (He wasn't exactly lying—the United States Attorney General was personally handling his case.) "They got some new evidence that can free me any day now."

"Word? That's what the fuck I'm talking about! They can't keep the god down, bro," Gangsta Black said, stroking Samson's ego. Samson was God-Body, an adherent of the Nation of Gods and Earths, a sect known as the Five-Percenters. While most of the Crescent Crew were orthodox Muslims (in theory) a small contingent of the gang followed King Reece and were die-hard Five-Percenters just as he had been. It was hard to disagree with their belief in themselves when they were living like gods on earth.

"Hell naw, they can't keep me down. I been working on my case since I've been in. I'm not going to let them devils keep me here," Samson bragged. Oh, how he was embellishing the truth! He had been working on his case all right—working the right angle with the Feds.

Initially, Samson was okay with taking the fifteen-year sentence for criminal conspiracy and attempted murder for the beatdown of John Meyers, an executive at AMG records. He was gang-gang to the core and death before dishonor was their ethos. He was a loyal soldier to King Reece and looked for opportunities to prove his allegiance. The beatdown was no different, a simple example of Crew business. He knew the consequences of his acts. He fell on his sword so his King could continue to set them up for the next generation. With the case settled, the smoke would clear around King Reece so he could forge forward with their plan to dominate the music industry.

Samson continued to weave his tale, "I already knew I had a good case," he lied. "It was just a matter of finding the missing link."

Samson rushed to settle his case before the authorities

discovered his true identity as being the man on the tarmac the day King Reece was arrested. On that fateful day, King Reece had taken a gun from Samson and murdered a federal agent in broad daylight as they attempted to escape to Mexico to evade prosecution. The incident was all captured on video from the informant, Destiny, who was King Reece's then-girlfriend, and now deceased, baby mother. Fortunately for Samson, King Reece's move had afforded him the opportunity to escape and flee to Mexico on a chartered jet. The incident awarded him a spot in the Top Five on the FBI's Most Wanted list.

"No doubt. There's always a missing link," Gangsta Black agreed. "Bro, how was it living in Mexico? I heard them mothafuckas do not like the Black man."

While in Mexico, Samson underwent surgery to have his face altered to evade capture. He remained in the country under the protection of El Jefe. Samson's size made him stick out like an oak tree in a rose bush, and El Jefe quickly made use of his intimidating size. At nearly six and a half feet and three hundred-plus pounds, the earth shook when Samson walked. El Jefe added Samson to his security team, and Samson rushed to earn his keep.

On his first time out with El Jefe, Samson snatched up a news reporter who had been spewing negative rhetoric about El Jefe's organization. As the man attempted to run, Samson scooped him up and power bombed him into the pavement, snapping his neck. As the man clung to life, hopping around like a wounded chicken, Samson wrapped his mittens around his neck and hoisted him high in the air. He squeezed the remainder of his life out of him while he stared him in the eyes. Then he dropped him to the floor as if he were trash and walked away amid the stares. The sheer violence of the act immediately endeared him to his new circle of friends. Mexico was a notoriously violent country, but their brand of violence was rifles and long knives, not over-grown Black men with freakish strength. It was one thing to be a giant, it was another thing to behave like Andre the Giant.

"One thing about me, lil bro, I'm gonna demand respect wherever I go," Samson replied. "I don't give a fuck who like me as long as they respect me. In Mexico, they gave me the ultimate respect,"

It may have seemed as if Samson was capping, but after the move with the reporter, El Jefe's top two enforcers took a liking to Samson and put him down with their other hustle: abduction.

In Mexico, the poor lived off the rich, so the smart rich put their money toward employing personal armies. The not so smart paid on the back end—meaning they paid men like Chabo and Gil to go after the kidnappers and return their family members when they were abducted. Chabo and Gil played both sides of the hustle though. They would have their minions abduct a rich family member, then come in to save the day. After they put Samson down with their lucrative operation, their money flowed like wine. Samson would abduct the family member—in broad daylight sometimes. His size alone was intimidating enough that he didn't even have to brandish a weapon most of the time. However, absolute power corrupts absolutely, and Samson quickly became intoxicated with his power. In Mexico, outlaws were heralded with the utmost respect—the more outlandish the acts, the more praise was heaped on your name. Samson quickly realized this and sought to make a name for himself. When he abducted someone and the family refused to pay the ransom, Samson would make gruesome examples out of his victims. Beheadings were normal in Mexico, so Samson went beyond the norm. He imported Crew business and turned it up a notch, dismembering women and children—something the Crescent Crew eschewed—and littering the streets with their body parts. His actions quickly earned him the name *Monstruoso*, or "Monster" in Spanish.

"I bet they did," Gangsta Black said. "Shit, the Eses in the West even heard about you. They said you was living large in Mexico."

Samson smiled and pulled out his photo album. "Was I? Check this out, homie."

Gangsta Black leaned over Samson's massive shoulder and took a trip down memory lane with him. There were a bevy of Mexico's most beautiful women in all their splendor crowding the pages, none of them appearing to be older than twenty. Other photos were of Samson surrounded by the women. In these photos he appeared so massive that the women resembled children. Page after page of him flossing the status his money and power afforded him.

"Damnnnn, Big Homie, that's the shit I'm talking about!" Gangsta Black said, excited as if he were living the life himself.

"Yo, all you have to do is make it out and hold shit down for me until I come, and this is going to be your life too. Loyalty is royalty," Samson reminded him.

The irony of Samson's words was lost on Gangsta Black. He had no idea that the O.G. he was praising was the lowest of the low. He was a bonafide rat who had sacrificed his freedom for that of his comrades, and now he was nursing the ultimate mutiny—forming a new and improved Crescent Crew by using his strong Mexican connections.

"I got you, Big Homie. You can count on me," Gangsta Black promised.

Samson's phone buzzed to life beneath his pillow. He discreetly saw that it was his brother and answered the call. "Peace G!" Samson boomed with excitement. "What's good?"

"Maaan, you not gonna believe this," Hulk said. "Them niggas made a move on me."

Samson sat up on the bed so quickly his head almost hit the ceiling. "Who?"

"The Crew, man. They caught me slipping at my daughter's spot and tried to take me out."

Samson couldn't believe what he was hearing. "Are you sure it was them?"

"Hell yeah! I answered the phone after I took it from the lil nigga and I saw the Coat of Arms on the screen," Hulk explained. "It was definitely them niggas."

"And you sure they knew it was you?"

"Bro, what other niggas you know that look like me running around?"

Hulk had a point, but it still wasn't adding up to Samson. He had brokered a deal that guaranteed a peace treaty until he was released. Making a move against him and Hulk was like slitting their own throat.

"So what happened?"

"You already know what happened."

"So do they know it was you?"

"They do now."

Samson paused a moment to digest the news. He had given Hulk his blessing to go back to the Ville after he reached out to El Jefe to plead his case. Jefe had guaranteed no harm would come to him or his brother until further notice. Samson was biding time until Qwess's trial, where he was required to take the stand in exchange for his freedom. His statements were sealed now; only a select few could attest to the veracity of their existence. As far as the world knew, his honor was still intact. If he had it his way, when the world discovered different, he would be too strong for it to matter. He had plans of building a multinational crime conglomerate that would make what the great King Reece accomplished a mere afterthought.

But this strike against his brother concerned him. Someone wasn't playing fair.

"Okay, so you know what this means, right?" Samson asked.

"Damn right."

"Yep. We're officially at war. I'm going to send in some reinforcements. Oh, and I'm going to hit their pockets too," Samson plotted. "Let's see how loyal they are when the money get low."

"Okay, bro. I'm going to hunt them down, one by one. By the time you come home all we'll have to do is step into position."

Hulk's pledge was music to Samson's ears. This was going to be easier than taking candy from a baby.

Samson ended the call and dismissed Gangsta Black from his cell. As soon as Gangsta Black left, Samson called another number. Someone picked up the phone on the second ring.

"El Jefe? You not gonna believe this . . ."

Chapter 6

Wilmington, NC

The cream SLS AMG Mercedes rolled into the beach access road on Wrightsville Beach and parked right behind the BMW 650 convertible Maleek Money was driving. The lights flashed on the Merc, and Maleek Money slid from the Bimmer and walked to the passenger side of the coupe. The butterfly door glided up right in his face and stopped at his chest. Maleek Money peeked in, and there was Bone behind the wheel.

"As-salamu alaykum. Hop in," Bone instructed.

Maleek Money lowered himself into the cream leather seat and the door descended into place. Maleek was beyond nervous. The fact that Bone was in town was enough to have him unnerved.

"Wa alakykum as-salamu, what's the word?" Maleek Money returned the greeting with a nervous smile.

Bone stared straight ahead at the ocean in a daze. Although his cavernous eyes were hidden behind his gold Versace shades, it was apparent that they were laser locked on something. The future? The past?

"Yo, that move you authorized," Bone began. He was speaking so low that Maleek strained to make out his words. "It was ballsy, the right thing to do. It's what I would have done if I was in your position. We put the tag on his head, and it was on-site. He was food," Bone assured him. "Khalil just couldn't complete the job and he paid the ultimate price. May Allah brighten his face."

"Inshallah. Ma'shallah," Maleek Money interjected.

Bone shook his head. "We can't even have a proper burial for the brother because they took his body with them."

"Word?"

"Yeah, the chick told us she saw it go down."

"So where she at?"

Bone cocked his head and twisted his mouth in response. Maleek Money nodded in silence. He knew what that meant.

"So, you did good, Akhi, but . . . you also fucked up too. Big time."

Maleek was confused. "Huh?"

Bone nodded. "Yeah, it's complicated."

The men sat in silence staring at the ocean. A thick white chick in a yellow bikini walked past them headed to the beach. She stared at the German automobiles as if she had x-ray vision, but the five percent tint on the widows of the Mercedes was impenetrable.

"How is it complicated? That nigga don't want no smoke with the crew! We growing every day; he can't even come into town. We gonna catch him and eliminate the complications," Maleek Money vowed. He was amped and ready for action, ready to right his wrong.

"It's bigger than that, though, Akhi. I mean, you may have

just cost us the plug," Bone shared. Saying it aloud didn't even sound real.

"Cost us the plug? How the fuck is that?" Maleek Money demanded.

Bone squinted his eyes and attempted to peer through the back of Maleek Money's car. "Yo, somebody in your shit?" he asked.

"Huh? Oh yeah, Keisha in there. I'm keeping her by my side until this shit die down."

Bone grunted and scanned the area for any opposition. He was riding with a life sentence in his lap in the form of a fully automatic assault rifle equipped with a 100-round drum. He could see both of Maleek's weapons tucked in the waistband of his khaki shorts, and he was quite sure Maleek had a chopper in the trunk. They were riding dirtier than UGK.

Bone pushed the red button in the center console and the Mercedes roared to life. He tossed his rifle to Maleek Money and turned the car around, peeping the scene. He slowly pulled from the beach access road and cruised the strip.

As Bone eased down the strip with all eyes on him, he decided to hip his number two to what was going on.

Bone held up his slender finger. "First of all, don't ever put your *zawj* in your business. You may think you protecting her, but you really exposing her to more danger. The more she knows, the more of a target she becomes—and the more of a liability she becomes to us. Feel me?"

Maleek Money nodded. He understood exactly what Bone was insinuating. If Keisha knew too much, they would have to eliminate her.

"And on that other shit," Bone said. "I had a meeting with El Jefe recently. He doesn't seem to believe that rat nigga is sour—"

"What? That's crazy! We have the paperwork!"

"I know, but he wasn't convinced. Asked me to hold off on making a move on him until *he* figured things out."

"What? He doesn't run our shit!"

"Yeah, but he is responsible for our shit running in a way. So if word got back that we made a move on the rat's brother, I don't know how it's going to play out."

All Maleek Money heard was that he may have cost them the plug. His first thought was that Bone would kill him. Then he realized that Bone had actually given him his weapon. He still wasn't convinced though—that move could be the ultimate setup. Maleek Money watched the rearview mirror like a hawk. He wasn't watching for the cops, he was watching for any opps. Bone may not pull the trigger on him; he may have been plotting to have someone else ambush them while they drove like it was rumored Suge did Pac.

"So, what does that mean?" Maleek Money asked. He managed to say his words with resolve, although he was shaking in his boat shoes.

"It means we have to wait and see how this plays out."

Maleek Money saw his riches sweeping away, and maybe even his life. "Big bruh, I'm sorry, man. I thought I was making the right call. I know we had put the green light on him because of him snitching on Qwess, our O.G . . ." His voice trailed off. "I thought I did a good thing."

"You did," Bone assured him, but he caught something in Maleek's soliloquy. "Aye, you understand this isn't just about Qwess, right? See, if Qwess gets convicted, he loses all the legal power he gained in the industry. Then that puts the spotlight on all of us. Dude cleaned our image up and tied the street shit to the entertainment industry. So they don't know what's what. Now, if he get cleaned out on this, then we all sour. So that's the main reason why we have to do whatever we can to make sure he walk."

Bone's words gave Maleek Money a better grip on things. One thing was for sure, Bone wasn't going to kill him—he needed him.

"I understand," Maleek Money said. "Like I said, when I gave you my *bayat*, whatever you need me to do for us to win, consider it done."

Bone nodded. "I don't doubt you, Akhi. I don't doubt you one bit."

Bone wheeled the car back to where the BMW was parked. As he pulled into the beach access, he saw Keisha bending over, taking something out of the trunk. Her short shorts were crammed in the crevices of her wide ass and her smooth skin was glistening with oil. As soon as Bone registered that it was her, he immediately turned away. His brother's woman was off limits and to him, it felt like he was sinning just to look at her, but as Keisha closed the trunk and turned to face them, he had to admit, Keisha was fine. He could see that his brother had polished her into a shining jewel. She exuded the aura of a rich, kept woman, and Bone inwardly smiled because his prediction was correct. He knew when he first saw her that Maleek Money could turn her all the way up.

"You did good, Akhi," Bone said, nodding at Keisha. "You turned her up, bro. Keep treating her right and she'll be loyal to you. We may need her later. I can see it in her, you got a winner. She'll jump off the moon for you."

"You think so?"

"I know so."

Maleek Money smiled, but he did have another question. "Aye, Akhi, I have a question."

"Shoot."

"Why you don't have a woman? I mean, I'm assuming you don't because I never seen you with one."

Bone chuckled. "Maaan, early on a bitch burned me," he said. "I was married during my first bid, and my wife was my

Co-D on my case. I took the case so she could go free, and I left her everything. Cars, jewelry, money . . . everything. Now, during this time, I was nowhere near where I am now, of course. I even left the bitch my record label to run. I had a fire-ass artist out of the Metro that was going to be the next biggest thing."

"So what happened?" Maleek Money asked as he admired Keisha from behind the tinted windows.

"She crossed me. First, she wouldn't send me any of my money. Had me walking around the yard in State bo-bo's while she was living it up on my dime. Short story shorter, the bitch ended up fucking my little man—and my artist. Then she signed over my record label to my little man, had him driving around the city in my 'Vert, wearing my clothes. She eventually divorced me while I was inside and married him. This nigga even had my record label tatted on his arm."

"What?"

"Hell yeah!"

"That's crazy!"

"Nah, *I* was crazy for believing in her. She taught me a lesson though, and I ain't never forget it."

Maleek Money sent a text to Keisha and told her that he loved her. "What's that?" he asked Bone.

"She taught me that a bitch always gonna do her. I don't give a damn how good you treat them, how good you think you fucking them, it don't matter. You can hook her waist to a dump truck, and if she want to get light on your ass, a whole tank of gas won't stop her."

"Damn," Maleek Money said. Then a thought occurred to him. "Aye, if that's how you feel, why do you tell me to put so much faith in Keisha?"

"I don't; I tell you to make Keisha have faith in you—there's a difference. But at the end of the day, it's a sad bird that only has one nest to fly in."

Maleek Money was confused. "What does that mean?"

"It means, trust in Allah, but tie your camel."

"Bet."

Maleek Money raised the door and prepared to step out. As soon as his loafer hit the ground, Bone's phone shrilled to life through the speakers.

Bone looked at the screen and sighed. "Yep, I guess we'll know what's up soon enough. This is him calling now."

Chapter 7

Qwess stepped onto the rock and surveyed the scene. After he blew his bail hearing, he fought for them to move him to GP (General Population) with the rest of the inmates. He was tired of being confined to his cell in Seg for 23-and-1 as if he were a coward or a miscreant. He understood where they were coming from. They were trying to protect him because of his celebrity status, but they didn't realize he liked it in the trenches. This was where he felt most comfortable, with his ear to the ground. If he wasn't going anywhere for a while, he needed to be comfortable. He put his big dog on the mission, and after much haranguing (and signing a waiver), Malik Shabazz managed to get him pulled over to GP. Granted, GP at this facility wasn't exactly the trenches, as most of the federal prisoners on this side were big men in their own right. Still, there was only one Qwess in the world.

Qwess's attention was drawn to the middle of the rock where a chess game was taking place between two men. One man was an older Black man, and the other player was a man of Arab descent. Qwess couldn't make out what country he was from because his features, while clearly Arabic, were indistinct otherwise. This was Qwess's third day in GP, and each time he came on the rock his attention was drawn to the same table. There was something about the energy of the men that seemed familiar to him, but he knew that he didn't know them. Thus far, Qwess only observed the rock from atop his perch on top of the cell block. He liked to get the lay of the land and survey the ground before he engaged. Plus, with everything weighing his mind down, he didn't feel like playing jail politics.

Qwess had a visit that morning that left him with bittersweet news. Because of how the judge behaved at his bond hearing, Malik Shabazz filed an appeal motion on the grounds of bias. He requested a change of venue to receive a new judge to hear his case. Malik Shabazz was confident that the government would grant him a release because they couldn't stand the media blitzkrieg he was preparing if they didn't release him. This news had Qwess in good spirits. However, there was always a little rain with the rainbow, and Qwess's rain these days was all about the money.

Qwess's wife, Lisa Ivory, was with Malik Shabazz that morning, and after Malik Shabazz lifted his spirits, Lisa crushed them again when she informed them of their financial status.

"Baby, we're almost broke," Lisa informed him with sadness. Of course, broke wasn't broke in the traditional sense. For them, broke meant they couldn't maintain their opulent lifestyle. Broke meant, they had more money going out than they had coming in.

"That can't be," Qwess denied. "What about that other thing? Have you gone to see the King?" Qwess asked cryptically.

Qwess had acquired King Reece's handsome estate in his death. He quickly "invested" a lot of the money into his business to legitimize it, but there was also a surplus of cash that couldn't be accounted for. Qwess had stashed a lot of this money inside King Reece's mausoleum so it couldn't be accounted for. This was his emergency fund for when things went south.

"No, I haven't gone to see the King yet," Lisa said. "It's not that bad yet, but we're close."

Qwess shook his head. "How?"

"Baby, we put everything into Wave, and it's not making a return yet."

"And what's up with that?"

"I mean, the early numbers look good, but it's not a smash like we initially intended. We're getting some push-back from some of the licensing companies overseas."

Qwess knew this would happen, but his partner Liam was supposed to have things like this under control. He'd swooped in with promises of being the man, but thus far he was lacking.

"Tell Liam I need to see him immediately."

"Baby, he would never come here. You know that. We have to get you out of here so you can handle all of this."

At this point, Qwess looked at Shabazz. Shabazz assured them that the nightmare would be coming to an end soon. The visit was terminated shortly after, but the words spoken echoed in Qwess's head long after the visit was over.

Qwess needed something to take his mind off his troubles, and there was nothing like a good chess game to help him do just that. He walked down the stairs and posted up by the table where the chess game was being played. The Arab man glanced up at Qwess and offered a slight nod. His opponent, the Black man, said nothing. Qwess watched the game in silence, assessing each man's skill level. They were both good, matching each other move for move. Qwess figured that each man was thinking three to four moves ahead at a minimum—decent but not master level.

"Who got next?" Qwess asked.

The Black man sighed and grunted, "We playing a set."

"Okay, cool. Who has the next set?" Qwess asked. He hoped this wasn't a pissing contest. A lot of incidents in jail were started over games. Guys inside looked for a way to flex their muscle without appearing to be an instigator, so games always did the trick.

"Look, superstar, this is kinda a closed game. We do this all day, every day, with no interruptions," the man added.

Qwess smirked as he sized the older man up. Inside, you could never judge a book by its cover, or gauge a man by his age, so Qwess wasn't taking this old-timer lightly. He wasn't about to let him punk him either though.

"Okay, *I* got next," Qwess announced with a little more authority.

The man stopped pushing his piece mid-move and looked Qwess square in the eye. "Look here superstar, ain't no music being played in here, so you don't call no shots. Everybody equal in here. If you want to play chess, go buy your own game. This one here is ours."

Qwess could feel the anger rising in his stomach. He came out here to clear his head, not disrespect his elders, but the old geezer was trying his patience. Fortunately, before he had to reassert his manhood, the Arab spoke up for the first time.

"Hold up, James," he said. "This is a free country. After I finish whipping you, I'll whip him, and then you can get your usual beating again."

The comment lightened the mood a bit. "Man, you ain't whipping shit, Mahmoud," James declared with a chuckle. "Now move the piece or do I have to get the guard to make the move for you?"

Mahmoud smiled a cheeky smile. He pushed the piece and spread his hands expansively. "Check," he announced.

James made a move, and Mahmoud quickly pounced on him.

"Checkmate!" Mahmoud announced.

James slapped his forehead. "Aw man! Youngblood distracted me," he claimed.

"Uh, James, Youngblood wasn't here when I set you up ten moves ago."

"Ten moves?"

"Yes, when I gave you my knight, I was setting you up."

"Bullshit!"

"The game doesn't lie, James. Now, if you will kindly get up, I have to whip my young brother here."

James protested for a second, but Mahmoud narrowed his eyes, and James quickly relinquished his spot. Qwess peeped the move, and it piqued his interest as to who Mahmoud was.

Qwess settled into the seat and set up his board, careful not to make eye contact with his opponent. Mahmoud tapped the table and got Qwess's attention. When Qwess raised his head, Mahmoud was looking right at him.

"As-salamu alaykum, brother," Mahmoud greeted.

Qwess was stunned. How did he know he was Muslim? He didn't really wear his faith on his sleeve.

Mahmoud pointed to the charm dangling around Qwess's neck. It was a pendant that read *Allah* in Arabic. Inmates weren't allowed to wear jewelry inside except for religious jewelry, so Qwess still wore his necklace and charm. "That's a nice piece," Mahmoud complimented. "Although in my country, the wearing of symbols is *makruh*."

"Oh yeah? What country is that?" Qwess asked.

"I am from Afghanistan," Mahmoud stated with pride.

While the two men mentally jousted over the chess board, they made very small talk. Qwess learned that Mahmoud had been awaiting trial for nearly two years. They refused to give him a bail because he was a flight risk, according to him. He never stated what he was charged with and Qwess never asked. This was the law of the land.

Somewhere during the middle of the game, Qwess zoned

out and ruminated on his problems outside the wall. The lapse in thought was the break that Mahmoud needed to gain the advantage on the board. When Qwess returned his attention to the game, he was down a rook and two pawns.

"Ah, I got you, young brother," Mahmoud said, raising his eyebrows. "I caught you slipping. Where is your mind at? Outside of here?"

Qwess grimaced.

"Tsk, tsk, tsk, Akhi, you have to keep your mind in the present," Mahmoud advised. He stroked his long white beard and adjusted his tinted glasses. "Allah says in the Qur'an that with every difficulty, there is relief."

Qwess nodded knowingly, "Yes, yes, I know. Surah Tin."

"Hmm mmm," Mahmoud confirmed eagerly. "You are correct, but it's one thing to know Islam, you have to live it though."

Qwess nodded his understanding. "I know, brother. Allah has been more than generous to me, and I fail all the time," he admitted.

Mahmoud pushed his rook all the way across the board and stole another pawn. "Akhi, you have to be more merciful to yourself," he said. "Allah says that if we didn't commit sin, he would destroy us and create a people who did, just so they could worship him. So, Allah only commands us to be Muslim; he didn't say he will penalize us for not being good at it."

Qwess chuckled at the truth of the statement. In fact, in Islam, one should never fret over a sin as long as he had time to offer the two ra'ka salaat of repentance called, *Tauba*. Still, Qwess was an all or nothing type of guy. So, when he fell off his *deen*, he did it hard. There was no in-between for him. Either he was making all five of his daily prayers or he wasn't making any of them.

Qwess moved his knight in position to capture a bishop.

"I can feel that," he agreed. "Honestly, it's hard to focus on all that when your schedule is as hectic as mine though." For some reason, Qwess felt comfortable talking to this stranger.

Mahmoud smiled, "Well, sometimes Allah *subhanah ta'ala* sits us down for a reason, maybe to get us back to the basics."

As soon as the words passed Qwess's ears, he knew it was a jewel.

The basics . . .

The basics for Qwess were himself and Flame. Unfortunately, the two most important pieces of his puzzle were in precarious positions.

But could they bounce back?

The water was always refreshing. It was the one place he felt alive and free. Gravity was altered in the water, so his handicap was nonexistent there. In his Olympic-sized pool, he was the old Flame, with control of all his faculties.

When Flame purchased his home and overhauled the pool, he imagined pool parties that turned into orgies filled with some of the most beautiful women in the world. He imagined lavish fourth of July blowouts with the who's who of the entertainment industry. He never imagined in a billion years that he would need the pool for therapy sessions just to survive.

Flame floated in the pool with his arms outstretched as if he were being crucified. His feet scraped the bottom of the pool, but he never knew it because he had no sensation in the lower half of his body. That was fine though, because he still felt the cool water on his naked torso. His head was tucked just beneath the surface of the water as he peered down at the fire logo emblazoned on the pool floor, reminiscing on better days. Oh, how he would give anything just to walk again.

Flame heard someone call his name, but he was so lost in his sorrow he didn't bother to look up. He was just floating

and living the good life in his head. He floated around the
pool with his arms outstretched until he felt his hands touch
someone. He slowly raised his head and looked at Kim.

"Come on, honey," Kim said. "Snap out of it. It's time
to get some work in."

She pulled Flame up from under the water by his arms.
Gently, she guided him to the edge of the pool and allowed
his feet to touch the floor.

"Can you feel that, Joey? Your feet are touching the
floor. How does it feel?"

For a second, Flame could've sworn he felt the gritty
pool floor on his feet. He lit up with joy! He told his mind to
move his foot, but nothing happened. It was all in his head.
His two seconds of joy was replaced with more sadness.

"I can't feel anything," Flame croaked.

Kim patted him on the back. "That's okay; you can't feel
anything today. Don't worry though, you will soon enough."

Kim guided Flame to the shallow area of the pool and
proceeded to take his body through the motions, lifting his
leg, bending his knees, and moving them to make him simu-
late walking.

"It's all in the head, Joey. It's all about muscle memory.
Your brain controls your body," Kim coached as she worked
him out. "You have to tell your body that *you* are in control.
It'll listen to you."

Flame loved having Kim around, but her presence was
bittersweet. Every time she did something great for him, he
felt even more guilty. He had done her so wrong, yet she
was still here for him.

Kim faced Flame and placed his hands on her shoulders.
She stared him in his eyes and wrapped her arms around his
waist. "Now," she said. "Walk toward me."

"What?"

"You heard me, walk toward me."

"You know I c-can't do that."

"Sure you can; you're Joey Devon, you can do anything you put your mind to."

Flame allowed her words to seep into his psyche. He felt strong. Powerful. He felt like he could do anything. He told his brain to follow her lead and raise his legs. He tried to will his brain to do his bidding. In his mind, he raised his legs and . . .

Nothing.

He tried it again. He focused all his energy on telling his brain to tell his legs to move and in his mind he felt his foot shift a bit.

"Oh my God! Did you feel that?" Kim screamed.

"What?" Flame asked.

"Your foot moved. You didn't feel that?"

"Did it?"

"Yes!"

Flame was a nervous wreck. He thought he felt his foot move, but he wasn't sure. He'd thought he felt it move so many times before and it actually hadn't. Now, Kim verified that his leg moved, so it had to be real.

Flame couldn't believe it. "Oh man . . . oh man . . ." he whispered.

"Oh God!" Kim corrected him. "This was God's doing."

Flame smiled, "True."

"Now are you ready to trust me?" Flame nodded. "Good. So now are you ready to do what I suggested?"

Flame sighed and shook his head. "I-I don't know about that, Kim. I'm not ready to get back in the studio yet. That music shit is what got me in this position in the first place."

"First of all, watch your language. Secondly, it wasn't the music that got you in this; it was YOU living up to your image that got you in this position," Kim reminded him. "What I'm talking about is a different kind of music, a way for you to give glory to God for bringing you back from all that you have gone through. This is a way for you to right your wrongs and bring the world closer to him."

Flame weighed her words. "I don't know, Kim. I'm not ready. I'm still broken."

"Joey, this is what your healing looks like. Think about it. Your two favorite loves are music and God. You get back to you by focusing on what you're passionate about. Plus, you can give God the glory and not yourself."

Flame had to admit that Kim had a point. In theory, what she spoke of made sense. Getting back in the studio would be a great way to exorcise his demons and keep his mind occupied off his misfortune—and give God the glory for saving his life.

"I don't know, Kim."

"I do! Just think about it?"

"Okay, I'll think about it . . ."

Chapter 8

The stripper anthem quaked the walls of the building as dollar bills rained to the floor like confetti. Kaleidoscopic lights zipped through the room like laser beams, tasing the crowd with vibes. The house was packed with hustlers and working men ready to drop their hard-earned cash on the dancers. The famous porn star Navaho was headlining the club for the night, and the whole city was buzzing about her appearance. This was her first appearance back in the Carolinas since she had gone on the lam with her paramour.

A tall, dark-skinned man sat at a table right in the center of the club. He could see everything, and everyone could see him too. He made sure of it. His dark, silky hair was snatched back in a ponytail away from his slender tattoo-filled face. A short diamond necklace dangled from his neck and a green rag hung from his brown khakis damn near down to his green Chuck Taylors. His eyes were fixated on the slim red-bone doing tricks on the pole. Each time she slid down the pole he threw bundles of cash at her and egged her on as if he were her personal fan club. He stood and walked to the edge of the stage to get a good look at her. A twenty-inch weave cascaded down her lithe back and glitter covered her skin like leopard prints. She was topless, showing her round C cups and Hershey Kiss–colored nipples. A black velvet G-string bisected beautiful, tattooed ass cheeks. She eyed the tall stranger seductively, and he returned the gaze.

The man gestured for her to come to the edge of the stage and show him some love. She slithered over like a human slinky, licking her lips like she was fiending to feast on him. She rolled over on her back and bust it wide open to the beat of the stripper anthem. He reached out to tuck a bundle of cash into her garter, and she moved his hand up toward her center. With her free hand, she slid her G-string to the side and showed him her beautiful monkey. He threw a gob of money right at her jewel and swigged his champagne.

Gangsta Black had just come home, and he was ready to party and put in work.

Miami, Florida

Bone and Maleek sat in the back of the Escalade as the executive limo pulled up to the gate of a mansion nestled behind lush shrubbery. The limo had met them at the airport and whisked them here for their meeting with El Jefe.

El Jefe had summoned Bone weeks ago, demanding a meeting as soon as he returned to the U.S. Then, this morning, he had instructed Bone to go to the airport and await additional details. When Bone arrived with Maleek in tow, a private jet was waiting for them. They boarded the jet and flew to Miami from Wilmington. Now they were here to discuss the details of their future.

The gates glided open, and the Escalade slid through and pulled around the circular driveway of a huge mansion. The driver helped them out of the truck and into the home. Once inside, another man, this one a Mexican, guided them down wide hallways with marble floors to a formal dining room. He settled them in the room, then left them alone.

"He will be with you guys shortly," he said.

Bone nodded, "Gracias, hermano," he said in perfect Spanish. He wasn't flexing, per se; he just wanted them to know that he spoke Spanish too—just in case they wanted to speak above their heads.

As they waited, Maleek stared around the room in awe. He estimated the dining room table had to be at least twenty feet long, and was made of wood so thick it was as if they had chopped down an oak tree and stuffed it inside the mansion. However, the wood top was shiny and cleaner than the floor. All around them, huge windows allowed them to see the beautiful ocean everywhere they turned. The sun was just beginning to set in the sky, gifting them with radiant hues of light cascading through the windows onto the gold and rose-colored furnishings in the room.

"Yooo, this shit is player," Maleek whispered. "This how I'm going to live one day."

Bone frowned a bit at his protégé. He suspected that they were being watched through the cameras, and he didn't want it to seem as if they were in an unfamiliar territory of wealth. They needed to act like they've been there before, even if they hadn't. Of course, that was easy for Bone to say, he was living like this. He owned multiple homes to his taste, and his mansion in Charlotte was just one. Granted, he didn't have ocean views, but uh yeah . . . everything else, he owned his share of it.

"Chill, bruh," Bone hissed. "Act like you been here before. Remember Law number thirty-six," he reminded him.

Bone was referring to Law #36 of the classic book the *48 Laws of Power.* Just as King Reece had done for them, Bone had drilled that book into Maleek Money's head. It was one of the bibles for the Crescent Crew. Law #36 stated to "Disdain the things you cannot have." In this case, Bone was telling Maleek Money to act like his name suggested and not be impressed by all the trappings of success surrounding them.

Maleek Money accepted his admonishment and piped down a bit, but he still admired El Jefe's lifestyle and wanted to live just like it. After all, that's the reason he became an outlaw, to live life enormous instead of dormant.

Bone checked the time on his Rolex and saw that it was almost time for salaat. "Aye, yo, I need you to watch my back while I perform Maghrib," he told Maleek. "Then I'll watch yours while you get yours in." Although, Bone was eye-deep in the crime life, he never missed one of his five obligatory salaats. He actually felt as if that was the secret to his longevity.

Bone dropped to the floor on his knees and patted the floor to gather dust on his hands. He clapped his hands together then washed them over his face. Then he repeated the same ritual over his arms, legs, and feet, finishing off with his head. The ritual was called *Tayammum*, a form of purification for prayer. Once he was done, he removed the long thobe he wore and placed it on the floor as a makeshift prayer rug. He faced what he knew as the East and began to perform his prayers.

Maleek Money stood directly behind Bone and watched his back as Bone chanted the Qur'an in his prayer. As soon as Bone kneeled over and prostrated on the floor, in walked El Jefe . . .

Gangsta Black was having a blast inside Bone's strip club. By now, he was joined by a few of his partners and they were all having a blast, showering the dancers with money and throwing back champagne.

The DJ announced that Navaho was about to take the stage, and Gangsta Black rushed to the front to get the best view in the house. Like most men inside prison, Gangsta

Black was mesmerized by the former porn star. She was a bonafide legend behind the wall. There wasn't a prison yard in America that didn't have her plastered all inside the lockers and taped to the walls. Her legend had grown even more when it was rumored she had hooked up with a regular street nigga and helped him go on the run from the authorities. This made her even more beloved, and Gangsta Black was planning to shoot his shot too.

The lights went low, and the DJ announced, "Coming to the stage . . . she isn't *a* hoe; she is Navaho!"

Men and women swarmed the stage to get a better look and Navaho didn't disappoint. She slid from behind the curtain wearing nothing but a red sheer bodysuit and a red thong. Her luxurious hair fell down her back and stopped just above her famous ass. Her makeup was flawless. Her skin glistened. Her toned body shined with oil and her thick thighs flexed when she walked. She stalked the stage like a panther on the prowl, giving the audience and her videographer the show of a lifetime.

Navaho sauntered right over to where Gangsta Black stood by the stage. She noticed him from behind the curtain before she came out. She saw that he was the big shit this night, and she was ready to separate him from his coins. Navaho stood directly in front of Gangsta Black, so close that her pussy was practically in his face. Like a cobra, her hand lashed out and gripped the back of his head. She paused a moment, then snatched his head forward right into her crotch and grinded her pussy all on his face.

Money rained on the stage like a tornado!

But Navaho wasn't done.

Seeing that she had a good sport, Navaho decided to pull Gangsta Black on the stage to be a part of her set. She led him to the chair in the middle of the stage and sat him down. While Gangsta Black got comfortable, Navaho entertained the other members of the crowd, traipsing around, collecting her funds. When her garter was good and stuffed, she returned to Gangsta Black.

Navaho danced around Gangsta Black, teasing him with her mounds of curvy flesh. She bent over in front of him, and her famous ass flared open, revealing a clean shot of her vagina. Her lips were so fat they were busting out the seams of her panties, and Gangsta Black could've sworn he saw creamy moisture. Navaho smacked her cheeks, and the sound echoed above the music as if a gun had been fired. Then she gently lowered herself onto Gangsta Black's lap.

That's when she felt it . . .

El Jefe froze when he saw Bone prostrating on the floor in his dining room. There wasn't a Mexican drug lord alive that wasn't superstitious or at least aware of the practice of summoning spirits to aid their criminal pursuits, and El Jefe was no different. Seeing Bone prostrating on his floor, he initially thought Bone may have been attempting to cast a spell. This made him uneasy. El Jefe slowly walked into the room to show respect until Bone completed his prayer. Once Bone stood, El Jefe greeted him.

"Hola, Jefe," El Jefe greeted.

Still feeling euphoric from the salaat, Bone returned the greeting with a smile. "Hola."

"May I ask, what was that you were doing?" El Jefe said.

"That was my prayer. As a Muslim, I am required to perform five obligatory prayers a day," Bone explained.

El Jefe clasped his chin. "Interesting . . ."

"Interesting?"

"Yes, I find it quite odd that someone who handles so much illegal activity is still such a religious man," El Jefe said. "But I guess the world is full of contradictions."

"There are no contradictions," Bone snapped. "The people who use the shit we sell are non-believers, so it's on them."

El Jefe took a seat at the head of the long table and extracted a long, thick cigar from the inside of his sport coat. "How can you be so sure they are non-believers?" he asked.

Bone shrugged. "Because no true Muslim would use this shit."

El Jefe caught that Bone was getting offended. "I don't mean any offense," he said. "Personally, I don't have a religion, and my wealth is my God. I was just curious as to how this works for you. However, I did not summon you here to discuss religion; we need to discuss politics. Take a seat."

Bone and Maleek took a seat at the long table.

"Aht, aht . . . not him," El Jefe said, pointing to Maleek Money. "Just you and I, like always. I remember him well, so of course I trust him, but this is our business."

On cue, a man entered the room and escorted Maleek Money away. The door closed, and El Jefe got right down to business.

"Jefe, last we spoke, I thought I made it clear that you weren't to cross certain relationships," El Jefe reminded Bone. "I've heard some things that have me very worried that you disobeyed my instructions."

Bone didn't know how to respond. For one, he took exception to the way El Jefe was talking to him, as if he were a peon. Secondly, if he wanted to maintain respect, he couldn't let it be known that Maleek Money had made the call to terminate Hulk without his approval. This would make it seem as if he didn't have control of his family.

"El Jefe, sometimes things aren't as they seem," Bone attempted to explain. "Out here, things aren't always black and white; they're shades of grey. The grey area is where things get murky."

"I don't like grey, except the grey inside the green! Now I gave you explicit instructions not to touch him."

"Hold up now, you don't instruct me to do shit. I'm not from Michoacán."

El Jefe shot to his feet, ran down the long table, and leaned right in Bone's face. "What did you say to me? You come into my home and disrespect me? After all that I have done for you?" El Jefe was breathing in his face so hard, spittle nearly clipped Bone's cheek. "You disrespect *me*?"

Bone bit his lip and piped down on his pride. "All due respect, El Jefe, I'm simply stating that you run your organization over there how you see fit, and I'll run mine how I see fit. These guys are a threat to our livelihood, and yours too actually. I was just trying to protect us all."

"So are you admitting that you defied my order?"

"I'm saying—"

"Careful . . ."

"I'm doing whatever I need to do for my family to survive these tumultuous times."

El Jefe eased back a bit. He stood and lit his long cigar, then paced the floor in silence.

While Jefe paced, Bone stared at his back with a sinking feeling in his gut. He replayed everything in his head, silently cursing himself for being so foolish. He thought back to the ride on the private jet and the Escalade limo that whisked them there. He now realized just how vulnerable he was—and stupid. El Jefe had been playing him all along. What Bone thought was a money flex was actually a power flex. The ride in the jet and limo was a way of ensuring Bone didn't come to the meeting packing heat. El Jefe had controlled all the options, and now Bone was at his mercy. If he decided to have his soldiers take him out, there was nothing he could've done except put up a regular fight against an army of guns. He thought of Maleek Money outside the room and wondered if they had already taken him out.

"You know," El Jefe said with his back to Bone. "The irony is that you are only in your position because Monstruoso put you there. You were supposed to be his stand-in until he is released. He's the reason why I have continued to supply your organization." He turned to face Bone and shrugged. "And now he is on his way home, and he wants his position back."

"How? Don't you see? He's sour! He's a snitch! How else would he be on his way home?" Bone ranted.

El Jefe shook his head in pity. "You have been good for business, but I told you that business is about relationships. He and I have a relationship that is above any money we have made together. I am a man of principle, and I must stand by that. I must give Monstruoso the benefit of the doubt until something changes."

Bone couldn't believe what he was hearing. Samson had flanked him and gotten the upper hand. He kept waiting to hear the report from the inevitable gunshot, for surely there could only be one king. There was no way he would allow him to walk away. For one, he knew too much. Two, he had to know he wouldn't take this sitting down.

"So what now? You kill us and then wait on Samson to get out to resume business? You're leaving all that money on the table?"

El Jefe blew ringlets of cigar smoke high into the air. "Kill you? I'm not going to kill you," he said. "At least not physically. However, I can no longer supply you your material."

"Wait a minute, now. I've been loyal and never shorted you a dime. That's got to count for something. I have a whole family that depend on me," Bone protested.

"Well, I have a country depending on me."

"Right, and you're going to let millions of dollars a month slip through your hands?"

"Not exactly," El Jefe smirked. "Perhaps you're not grasping the magnitude of what's going on."

As he said the words, it finally clicked for Bone. He realized what was happening. He had been double-crossed from inside. He was being squeezed out of the game. Neutered.

El Jefe said, "I already have your replacement . . ."

Gangsta Black gripped Navaho's ass as she sat on his lap. She squealed and tried to raise up, but he pulled her back down. In the blink of an eye, he wrapped his arm around her neck and whipped out his P-89 Ruger. He jammed it to her head and stood up beneath the lights.

"You know what it is!" Gangsta Black yelled, aiming his weapon around the room.

At first no one heard him, but it quickly registered that he was holding a weapon to her head. Then total pandemonium ensued as everyone scattered to make a break for it.

The two Mexican men that came in with Gangsta Black stood from their table and sprayed the room with automatic gunfire, aiming at the patrons as they attempted to escape. Bodies toppled over each other like bowling pins. As each body fell, the Mexican men stood over them and gave the final blows to their heads.

On stage, a crazed fan lunged at Gangsta Black before he could pull the trigger on Navaho. The move saved her life, but it cost him his own. Gangsta Black popped him in the chest twice and caught his first body on his second run at life. Seeing the body fall awakened the monster in him. He had violence on his mind and murder in his heart. He spun around looking for Navaho, but she was already gone.

Navaho had dashed to the dressing room to make her getaway. She recalled there was a back door that led directly to the parking lot where her Mercedes was parked. She stepped over fallen bodies of dancers and customers, leaned against the wall to hide, and dropped to the floor near the entrance of the dressing room. She crawled and kept her head low until she managed to cross into the dressing room.

She raised her head only high enough to locate the back door before tucking it and quickly crawling to the door. As soon as she made it to the metal door, it flung open. A gust of air rushed in and attacked her face, and she shielded her face from the wind. When she removed her arm from her eyes, she was staring at the top of a huge crocodile-skinned cowboy boot. Damn, she was caught.

Navaho's eyes slowly traveled up the man's boot, to his legs, to his waist, to his chest, to the . . . lights. *Damn, he is big!* That was her last thought before the boot crashed into her face and stole her consciousness.

Hulk stepped over Navaho and walked through the dressing room to the floor to survey the damage. What he saw made him smile. Bodies were strewn about the floor, and people ran around panicking. He spotted the other members of his team holding court, taking out security and partygoers. The sight warmed his heart. The carnage he was witnessing would guarantee the club would be shut down, which was their plan.

They were squeezing Bone from every angle, first taking away his supplier, and then shutting down his businesses around town. With no product to supply his gang, and no businesses to sustain his income, they estimated he would be broke in no time. Then his own team would turn on him. If he couldn't feed his wolves, they would put him on the menu and switch sides quicker than a broke man in a bank with a gun.

Hulk FaceTimed his brother and showed him the damage in real time . . .

Hundreds of miles away, Samson stared at the phone with a huge grin. He was using his brother and his new gang—defectors from the Mexican Mafia—to execute a hostile takeover of the Crescent Crew. Those who didn't get down would lay down. If all went according to plan, by the time he was released, the streets would be paved in gold for him. He had built the Crescent Crew along with King Reece—it was rightfully his, and he was reclaiming ownership of his band of brothers by pulling off a violent coup from behind bars. He was proving to be a deadly, contradictory foe, a murdering, gangster snitch. However, he didn't see it this way. The only thing he knew was that he would not lose.

Chapter 9

Qwess pushed the pawn to the other side of the board and smiled triumphantly. "Let me get that Queen back, brother," he said to Mahmoud.

"Ahh *astigfirallah!*" Mahmoud cried. "I didn't see that one."

"Unt unh, don't put Allah in this," Qwess joked. "You're getting this work."

They were in the critical fourth game of a five-game set, and Qwess had just taken the advantage by promoting a pawn to a Queen. This had become their norm, playing chess to past the time. Some days Qwess was the statue, some days he was the pigeon, but it was all in fun. He and Mahmoud actually bonded over the chess board, and he looked forward to their daily games that doubled as therapy sessions for him. He learned that Mahmoud was very knowledgeable about Islam and life in general. He approached life from a very basic standpoint, something that living the high life had taken away from Qwess. Qwess had been calling shots for so long he couldn't relate to life at the lower tier. He was off-balance, and that's where Mahmoud helped him. He helped

Qwess remember that the simple things in life were the most important things.

Qwess moved his newly crowned Queen into position to finish Mahmoud off. He looked at Mahmoud to tease him. This was the fun part, boxing your man in and knowing he was helpless. Mahmoud chortled a bit and it tickled Qwess. Qwess gripped the piece and slowly pushed it into position while eyeing Mahmoud the entire time.

Suddenly, something caught Qwess's attention on the TV over Mahmoud's shoulder. There was a breaking story on the news. The words at the bottom of the screen read, *"Crescent Crew War Claims 9 Lives."*

Qwess abandoned the chess board and walked to the TV to hear the full story. He wasn't the only one interested either. The whole room was watching the news while cutting glances at him. The brunette-haired reporter spoke:

> *"Gunfire erupted in a popular strip club last night, claiming nine lives and sending over twenty victims to the hospital with serious injuries. The club is owned by an alleged member of the notorious Crescent Crew crime organization. One of the organization's founders, legendary rapper and entertainment mogul Salim 'Qwess' Wahid, is awaiting trial on federal charges that could land him on Death Row. Sources say this latest shooting is directly related to that case.*
>
> *"Now if you remember, a few years ago, the group's other founder, Maurice Kirkson, better known as 'King Reece' was involved in a nasty scandal involving a disgraced FBI agent that rocked the bureau to its core. Kirkson and the former FBI agent were brutally murdered by a Mexican drug cartel . . ."*

Qwess couldn't bear to hear anymore. This was not good. Here he was battling for his freedom, and the streets appeared to be waging a war with his name all in it. He hadn't heard from Bone in months; he'd only heard about the thwarted attempt on Hulk's life. Even then, the details were sketchy. Now with the latest attack, he didn't even know if Bone was dead or alive. He didn't know if Bone was still on his side or if he was going renegade.

Qwess had too much on his own plate to digest. He sat back at the table with his mind befuddled and attempted to finish Mahmoud off. He believed he was always under federal scrutiny, so he couldn't allow them to see the latest news affecting him. But it did . . . tremendously.

"You *tayyib*, Akhi?" Mahmoud asked Qwess.

"*Inshallah*, I'll be okay," Qwess assured him. "Just a lot going on out there, and I'm trying to stay low."

Mahmoud nodded knowingly. "Ma'shallah," he said, which meant, *It is as God wills it to be.*

Qwess and Mahmoud resumed the game in silence, pushing pieces and grunting, both attempting to avoid the elephant in the room. Other inmates were milling around the chess board, ogling Qwess. The news had flashed a picture of Qwess during their report, and now all eyes were on him. Some of the inmates already knew who he was, and others didn't; they simply knew he was important. Now, after seeing him on TV, they knew they were among the world's elite.

"So, I'm not getting into your business, brother, but I must give counsel perchance it may profit the listener," Mahmoud said. "Years ago, when I was ensnared by these *kuffar*, my whole brotherhood turned against me. I had risen to the top of the world—I felt invincible! I had four wives—and switched them out every three years—homes in Dubai and Makkah, Lamborghinis, Ferraris . . . all of the things of this world. I thought that I was doing it the right way, for surely Allah rewards the believers, right? Well, as you know,

Allah will give us what we want for a time, and then he will give us what our deeds call for."

"Destruction," Qwess said.

"Exactly. My destruction was losing it all—family, money, respect, and faith."

Mahmoud had never shared any of his story with Qwess. For weeks, they played chess together and made small talk, all while building about Islam. Qwess didn't pry and Mahmoud didn't offer. It's just the way of prison. Now, it appeared Mahmoud was laying it all on the line and opening up to Qwess.

"But Allah is oft-forgiving, most merciful," Mahmoud recalled. "So I was given a second chance."

Qwess perked up. What was Mahmoud trying to tell him?

"Wait, did you beat your case and you're about to go home?" Qwess asked.

Maybe this is why the brother was opening up. Maybe he was preparing to leave. He hadn't heard any news of Mahmoud being released though. As important as Mahmoud was to the jail, Qwess would've heard something.

"No, brother, I'm talking about before this," Mahmoud clarified. "Fortunately, I was able to maintain my resources after I lost everything. I shifted my focus and made everything *fisabilallah* (in the cause of God). Once I shifted my focus, I persevered. I gained everything back and then I was sent here, but this is part of my new jihad. *Inshallah*, my reward is near."

Qwess nodded. "*Inshallah*."

"So, for you, young brother, you are going through your troubles right now because Allah is striving to get your attention. Once you shift the focus, and make your striving, *fisabilallah*, then things will change. And no matter how this turns out for you, *inshallah*, I will be there for you to help you in any way I can."

Mahmoud's offer of assistance held considerable weight to Qwess. He understood that in Islam, you wanted for your brother what you wanted for yourself, but in his experience, a lot of Arab Muslims weren't quick to extend that right to non-Arab Muslims. Qwess was humbled by the gesture yet apprehensive.

"I appreciate that, Ahki. I'll keep that in mind," Qwess replied.

They finished the game and played one more to finish the set. On this day, Qwess was the statue.

After the game, Qwess retreated to his cell to reflect on everything. He had to save face on the rock and appear unaffected, but inside, he was a ball of nerves. This latest incident could not be good for his case. His name being attached to violence in the streets while fighting to get a bond in a murder case was akin to climbing up Mount Everest with a boulder strapped to your back. Qwess still couldn't believe his life had come to this. He had done all the right things. Chose his career over the game. Tried to get his team out the streets. Helped his community. Married well. Brought his father home from prison. Remained true to the game, through and through. Yet *he* was facing the needle. It just didn't make sense to him, in reality or from a spiritual side. Surely life couldn't be that cruel.

He thought about what Mahmoud had shared with him, his story. He juxtaposed Mahmoud's story against his own life. Had he made his decisions, *fisabilallah*? Did he leave the streets and give back to his community for the cause of Allah, or did he do it to be recognized? Was his intent righteous or was he putting on for the world? He had been so consumed with life and attaining the things of this world that his *deen* had taken a backseat. Now he had been humbled to his knees on a humbug. As his father always preached, Islam comes after everything else has failed.

Qwess walked over to the sink inside the cell and performed *wudu*. He planned to offer two units of prayer. He knew the answers to his problems were within. *Why was he here? What was the lesson he was supposed to learn? What was Allah trying to tell him?* Qwess knew the answers were inside his prayers.

Qwess offered his prayers in long chants with perfect enunciation of the Arabic. When the Arabic was rolling off his tongue fluently, it felt as if his prayers penetrated his soul deeper. He concentrated deeply, rolling his *R*s and holding the vowel sounds out for extended seconds. He burrowed into his groove, and he wasn't even in jail anymore; he was in *Jannah*, seeking the pleasure of his Lord.

Qwess finished his prayers fifteen minutes later, but he remained sitting on his prayer rug in deep contemplation. Suddenly he heard keys jangling outside his door. He looked up just as the guard tossed pieces of mail on the bed. He was eagerly anticipating a letter from his wife to bring him up to speed on his business dealings, so he abandoned the floor and rifled through the stack of mail. He saw a few pieces of mail from Lisa, but there was another piece of mail he didn't recognize. He knew it wasn't fan mail because he hadn't had time to update his address to the world. The envelope was missing a name, but it was stamped from Houston, Texas. Qwess thumbed the envelope, and it felt as if pictures were inside too.

Qwess opened the letter and, sure enough, photos tumbled onto the floor. He picked the photos up one by one and saw various images of the same person: a little girl who looked to be about nine years old. She was a beautiful tone of brown sugar with long, wavy hair and hazel-colored, almond-shaped eyes. In one of the photos, the little girl was on a stage singing her little heart out. Qwess had no clue who she was. He turned one of the photos over and read the words on the back: *Aminah Beaufont.*

Qwess had never heard the name before, but he was about to learn all about Aminah.

Flame sat behind the mic in his wheelchair, staring at the phone in his hand. On the screen were the lyrics to a song he had written just this morning. He had been sitting in the same spot in his home recording studio for over an hour with the headphones smashed on his head.

It felt weird to be back in the studio, foreign even. This was his first time near a mic since getting powerbombed to Hades, and a well of emotions flooded him. Guilt. Shame. Fear.

During his career, he had breached the upper echelons of society with just his mouthpiece. Not bad for a ghetto kid. All he needed was one mic to become somebody, one mic to broadcast his struggles to the world. Before, it had been second nature; he could craft a hit in an hour with a pen and a pad. Now, he couldn't muster the courage to utter a word into the mic. He was traumatized and paralyzed with fear. Terrified of the unknown. What if he had lost his mojo? Contrary to popular belief, music wasn't like riding a bike. If you didn't use it, you lost it.

Or did you?

Flame heard sound inside the headphones. "Come on, Joey, you got this!" It was Kim, encouraging him as always.

"Stop thinking and just DO this. God got you," she coached.

Kim pushed a button on the control board and pushed the music through Flame's headphones. He closed his eyes and memorized the first lines of the song. He allowed the beat to seep into his soul and permeate through his pores. He dug down deep and rode the beat:

> *"When I was down on my knees, you taught me how to walk again/ Poured your grace on me, and blessed me with a best friend/ Acting like a heathen, instead of a thespian/ but you still didn't leave me alone—Amen!"*

His cadence was slow and articulate, strong and deliberate, his words part rap, part singing—the perfect mix of his skill set. He was feeling himself and began freestyling the rest of the track.

> *"I did it my way and see how that turned out/ Left for dead on the asphalt and clawed my way out/ Flat on my back, legs numb, asking God why/ Then a voice inside told me look to the sky/ There I saw an angel in the form of a girl/ She came into my life and changed my world / She dried my tears when I cried, introduced me to the Most High/ Taught me how to pray and that's where power reside/ Now I'm a better man, with better plans, a veteran/ But nothing without the grace of God in my hand!"*

Flame spit the last line and had to gather himself. Chills zipped down his spine with each line. He felt the words sizzling in his spirit. The content was fresh for him, *and* it was a freestyle, so it was birthed from his heart. Gone were the freaky lyrics about licking women in their crevices, replaced with lyrics praising God. He didn't expect this to come out. He just rode the beat and let it flow.

The beat finally stopped and silence echoed in his ears. Then he heard Kim's voice.

"OH MY GOD! That was brilliant. I knew you could do it."

Flame was speechless. If he hadn't heard the words he wouldn't have believed that he'd done it himself. Feelings of euphoria covered him. He had *that* feeling again, the joy that recording music gave him in the beginning. The unparalleled thrill of being in the zone. What LeBron James felt on the court, he used to feel in the booth. Now it was back. He had just recorded a verse for the first time in his new lease on life and it felt better than old times.

Chapter 10

Maleek Money drove down Carolina Beach Road in his Range Rover Autobiography edition. Keisha rode shotgun and one of his lil soldiers rode in the back. He was headed to Buffalo Wild Wings to watch the game and devour garlic parmesan wings and street tacos. It was their weekly tradition, a request of Keisha's.

Being a small-town girl, Keisha enjoyed the simple pleasures of life. For her, Buffalo Wild Wings in Wilmington, North Carolina, was akin to Pappadeux in Atlanta. She grew up in the projects and could recall when, as a child, they didn't have enough money to buy separate meals. She vividly recalled how other patrons gawked at them as they shared small chicken wing meals. Now, rolling with Maleek Money, Keisha could afford to buy her whole project chicken, and this weekly tradition was a small conquest for her.

Maleek Money bust a left onto College Road, and Keisha gripped his thigh. "You okay, babe?" she asked.

Maleek Money nodded. "I'm good, thickness. Just a lot on my mind." He didn't know how to explain to her that unless they found a plug quick, their beautiful lifestyle would be coming to an abrupt halt.

"Well, babe, what is there to worry about? We're young, black millionaires," she half-joked.

"Hell yeah," Skull added from the backseat.

"This type of money fixes everything. Remember you told me that?" Keisha reminded Maleek Money. She was young and naïve and thought that money could quell all woes. If spent in the right manner, it possibly could. But Maleek Money wouldn't have lived up to his name if he was smart with money.

"Damn right, this money fixes everything," Maleek Money affirmed. He was still all the way up by around 1.5 million, but he was in full flex mode, stunting for the Port City so his funds dwindled fast like the sand in an hourglass. He couldn't let them see any chinks in his armor. If they did, they may not have respected him the same.

Maleek Money coasted down College Road, one of the main strips in his adopted city, checking out the sites. Compared to Fayetteville, Wilmington was like a different state all together. Fayetteville's vibe was Black and more inclusive, due to the military base playing a major part in the city. Wilmington, on the other hand, was more old, White money. The older guard of the city might have racist tendencies, but their children were all about giving the brothers reparations in the form of sex. White women in Wilmington loved Black men! They especially adored rich, flashy men like Maleek Money. He had a few college co-eds he was knocking down in his spare time that attended the local college, and they were treating him like royalty. They didn't ask much of him, and he didn't give them anything except his hard wood.

Maleek Money stopped at a red light at the intersection of College Road and New Center Drive. A grey GMC Yukon pulled up beside him on his left. The window on the truck was pulled halfway down and ranchero music poured from the vehicle into the night air. Maleek Money could see the passenger staring at his Rover, trying to peer through the dark tint. Maleek Money slid his Sig Sauer pistol from beneath his thigh, ready for some action. He didn't know if they were simply admiring his hundred-thousand-dollar vehicle or bringing him a move.

Suddenly the passenger window glided down, revealing a swarthy faced, slick-haired man.

The man stared through the dark window.

Maleek Money flipped off the safety latch.

The man raised his right hand slowly.

Maleek Money raised his left hand with the pistol in it.

The man placed his hand on top of the windowsill and gave Maleek Money a thumbs up.

Maleek Money breathed a sigh of relief. He was just a fan.

"Damn, that Yukon was bumping," Skull said. "You see that shit?"

"Yeah, I saw it. Did you?" Maleek Money asked, frustrated that Skull wasn't even on point. He should've been the one ready to dump if things went South.

"Yeah, them Mexicans living like Black folk," Skull said. "They copying our whole style and putting their *mira* twist on it."

Maleek Money laughed and whipped the Range into the Buffalo Wild Wings parking lot. He backed the truck into a parking spot in the front and gathered his things from the center console. He looked up and saw the same grey Yukon slide in front of them. He recognized what was happening a split second before it happened.

"Get down!" Maleek Money roared.

He reached over and shielded Keisha as automatic gunfire peppered the windshield.

Pop! Pop! Pop! Pop! Pop! Pop!

Keisha screamed and covered her ears from the thunderous reports echoing through the air. Bullets tore into the leather seats just beside their heads, and Maleek Money pushed them further down into the seats just as another shell tore into the headrest.

Skull managed to return fire from the backseat, and the shots deafened the confines of the car. He leaned forward and bust his .45 straight through the windshield. Shards of glass flew everywhere. His return was enough to momentarily pause the shooting from the Yukon, and Skull used the opportunity to get on the offensive. He hopped out and ran up on the Yukon to finish the job.

With the action stalled, Maleek Money peeked up from his position to see if the coast was clear and prepare their escape. As soon as he peeked over the dashboard, he saw Skull's head explode like a melon. His dead body crumpled to the ground mercilessly.

"Nooooooo!" Maleek Money roared. He unloaded his whole clip through the windshield recklessly. However, luck was on his side this day. A lucky shot caught the passenger of the Yukon and his head fell forward and clunked the dash. A split-second letter, the driver skidded off into the night.

After the coast was clear, Maleek Money slowly pulled himself out of the floor on the passenger side. He reached down to pull Keisha up.

That's when he saw the blood inside her blond hair.

Bone opened the heavy gate and walked onto the grounds. He hadn't come in a while, and judging by the disrepair of the property, no one else had come in a while either. When the Crescent Crew were at their height, everyone flocked to King Reece's grounds to pay their respects. However, as the old saying goes, out of sight out of mind. The King had been out of sight for a while, and Bone had filled his shoes lovely, putting on for the city and keeping the spectacle of the Crescent Crew alive. In the streets everything flipped over, so when people saw Bone repping the Crew they tended to forget about the founders. But that was never Bone's way. He was loyal to the death and beyond. He understood that if it wasn't for King Reece he wouldn't be in the position he was in. If for not King Reece setting the tone, then Bone wouldn't have gone to bed as the richest nigga in the city.

When things were going rough for Bone, he came here to bow before his King. Each time before, when he prostrated on these hallowed grounds, it was if he could HEAR King Reece speaking to him. When Bone heeded the words, he flourished. So in theory, it was as if King Reece was guiding Bone from beyond the grave. Bone hoped that King Reece would show up this time as well, because he definitely needed some guidance.

Bone bowed down on the hallowed ground, breathed deeply, and focused. Just like the other times, the voice of King Reece echoed in his ear as if the trap Lord was right there in front of him:

> *"You let them play you out of pocket, lil homie, but don't worry about it; with every difficulty there is relief, and your relief is closer than you think,"* he said. *"Remember those are the niggas that killed me off. Don't ever forget that! They tried to kill you and our legacy off so you got to go even harder now. Hold onto your bread and wait for the relief to come. Then, ride on them niggas!"*

Just as the words riled Bone up, the connection disappeared. He attempted to regain the connection, but was unsuccessful. Just as quickly as the voice had come, it disappeared, but it was enough for Bone. The God had spoken, and Bone felt better about things, despite the hurdles he had been running into lately.

After returning from Miami, Bone reached out to a few

distributors he had befriended throughout the years, guys who had their own international suppliers, but he came up empty there as well. There was a startup crew making noise in Atlanta called the SKG whom Bone was familiar with, but their light was quickly extinguished when they banded with a crew of violent Africans. Needless to say, money and violence don't mix, and they found that out the hard way. So they were out of the picture as well. Bone hadn't realized just how far up the ladder the Crescent Crew had climbed. He was so busy building and maintaining the kingdom, he hadn't realized how expansive it had grown. When things were good, that was a great thing—it felt good to be king. However, under current circumstances, being the head of the kingdom was bad; there was no one that could supply their needs. However, the God King Reece said relief was right around the corner, so Bone believed it.

Bone stood and returned to his G-Wagon truck. He climbed inside and settled on the plush red leather interior where he collected his thoughts. Worst case scenario, he had enough money to go to Dubai and live a great life with all his millions. Maybe he could find a wife or two—or three—and live his best Islamic life in opulence. He could decompress and really leave this life behind. He held a lot of reservations about the life he lived . . . the murders, the drugs, and poisoning his community. It all went contrary to Islam. For so long, he had denied the truth while still praying to be guided to the straight path. Maybe sparing his life and removing his plug was Allah's way of guiding him to the straight path? Surely he could've died in Miami. Yet his life was spared, along with his riches. Bone was the man he always wanted to become. Should he just walk off into the sunset now?

Bone's phone shrilled to life through the screen. A picture of Maleek Money flashed on the screen. Bone sighed and answered the call.

"As-salamu alaykum!" Bone greeted.

"They shot her, Akhi! They wet her up!" Maleek Money screamed. "I'ma murder these niggas bro!"

"Wait! Calm down. They shot who?"

"Keisha man! They shot my wifey," Maleek Money replied and broke down in sobs. "They followed me and set us up. And they killed Skull."

"Where are you?"

"I'm in the Port."

"All right, reinforcements on the way."

Bone ended the call with a sigh. This was his dilemma. He could roll off into the sunset and disappear, but what kind of boss would he be to leave his crew? He glimpsed the tattoo circling his forearm. It read: *Death Before Dishonor.* These words were more than a statement; they were a lifestyle, and he swore an oath to rep them till his death.

Apparently, El Jefe had done more than just cut them off. It appeared he had declared war on the Crescent Crew, and Bone was ready to make his namesake.

Chapter 11

Qwess hadn't been able to think about anything since he received the letter a couple weeks ago.

A daughter. He had a daughter.

The statement didn't even sound right passing his lips. Yet he'd read the letter no less than a hundred times and looked at the pics twice as many times. The little girl bore an uncanny resemblance to him. That fact was undeniable. And he'd definitely had a dalliance with Sasha, but this could all be some type of farce. After all, the letter came from a bogus sender.

Qwess rolled from his bunk and peered through the thin glass out onto the tier. The usual happenings were going on, but things seemed different for him now. Everything changed for him the day he received the letter. He hadn't played chess or even cut laps around the dorm like he usually did. All his time was spent trying to put the pieces together. The letter was simple. Two lines: *Say hello to your daughter. Aminah Beaufont.* However, it might as well have been the length of a novel.

The letter left so many questions lingering in Qwess's head.

Who sent the letter? Did Diamond know? Was this the basis of his and Diamond's beef? Where was Sasha? Did she send the letter? What would he tell his wife?

For days, Qwess eagerly awaited a follow-up letter, something to give him more information, but it never came. So he was simply left with his thoughts—the deadliest thing an incarcerated man can have.

Qwess spotted Mahmoud on the tier. He was cutting laps around the dorm with his hands clasped behind his back. His chin was stuck to his chest, and he appeared to be mumbling. Qwess thought this was odd. Mahmoud usually strutted around as proud as a peacock, not in arrogance but confidence. He had carte blanche in the jail, so he had no worries while he awaited trial. Qwess concluded his brother was stressed, and a brother in need is a brother indeed.

Qwess stepped out onto the tier and joined Mahmoud as he cut laps.

"As-salamu alaykum, good brother," Qwess said, interrupting Mahmoud's routine. "You look like you have a lot on your mind. You good?"

Mahmoud sighed, "Ah, Ahki, you know how this thing goes. Sometimes you're good and other times, not so much." He shrugged.

Qwess was still lost, but he knew something was wrong. So he pressed further. "You know you can talk to me about anything, right?"

Mahmoud glanced at him and smiled. "What if I told you my friend and brother was leaving me soon?"

Again, Qwess was confused. He took a stab at it. "Your brother is sick and dying?"

Mahmoud shook his head and chuckled. "No, actually he is getting a second chance at life," he replied cryptically.

This time the confusion was evident on Qwess's face.

Mahmoud stopped walking and faced Qwess. He placed his hands on his shoulders and bore his gaze into him. "I'm talking about you, Akhi," Mahmoud said. "You're going home today."

Surely Qwess's hearing was playing tricks on him. "What you say?"

"I said, you're going home today. You made bail."

"Ahki, what are you talking about?"

Mahmoud beamed a smile at him. "Allah has granted you mercy, brother. Surely, Allah is the most gracious, most merciful."

Qwess couldn't believe what he was hearing! He had been granted bail? Of course, he knew how Mahmoud knew of the information before him; he was an Oracle—he knew everything inside the walls.

"When?" Qwess wondered, nearly unable to contain his excitement.

Mahmoud glanced toward the sally port. "Should be any minute now," he said.

Qwess sighed with relief. Shabazz had done it. He had worked his magic and was bringing Qwess home. With his life in shambles, Qwess was beginning to wonder if his powerful attorney had lost his mojo.

Mahmoud and Qwess resumed their walk around the dorm.

"Brother, there is a storm brewing out there for you," Mahmoud warned. "Everything you knew about your life before coming in here has changed. As you fight this case, your money will be funny, your resources will be stretched thin, and most importantly, your reputation is under attack. There is a small chance you may have to go back to what you are familiar with." Mahmoud paused to let his words sink in. "Two-one-five, three-two-three, nine-seven-six-five. Memorize that number. If you are ever in need—with anything—call that number and allow me to help you. Don't

let these *kuffar* define you, don't let them make you fail by
shaming you. You have to live life on your terms. Understand?"

There were a thousand thoughts racing through Qwess's
mind. He had been inside for nearly a year. He was going
broke. His wife had been holding things down, but he
couldn't draw blood from a cactus. He couldn't fathom what
his life would be like outside these walls, but he could guarantee one thing: he would not lose.

"I understand, Akhi," Qwess replied.

Mahmoud pointed at the door to the dorm. "Here they
come. Get ready for your new life."

Qwess saw two officers coming in the dorm. With them
was a familiar face that Qwess had no desire to see or speak
to. It was Agent Roberts from the Hip-Hop police, the same
man who had tried to flip him in New York. Now here he
was in North Carolina on the day he was getting released.

"Qwess!" The officer working the unit called out. "Bag
your baggage!"

Qwess returned to his cell to gather the things he had ac-
cumulated while inside. He quickly rummaged through the
food and toiletries and tossed it into a pile in the middle of
the floor. He corralled all of his legal documents and tossed
them inside the legal box. Just as he slid the lid on the box,
he felt someone enter the cell. He didn't even have to turn
around to know who it was.

"Congratulations on your freedom, Superstar," Agent
Roberts said. "Niggas always find a way to get out of some
shit, yo," he mumbled.

The energy was all off. Qwess peeked over his shoulder
to get a good look at him. Agent Roberts was dressed like a
music mogul. He wore a two-piece charcoal grey suit and a
cream V-neck sweater. An Audemar Piguet dripping in diamonds adorned his wrist, and an iced-out Cuban link dan-

gled from his thick neck. His bushy beard was so long that it covered part of the chain.

Qwess stood and turned to greet him. "Agent Roberts, how's it going?"

Agent Roberts walked into the cell and pushed the door closed. "You know, your boy Diamond is back in the States roaming free. After what he did to your lil man . . . after what he did to THE Sasha Beaufont . . . after all the drugs he sold and people he killed . . . he's roaming around like it's all sweet."

As soon as he mentioned Diamond's name, he had Qwess's attention. However, Qwess knew he hadn't made the trek to the Dirty South to brief him on Diamond's whereabouts. So he remained quiet and let the Fed speak.

"Then, you, here you have been sitting here in this damn cell refusing to tell anything about this fucker. You supposed to be this man of the people, a guy who is a leader in the community and shit, but you steady protecting this nigga. You wrong, dead wrong, don't stand for shit. Yet you about to get out of here to a fucking parade probably." Agent Roberts shook his head. "Sometimes I hate my job."

Qwess smirked and began gathering the rest of his things. "You know, it baffles me how brothers like yourself work for the same system that has been killing us for years," Qwess said. He closed the lid on his legal box and walked right in the face of the agent. "Then you the worst kind of brother too, because you planted yourself inside the industry that was the only way out for some of us. You laying in wait like a snake on the path of the righteous, waiting to trap your brother off while he enjoying the best time of his life. You passing yourself off as one of the members of the culture. All the while, you a culture vulture."

"You may think I'm one of them, but I'm one of us. I even came all the way here to help you," Agent Roberts claimed.

"Bullshit!"

Agent Roberts shrugged his shoulders. "I came to warn you, but you don't want to play ball."

"Look man, we don't talk to police; if you been studying me long enough then you know that. Now, if you'll excuse me, I have to get back to the world." Qwess scooped his legal box and brushed past him.

Agent Robert placed a palm on Qwess's shoulder. "Maybe you can finally meet your daughter," he said.

Qwess froze. "What did you say?"

"I'm talking about Aminah. Your daughter from Sasha?"

Qwess narrowed his eyes. "What do you know about that?"

"I know everything about that. Who do you think sent the letters to you with the pics?"

"Wait, that was you?"

"You asking the wrong question. The question is how did I get the pics and info?"

His words struck Qwess. He couldn't even hide his surprise.

Agent Roberts nodded. "Exactly."

Qwess was done with the games. The world was waiting on him. "I see you have a few aces up your sleeve," he said. "You gonna spill the beans or do I have to find out on my own?"

Agent Roberts smiled and shrugged. "You not gonna play in my game, I'm not gonna play in yours. Just be careful out there."

"Anything else would be uncivilized."

Qwess walked out of the cell, ready to be a free man. His heart was heavy, his mind was overflowing. He had beaten the odds repeatedly, and he planned to do the same this time. He had to—his life was on the line.

Chapter 12

Bone sat behind his desk inside his office at his funeral home counting money. This was the only place he felt safe now. His enemies were on the offensive, attacking all of his legit businesses, effectively putting him on the run. He had become a prisoner in his own city, a city where he had kept the streetlights on. So far, two of his businesses had been ransacked and shut down, and a war was raging on the streets between the Crescent Crew and their unknown rivals.

In Fayetteville and Wilmington, they were being hit the hardest, being attacked on all sides by unknown enemies. The attacks had one thing in common; they were all calculated.

Bone realized this war had been planned since he and Maleek Money first flew to Miami. El Jefe had used their absence to move his people in place. The shot heard around the world had been when Maleek Money was ambushed, and Keisha had been shot just a few days prior.

Fortunately, Keisha survived the ambush. She had been hit in the shoulder, and a hot round grazed the side of her face. She earned a new crease on the side of her scalp, and she was traumatized a bit, but she was alive. After checking her out of the hospital, Maleek Money hid her away in the boonies until the smoke cleared.

Then the Crescent Crew went on the offensive.

Bone gathered his gang together and issued an edict. If they weren't Crew, they were food. Anybody in the Carolinas that weren't down with them were getting laid down. He also added a caveat to their mission: take the money and drugs along with their lives. The request was odd and thus signaled a turning point for them. In the past the Crescent Crew weren't concerned about money or work from anyone outside their gang. Such were the perks of being the plug. Now, with the tides shifting and their drugs running low without a definite supplier, Bone figured they would kill two birds with one stone on their attacks. Take out the competition and replenish their stash. He figured if the Crew couldn't get any woman, neither could anyone else.

Bone wrapped a rubber band around a stack of money and placed it with the other stacks piled high on the table. This was the weekly take from the Crew, money scooped up off the streets of the Southeast. Despite their current uncertainty, the Crescent Crew were still strong and the hundreds of thousands of dollars on the table confirmed it.

Bone shuffled another pile of money, straightened the bills, and fed them through the golden money counter. The wind from the bills whipping through the machine was money to his ears. He closed his eyes and let it sing as it tallied up the count. The sounds of Jay Electronica serenaded him into his comfort zone.

Suddenly the buzzer to the back door came to life. Bone's eyes snapped open and zoomed to the huge television on the wall. On the screen, he saw a black SUV backing up to the door. The back door to the funeral home swung open, and a tall figure stepped out the SUV wearing all black. The back hatch to the SUV opened, and the man reached in and slid two bodies out. He quickly dragged the bodies inside, and the SUV drove off into the night.

Bone grabbed the gold-plated AK-47 leaning against his desk and trotted downstairs to the crematory. He made it just as Rasul was dragging the last body into the room.

"Who is this?" Bone asked.

Rasul shrugged, "I don't know. The nigga a Mexican, and he was on that side of town, so he food. He had a few bags of *boy* on him that told us he knew something," he explained.

Bone examined the man closely. Upon closer inspection, he saw that he was still breathing. "Hold up bruh, this one still alive," he noted.

"Yeah, we knocked the first one off, but kept him alive so we can interrogate him. We need to know what he know so we can plan our attack on them and get back to the money."

Bone patted Rasul on the back. "Good thinking," he said.

Bone was ready to get to the bottom of things as well. War was bad for business. He pointed to the dead body. "Put him over by the furnace so we can slide him in and wait on this one to wake up."

While Rasul slid the dead body over, Bone prepped the retort for the cremation. He wasn't wasting any boxes or materials on this job. He was sliding him in raw dog. He preheated the chamber and waited for Rasul to bring the body.

"Aye, dude waking up!" Rasul yelled, looking back at the other man as he passed the first body off to Bone.

"Good. He's just in time," Bone said. "Cuff him with those handcuffs over there, and put the chains on his feet, then drag him over here."

Bone hoisted the dead body onto the slab of metal at the opening of the retort and watched the flames flickering awaiting their meal. He pushed the body toward the opening and paused.

"He up yet?" Bone asked.

"Almost."

"Damn, what did y'all do to him?" Bone chuckled.

"Clunked him over the head a couple times til he stopped resisting."

"Ohhh, you gave him the police treatment. Gotcha."

Suddenly, the man groaned and shook the stupor from his head. He moaned a bit and Rasul was right on him.

"Wake up, motherfucker!" Rasul barked. He slapped him in the mouth and the man came to life sputtering.

"*¿Qué pasa? ¿Qué quieres?*"

Rasul looked to Bone for answers. "What he say?"

"Don't worry about it. He'll see what we want soon enough. Stand him up so he can see this shit."

Once Bone saw that the man could see him clearly, he went into action with his performance. He walked over to the weak man and smacked him.

"I'm going to ask you one time," Bone said. "Who is sending these hits? Is it El Jefe?"

The man sputtered, "*No se tú dices! No hablo Ingles!*"

Bone smacked him again out of frustration. "*¿Quien es su caudillo? Digame!*"

Surprise registered in the eyes of the man. He didn't expect Bone to speak Spanish. He raised his eyebrows and doubled down, "*Yo no sé!*"

Bone wrapped his hand around the man's neck and dragged him to the slab of metal in front of the retort.

"*Mira!*" Bone barked. "*Tú eres proximo!*"

Bone slowly rolled the dead body into the furnace feet-first. The flames quickly incinerated the dusty boots and sank into his flesh. The stench quickly claimed the room, and the man quivered in fear. Bone issued him a dead stare while continuing to push the body inside the furnace. The more he pushed inside the furnace, the stronger the stench became. As the scent grew stronger, the other man became more and more uncomfortable. He began to whimper as his comrade's body disintegrated beneath the flames.

"Nah, don't cry now," Rasul said.

"*Tú eres proximo*," Bone assured him as he pushed the remainder of the body into the fire.

Sure enough, once the first man's body was incinerated to bones, Bone prepared to hoist the other man onto the slab. The man's feet didn't hit the metal before he started doing his best rendition of a *ranchera* artist, singing everything he knew.

"*No sé por seguro! El llamado, El Negro. Y no sé más!*" He screamed.

"What he say?" Rasul asked.

"He say something about someone called Black."

The man continued to blurt out info that seemed to be useless to them. Lots of info about a guy named Black and orders from the Mexican Mafia. It all sounded like gibberish to Bone and Rasul. His story wasn't adding up, so Bone and Rasul pushed him toward the furnace.

"*Espérate! Yo no sé no más! Por favor! Es la verdad.*"

The man continued to plead his case, but it fell on deaf ears. They pushed him to the brink of the fire then stopped.

"*¿Donde está la trabajo?*" Bone asked.

"*¿Qué trabajo?*"

Bone pushed his feet into the fire. Flames wrapped around his heel and he lost it.

"Okay, okay, I will tell you everything! His name is Black—Gangsta Black. He works for Monstruoso. He is his *carnal*, and calling shots from prison. La *Eme* and the Blacks have joined forces to eliminate your organization. Then they will take over your territory."

"Would you look at this; motherfucker speak English better than me," Rasul joked.

"Yeah, maybe he can speak it better in Jannah."

Satisfied that he had gleaned all he could from the man, Bone pushed his whole body into the furnace. As soon as the fire touched his body, he shrieked in pain. Bone and Rasul were oblivious to his cries. This wasn't their first rodeo. They had thrown more men in furnaces than Hitler. This was Crew business, and judging by what they just heard, business was about to get turned up.

Maleek Money pulled the sheets back on the bed and offered Keisha a sip of the tea. She pulled the sheets back up to her chest and winced.

"You cold, baby?" Maleek Money asked.

Keisha nodded. "Yeah, and these drugs got me all groggy."

Maleek Money gingerly touched the bandage on the side of her face. Keisha winced. "Ouch."

Beneath the bandage was a scar that was nearly three inches long from where the bullet creased her face.

"I know it hurts babe, but we gonna get that taken care of as soon as you heal. Gonna take you to the best plastic surgeon in the world!" Maleek Money promised.

Keisha pushed the tea aside and clasped her hands over her face. "I just keep seeing Skull's head explode and feeling my face catch on fire," she said. She attempted to shake off the memory.

"Don't worry about it, babe. We got them suckas back before Skull was buried. And they will never hurt you again. I kinda took your security for granted before, but never again. Never again, babe." Maleek Money cradled her head into his chest and pecked her on her sweaty forehead.

Maleek Money meant every word of his promise too. He had checked Keisha out of New Hanover Regional Medical Center and whisked her three hours away to his high-rise in Charlotte, North Carolina. The Queen's Quarter was a luxurious condo located in the heart of the city that overlooked

Bank of America stadium. It was the first piece of property Maleek Money purchased when he started getting some real paper. He used the condo to hide money and stash drugs. On occasion when he was getting his lothario on, he smashed a few of the Queen City's gold diggers there too. The building was secluded and secure, complete with a doorman and security codes required to enter. His neighbors were pro ball players, bankers, and some of the wealthiest businessmen in the city—and their mistresses. This was the last place anyone would look for a street captain of the Crescent Crew to reside. This is why it was the perfect duck-off for Keisha to recuperate.

"I'm just blessed to be alive," Keisha acknowledged.

Maleek Money pulled the covers back off her voluptuous body and smiled at Keisha. "Everything about you is blessed. Look at you."

Keisha blushed. "Stop, Maleek, you just saying that. I look hideous."

"Nah, my love, you can never be that. Get up out this bed and get your blood flowing a bit."

Maleek Money eased Keisha out of bed and walked her to the glass wall overlooking the city. He pointed to the skyline. "We on top of the world, Keisha. We beyond blessed, and nothing is going to change that. Them niggas got off on that one, but they awoke a sleeping giant. Them streets gon' rain blood for what they did to you."

Keisha sighed, "Baby, can we go without all this violence? I just want to look good, eat good, and live the good life."

Maleek Money stood behind Keisha and wrapped his arms around her waist. "Baby, we gotta die to go to heaven. The price of this life is bloodshed," Maleek Money advised her. "Don't worry though, we got something for that ass."

Maleek Money was speaking to Keisha, but the pep talk was actually for himself. The botched hit had shaken him up a bit. He was definitely with all the smoke; he had killed enough to validate his status in the game. However, it was a different story when the target was on his head, and he was being hunted. Truth be told, Maleek Money was scared shit-less. What part of the game was this? He had gone from being a capo in one of the livest gangs in the city to being on the verge of having no dope to sell and a price on his head. Maleek Money was trained to go, but even the toughest men harbored doubts from time to time.

Maleek Money guided Keisha to the plush couch and sat her down in front of the huge TV.

"Let's Netflix and chill," Maleek Money suggested.

As soon as they settled in front of the TV a special bul-letin popped up on CNN. It was a live broadcast from the detention center in Fayetteville, North Carolina. The ticker tape on the bottom read: *"Rap Mogul Accused of Murder Re-leased on $2 Million Bail."*

"Oh shit! That's my big homie! Turn that up."

Maleek Money blasted the volume just as the camera panned on Qwess leaving the building, walking with his high-powered attorney. They walked straight to a podium, and the attorney began speaking while Qwess stood beside him in silence with that prison glow.

"Today is the first step in a long journey for justice," Malik Shabazz announced as if he had won a trial already. "For nearly a year, this man's life has been on hold because of these aspersions. Now, because of the mercy of this court, we can now return him home to his family and the commu-nity he so proudly serves."

Questions bombarded the fancy attorney while Qwess appeared stoic at his side in his tailored suit.

"Do you expect him to be formally charged in the mur-der of Sasha Beaufont?" a reporter asked.

"Murder? First off, let's not go wishing death on that beautiful woman. We have faith that she is out there somewhere just waiting to be rescued and come home to her family and fans."

"Do the Crescent Crew murders have anything to do with this release?" another reporter asked.

At the mention of the Crescent Crew, Maleek Money cringed. Damn, his gang's war had gone national. He was officially big-time, as if he didn't know already.

"Wait, are they talking about us?" Keisha asked.

Maleek Money smirked, "I don't know." Although heat was the last thing they needed, he had to admit that the notoriety made him feel good. "This shit craaaazy!"

"That's nonsense," the attorney quipped. "Don't ever mention the Crescent Crew and this man in the same sentence again."

The attorney wrapped the press conference, and the cameras panned to the convoy of luxury vehicles waiting for their freed mogul.

"I'm confused," Keisha said. "Why do you call him your Big Homie if he not even acknowledging the Crew?"

Maleek Money stared at the TV in silence wondering the same thing. A conversation he and Bone had nearly a year ago surfaced in his mind. Would Qwess sacrifice the family he created for the good life he made? Or had he already put his family on the altar? He was facing the death penalty, yet here he was free on bail? This was unheard of!

Then again, Qwess was a very wealthy man, and in America money moved things. In America, money turned a murderous pro bowler into a free man. It was also America that turned a serial killer into a bestselling author and hero after he turned on his family.

Maleek Money had questions. Foremost: which America did Qwess use to gain his freedom?

Chapter 13

Qwess walked away from the podium to the convoy of cars awaiting him. A hunter-green G-Wagon was idling in the middle of a three-car convoy that consisted of Doe's BMW i8, and Malik Shabazz's Rolls Royce.

Qwess walked toward the vehicles. The air felt fresh on his face, as if he were just being born. He peered at the sky and exhaled. Even the sky seemed to be bluer than he remembered, and new scents seemed to explode inside his nostrils. After spending months breathing in the recycled air of jail, his senses were picking up everything. Even his sight seemed to be sharper than normal.

Just as Qwess made it to the curb, his wife Lisa Ivory burst from the driver's seat of the G-Wagon and rushed to him. She jumped in his arms, wrapped her legs around his waist, and peppered his face with kisses.

"Welcome home, my King!" Lisa said.

Qwess embraced her tightly. "Thank you, Queen," he returned. A beam of light captured his attention. He paused and swung Lisa around, away from the light. "Watch out."

Lisa peeked over her shoulder at the camera crew filming

her every move. "No baby, it's okay. They're with me. I hired them to film this day," she explained.

"And why would you do that?" Qwess asked. He'd made it clear that he didn't want to come home to a bunch of hoopla and attention. Sure, he had made bail, but this wasn't a victory. This was merely a change of venue while he mounted an offense for the second half of the fight.

"This is for a documentary we're doing about all of this," Lisa informed him.

Qwess placed his wife on the ground and waved to a few well-wishers. Then he briskly walked to the convoy.

"Surprise!" Lisa said, presenting the G-Wagon to him. "I got it for you as a coming home gift. A tank for my soldier."

Qwess shook his head slightly. Here he was worried about money, and she had just splurged on a hundred-and-fifty-thousand-dollar truck. More flash too while he was trying to keep a low profile. He was fuming, then he remembered that the cameras were rolling.

"Thank you sweetie!" Qwess beamed.

He instinctively walked to the back of the vehicle, since he'd had a driver for the better part of a decade. Then it dawned on him that his driver had turned into his number one enemy.

"I'll drive, Qwess. Hop in," Lisa said.

Doe, Niya, Prince, and Shabazz all gathered around Qwess on the sidewalk and showered him with affection. Qwess had made it clear there would be no parties for his homecoming, so they were paying their respects now. Besides, he had twenty-four hours to report and connect to his monitoring system.

"Qwess, I'll give you a day or two to catch up with your family, then I'll be over to set things up," Shabazz plotted. "We're going to have to make your home Central Base until I can get that leg monitor removed. See ya soon."

Shabazz disappeared in his Rolls while Qwess wrapped

things up on the sidewalk. He'd had enough of being on this street. He was ready to return to his familiar surroundings.

Qwess hopped in the truck and exhaled as he washed his hands over his face.

He was free. He was finally free. But how?

Flame powered off the TV in his home studio and mouthed a silent prayer of gratitude to God for bringing Qwess home. Like everyone else in the world, he witnessed the report on CNN. Like everyone else in the world, he couldn't believe the news either.

Seeing Qwess free was bittersweet to Flame. He no longer blamed Qwess for his misfortune. Constant praying had siphoned the hatred in his heart and replaced it with forgiveness. Constant study and reflection had instilled in him accountability, and as such, he has taken full responsibility for his misfortune. He was living like a savage. No one told him to sleep with Sasha Beaufont. If anything, Qwess had warned him against it. Flame believed that if he—a wretched fornicator—deserved a second chance, anyone deserved a second chance.

The door to the studio opened and Kim walked in wearing a long black silk robe.

"Hey handsome!" Kim greeted cheerfully. "How is everything going? You knocking these songs out, huh?"

"Yeah, somewhat."

Kim walked over to Flame, sitting in his wheelchair behind the mixing board. She leaned over him and cupped his face. "I am sooooo proud of you, Joey," she said.

"Me? Why?"

"Because you not letting anything keep you down. You trusting God and letting him use you."

"Ah, okay. You think so?"

Kim nodded seductively, "Hmm mm, I do. And now it's time for me to let him use me for you," she said.

Flame cocked his head. "Huh?"

Kim smiled mischievously and unfastened the belt on her robe. The robe opened wide and exposed her naked body. Slowly, she peeled her robe back and let it drop to her feet. The ambient lighting in the studio cast a soft glow on her dark skin.

Flame's mouth tumbled open. His eyes scanned Kim's flawless body. Her dark brown, taunt nipples pointed at him from her firm 36Cs. Her freshly waxed vagina was slick with arousal, and lust danced inside her eyes.

Kim straddled Flame and wrapped her arms around his shoulders. She kissed his neck, then sucked on his earlobe. Then she licked a trail from his ear to the top of his neck and moaned in his ear. "Our Lord is pleased with you, Joey. So now I'm going to please you."

Flame gazed up into her eyes and palmed her naked ass. He kneaded her flesh softly and spread her cheeks. He could feel the heat from her center seeping onto his fingers. In his mind, he thrust his hips up to meet her gyrations, but in reality, nothing happened.

Kim stopped gyrating on his lap and dropped to her knees. She pulled back Flame's joggers and gripped his flaccid dick in her palms. She looked up at him and gazed into his eyes. A look of lust and reticence stared back at her.

Kim took his soft dick inside her mouth and hummed. But nothing happened. She put a little spit on it and suckled the head. Nothing happened. She slowly took all of him into her mouth and played with his balls. She felt him grow just a little and she got excited. She had seen his monster-sized dick at its peak. It was a marvel that she was excited about seeing it again. Unfortunately, the great Flame couldn't get past a flicker.

Kim looked up at him from her knees, disappointment evident in her eyes. She sympathized with his plight, so she didn't want to make him feel uneasy, but her eyes couldn't lie.

Flame slowly opened his eyes and peeped down at her. He recognized the look of disgust on her face. "I'm sorry," he offered weakly. "It's just that I can't feel anything since the . . ." He sighed deeply and blinked back the tears. "I'm sure you're doing a wonderful job and all, but I'm . . . I'm . . . an invalid."

Kim's heart wept for Flame. She could hear the pain in his words, and she could only imagine how it felt to go from being a sex titan to being unable to even enjoy sex at all.

"Maybe this is God's way of punishing me for all my promiscuity in the past," Flame assumed.

Kim shook her head vehemently. "Noooo, don't ever say that! Our God is a forgiving God. You repented with a sincere heart, so you are good," she explained. "We'll just work on you getting better. Then everything will get better, especially this." She gripped his member and smiled.

Flame returned a weak smile, but inside he was crushed. He had been a king among peasants and a God among kings. In his heyday, women all over the world had wailed out his name in lust, sometimes in foreign tongues he didn't even recognize. Many of them were nameless, just beautiful faces and perfect bodies. They weren't special to him. Now, here he was with the woman he loved, and he couldn't even rise to the occasion, or feel if he rose to the occasion. Oh, the irony of life . . .

Kim slid off Flame's lap and stroked his back while he continued to mix his tracks on the soundboard. He may not have been back to his former self in the sex department, but he was on fire in the booth!

Chapter 14

The door exploded from the hinges and masked men poured into the room with automatic weapons. Barrels scanned the room for targets. Someone ran from the back room and automatic gunfire spit and lit up the room. The flashes from the muzzle washed the room in light and three other people in the room materialized.

Fifteen more shots from the AR-15 made them memories.

After the room was cleared, more men poured in to clear the house. When the smoke cleared, one man remained alive, lying on the ground and drowning in his own blood.

Bone walked through the front door, flanked by Rasul and Knowledge Born. As he surveyed the damage, a sinister grin spread across his face. He hadn't been in the thick of things for a long time. The scent of the gunpowder made him nostalgic as a burst of adrenaline coursed through his veins. He had an army at his fingertips to do his bidding. All he had to do was think of an action and it was done. From his palaces, he called shots and his soldiers executed his commands. They were so efficient he hadn't felt the need to come out . . . until now. Enemies were encircling his empire, trying to topple his reign, and he wasn't going for it.

Bone stood over the fallen man, staring at him as he chased his breath. "Sit him up," Bone ordered.

His soldiers stood the man up by his arms. Blood trickled from the small wound in his chest. His head fell to his chest, and he grimaced in pain, panting.

"I'm only asking this one time," Bone asked. "Who is Black?"

The man winced in pain. "Black?"

Bone dug his thumb into the open wound and twisted it. The man yelped in pain.

"Who is Black?" Bone repeated.

Sweat dripped from the man's brow. "B–Black?"

Boom!

The round from Bone's .40 cal ripped into the man's stomach. He yelped out and buckled over in pain. They let him crumple to the ground. Bone calmly stooped down and placed the barrel of the .40 cal against the man's sweaty temple. Bone tapped him on the head with the barrel.

"If you live, tell Black that we're coming for him. Tell him if he's smart, he will kill himself," Bone instructed. "Tell him we gonna break him then kill him."

Bone stood in the middle of the room with all eyes on him. "Search the house. See if there is any dope and money. Whatever you find, keep it."

Gangsta Black pushed his Black BMW 7-series down Skibo Road with the music on tilt. He was riding solo and bumping a Nipsey Hussle track that put him in his zone.

A few weeks after coming home, Gangsta Black was already living the life. Just as promised, Samson plugged him right in and he was calling shots. Samson had imported some Mexican muscle to assist them in their quest to eliminate the Crescent Crew, and Gangsta Black was in charge of them.

He had been a shot caller while with the UBN, but never of this magnitude. Mexican soldiers were cut different. They didn't talk back or entertain designs of being "the man." They didn't like to shine in the spotlight and look the part of a gangsta. Rather, they were nondescripts, resembling painters or farmers on the outside. However, their hearts were as cold as ice, and Gangsta Black had their allegiance at his fingertips.

Gangsta Black led a coordinated plan to shut down their legit businesses that doubled as the Crescent Crew hideaways and laundromats in Fayetteville where they cleaned their money, forcing them out into the open. With nowhere to hide, they were easy targets in the Ville. The war was in full swing with gun battles erupting all over the Carolinas. The Crescent Crew's tentacles stretched all over the Southeast, but they were legion in the Carolinas. In the Carolinas, Fayetteville and Wilmington were their strongest points, so that's where Gangsta Black concentrated his efforts. Of course, the Crescent Crew weren't hard to find with their loud green cars and ostentatious lifestyles. They had been getting fat for years, and it showed in how they flossed in town. They made it known they were the richest niggas in the city. And that was their mistake.

As Gangsta Black cruised down Skibo Road in a zone, his head swiveled like a sentry. Just last night, his spot was attacked and robbed, and they sent him a personal message that they were coming for him. Two of his soldiers were killed in the raid, and they purposely left one alive to tell the tale. Gangsta Black had to admit that was a gangsta move, and it gave him a weird type of pleasure to be heading a war against the Crew he lowkey idolized for years. In the game, it was all love, but as they say, all is fair in love and war.

Gangsta Black was on his way to sow his royal oats with a thick Carolina girl. He was loving the girls in the Carolinas. They didn't build them like that in Cali, and being down for so long, he was making up for lost time with the felines. But while frolicking in the streets, he was on alert for anything green.

It appeared today was his lucky day.

In the McDonald's parking lot on his left, Gangsta Black spotted a green Mercedes G-Wagon sitting on chrome rims waiting in the drive-thru line. Gangsta Black concluded this had to be a member of the Crescent Crew. Judging by the car, this appeared to be a high-ranking member, because the truck he was looking at was at least a hundred thousand dollars—before the customizations.

Gangsta Black whipped the Bimmer around and slowly crept through the parking lot. Ducked low in the seat, he circled around to see if he could gain a better view of the vehicle's driver. The tint was too dark to allow him to see inside, but the chrome vanity plate on the front of the bumper told it all.

Gangsta Black reached in the backseat and grabbed his Mac-10. He chambered a round and slowly crept around the drive-thru again. True to McDonald's form, the G-Wagon was still idling in the line, sandwiched between a Toyota Prius and a Dodge Charger. Gangsta Black wasn't concerned with the driver of the truck. All he knew was the truck flew the Crescent Crew flag, so in his mind, whoever was driving was marked for death.

Gangsta Black pulled up alongside the right side of the G-Wagon. He pushed a button to put the car in park and waited. He yanked the slide back on the Mac-10 and hopped out firing.

Brrrrraaaatttt! Brrrraaaattt! Brrrraaattttt!

The automatic machine pistol spit rapid fire in broad daylight, the .45 slugs slamming into the side of the Mercedes truck. He fired until the slide locked back. He didn't miss a beat. He slammed another extended clip into the butt of the gun and emptied it into the vehicle before the truck could move.

Spectators yelled and screamed, dashing for cover. The Prius in front of the G-Wagon couldn't start quick enough, so the driver abandoned his vehicle. The Dodge Charger jumped the curb and barreled out of the parking lot, careening toward the Bimmer, just missing the rear bumper.

Oblivious to the melee he created, Gangsta Black advanced toward the stalled G-Wagon, intent on finishing off whoever was inside. When Gangsta Black was ten feet away from the truck, the passenger door swung open, and someone returned fire.

Pop! Pop! Pop! Pop! Pop!

Gangsta Black stumbled back and tumbled to the ground. He managed to swing the Mac-10 up as he tumbled and fired off another volley of shots. Six slugs tore into the back of the Prius.

The G-Wagon rammed into the back of the Prius and pushed it forward. The bottom of the bumper touched the top of the Prius and locked into place. The engine revved and 500 horses pushed the Prius aside, clearing a path for the exit. The G-Wagon plowed through the wreckage with the biturbo engine roaring and tires screeching.

Suddenly the G-Wagon stopped moving. A split second later, Maleek Money stood through the open sunroof with two Sig-Sauers in each hand. He quickly spotted Gangsta Black retreating back to his BMW. He screamed, "Allahu Akbar!" Then he let the Sigs sing.

Boom! Boom! Boom! Boom! Boom!

Gangsta Black scurried for cover, but not before a hot ball nipped his shoulder. He cringed and dived back into the Bimmer, firing recklessly to give himself some cover. An erratic shell went through his own driver's side window and shattered it. He managed to get behind the wheel and slam the car into drive. Ducking for cover, he maneuvered the Bimmer out of the parking lot and sped down Morganton Road in the wrong direction . . .

Maleek Money dropped from the roof and fell behind the wheel. He snatched Muhammad back into the car and smashed the gas. The G-Wagon hopped another curve and barreled out in traffic hot on the tail of the Bimmer.

"Get ready!" Maleek Money yelled at Muhammad. "I think that's that nigga, Black!"

Maleek Money zigzagged through traffic, tossing the heavy lunchbox around like a sports car. Up ahead the Bimmer ran a red light and nearly caused an accident. A burgundy Honda Accord spun a 180 and stalled out in the center of the intersection. Maleek Money barely missed the Honda when he zoomed through the intersection. The big Bimmer dipped through traffic and weaved in and out of cars, but it was still no match for the powerful engine in the Mercedes. Maleek Money caught up with the Bimmer and drew near the rear bumper.

"Shoot the tires out!" Maleek Money told Muhammad.

Muhammad was ready this time. He was reloaded with a CAR-15. He aimed out the open window and let it rip.

Tat-tat-tat-tat-tat-tat-tat-tat!

The staccato rhythm of the military-style weapon rang through the air. Bullets whizzed through the air and shattered the back glass. Another volley of shots took out the back tire. The Bimmer skidded to the right, swung to the left, then flipped over five times and slammed into a light pole and caved in at the center. A ten-foot plume of smoke quickly rose into the air.

"Yeah, nigga!" Muhammad roared, pumping his fist. "That nigga dead."

"Nahhhh," Maleek Money shook his head. If this was the guy who owned the audacity to hit his beloved Keisha and sent his wifey into hiding, he had to make sure he was dead.

He had to make sure they felt his fury. There would be no second chances. "Let's make sure we finish this nigga off."

Maleek Money abruptly turned the behemoth around and drove up right beside the disabled Bimmer. He hopped out the truck gripping both pistols and calmly walked to the smoking Bimmer. He fired three shots straight through the windshield just in case someone was still alive. Nothing moved except the spectators clamoring for safety.

Maleek Money walked to the open driver's window, pointed a pistol through the opening, and sprayed the inside of the car. When the smoke cleared, he peeked his head inside to confirm the death of the fool who tried him, but the car was empty. Gangsta Black had escaped.

Chapter 15

Qwess scanned the expansive grounds of his North Carolina property from the fourth floor of his mansion. In the distance, he saw deer drinking from the pond at the back of the grounds. Their position seemed so contrary to him. While they seemed free and so alive, he was trapped inside his home imprisoned by an ankle monitor. But home was still better than jail. After all, his home was 15,000 square feet.

Qwess walked down the long hallway to another room that overlooked the long road to his home and the circular driveway. He was expecting guests, and one by one they began to roll in.

The first car Qwess spotted was Amin's brand-new Bentley coupe. The shiny black car looked like Amin's personality. Sleek and opulent, yet understated. Qwess chuckled at the irony. Amin stepped out the Bentley in cargo pants, hiking boots, and a burgundy vest, and walked up toward the house out of sight from Qwess.

Next up was Doe's BMW i8. The blue-hued electric vehicle glided onto the property as if it were alive. The headlights glowed like alien eyes, and the frosted blue rims poked out from the side. Qwess imagined Doe leaning deep to the right as was his signature, but with the obsidian tint, he couldn't confirm anything. Doe parked beside Amin's Bentley, but he remained inside.

While Doe sat inside the BMW, a white Rolls Royce Ghost drifted down the long road. The vanity plate on the front of the car bisecting the Masonry body kit read *Allah* in Arabic. There was no mistaking who was inside this luxury boat. Malik Shabazz.

Qwess couldn't help but smile at the thought of his skilled attorney. His name should've been Merlin the Magician for the way he pulled tricks from his bag. Shabazz managed to do the impossible this time, obtaining Qwess a bail on a capital case. This was practically unheard of, yet the mastermind managed to work his mojo. In the end, it wasn't the legal wrangling that freed Qwess though; it was the folly of the judge.

The judge's remarks during the initial bail hearing were prejudicial. Shabazz argued that the remarks violated Qwess's rights to due process of law. He contended it was impossible for Qwess to have received a fair trial under such prejudicial conditions. It was a long shot, but it did the trick. A change of venue was granted, and the new judge was more favorable to Shabazz's arguments (and bribe). Much to the dismay of the government, bail was granted with conditions. The court imposed a two-million-dollar bail to house arrest. So Qwess was free yet still in bondage. But as a free man, he was now afforded the opportunity to restore his affairs in order. Since he couldn't go to his plush office and meet with his team, his team came to his new office: his home.

Qwess stared at the convoy of luxury vehicles below. Altogether, there were over a million dollars' worth of cars in his front yard. It was clear that everyone in his circle was winning and had done very well for themselves during his time away. Yet the burden weighing his mind down was his finances.

Qwess saw another car creeping down the road to his home. Slowly, the shiny red paint job of the late-model Toyota Camry came into view. There was only one more person missing from this little shindig, so Qwess assumed this had to be him. The Camry slowed to a stop right beside the Bentley, and Liam Cohen's tall, lanky frame crawled from the Toyota and peered around the property suspiciously.

As Qwess observed Liam's actions, it dawned on him the blatant paradoxes Liam presented. At one point, he was involved with nearly 70% of the top hip-hop artists in the industry, especially the gangster rappers. Yet here he was about to entertain a meeting with some heavy hitters in the game, some real live guys from the street, and he was as paranoid as a deer trapped inside a wolfpack. Qwess also noted how everyone else arrived in very expensive cars, and Liam arrived in a lowkey Toyota Camry, even though he was probably wealthier than everyone else in attendance, with the exception of Shabazz. Qwess shook his head at the irony of his culture and confirmed something he heard a long time ago by his father: Broke is loud. Wealth is quiet.

With everyone present, Qwess walked down the hallway to address his team.

"Yo, I just missed that motherfucker!" Maleek Money said, slapping his palm as he walked into the funeral home.

"That's okay, that nigga know we on his ass though," Muhammad said, patting Maleek Money on his back. "We'll get him."

They walked downstairs and found Bone siting behind his massive desk with his feet propped up on the table, watching the huge television on the wall. Bone saw the men and greeted them with a smile. "As-salamu alaykum! I see you've been busy!"

"Wa alaykum as-salamu!" Maleek Money returned.

"What happened out there?" Bone asked. "According to the news, you turned Skibo into Afghanistan."

"Shit, we was in the drive-thru and somebody started dumping on us in broad daylight," Maleek Money explained.

"Word?"

"Hell yeah! But Mu backed the niggas down with the Dessie and came up through the roof trying to rock the nigga like, *Boom-Boom-Boom-Boom-Boom!*" Maleek Money demonstrated with his hands. "The nigga got light, and we chased him till he crashed. Went to finish him off but he was already gone."

Bone gestured to the television. On the screen was the crumpled BMW, still smoking, with so many holes in it the doors resembled a cheese grater. "This it?"

Muhammad stared at the screen. "Hell yeah! I think it's that nigga Black."

Bone perked up. "So, y'all can identify him?"

"Definitely!" Both men screamed in unison.

Bone showed them his phone. On the screen was a photo taken from the club security cameras the night Navaho was performing. "This him?"

"Yup."

Bone smiled. "Bet. I got someone that can tap into the facial recognition cameras all throughout the state. Next time he pop up anywhere, we on his ass."

"Yo, you serious?" Muhammad asked.

"Hell yeah, Crew business gone digital," Bone affirmed. "We ain't playing around with these niggas. They trying to take food off our plate and destroy what we built? I'll go broke or die running these niggas out of town. And y'all better be on the same type of time."

Bone was laying down the gauntlet and raising the ante.

The heat was on, and the Crescent Crew was back in the driver's seat applying pressure.

Qwess sat at the head of the huge conference table. His team lined the table on either side of him. This was his first time seeing them all together at once in the same place. Each man played a specific role in the team that made up ABP, and their roles were as obscure as their connections. However, like a well-oiled machine, each department was predicated on another department working efficiently. Qwess had assembled everyone here to see the status of his life.

"Thank you all for coming here today on such short notice," Qwess said, addressing the crowd. "I want everyone to speak, but I want everyone to be on their most respectful behavior." Qwess's disposition was calm and resolute, clearly a byproduct of being in jail for so long. "I know this is some of your first time being in the same room together, so let's go around the table and introduce yourselves, starting with you, Amin."

While everyone introduced themselves, Qwess watched closely, trying to listen to the missing pieces in their respective puzzles. He had been inside, hearing things from their angles. Now he was here in the present to reconcile all sides.

After the introductions, Amin, being the CFO for ABP, began the financial briefing . . . and it wasn't good.

"Basically, there is no easy way to say this, but we are losing money rapidly, and we have been this way for a while."

While Amin spoke, Qwess listened to what was beneath the words. Constantly being on his prayers had him attuned to picking up energy. He also observed the reaction to the news of everyone around him.

"Of course, we all know that we have a lot of overhead to carry in general, and with no artists dropping music, things got tight really fast. Sustaining this while shifting our priorities to this new technology has tapped our money dry," Amin continued.

"How dry?" Qwess asked. "I need numbers."

"Well, on the traditional side, as a company, we're down to just over ten million, but I don't know what type of excess money we have because ol' *Lam* here isn't coughing up any numbers from his side," Amin taunted, jerking his thumb toward Liam, who was sitting right beside him.

"Actually, the name is Liam. *Lee*-Am," Liam corrected, clearly aggravated. It was evident he was upset with the taunt because his Israeli accent was more pronounced. "And I turned over some figures to you, but as I indicated to you when we spoke, Salim's and my business is a separate entity than your ABP thing. So, our figures shouldn't be lumped into that category."

"Our ABP thing?" Amin repeated.

"Yes."

"Let me guess, our ABP *thing* isn't anything special to you, huh?"

Liam turned to face Amin. "Ah-min, not really. That business model has been around for decades; I helped bring those types of labels to the forefront of popular culture. However, that model is a dinosaur now. *Wave* is the wave of the future—hence its name."

"It's Ah-*meen*, and unless we generate some funds, there will be no future for anything."

Qwess had witnessed enough. "Okay, that's enough," he interjected. "At the end of the day, we're all on the same side in here. There are no big Is and little Us in here. So, Liam, in order for me to gauge exactly what needs to be done moving forward, I need to know all the financials."

Liam scoffed.

"But," Qwess said, "we'll get back to that."

Amin finished his spiel, then Doe spoke next.

"Well, our record sales have taken a hit, but my wife's last album did some numbers. Also, since Flame has been out of his coma, sales on his old catalog have bumped up a bit. So that's a plus. We're also starting to see some traction in your old catalog since you've been released," Doe relayed. "Of course, that money won't be seen for another quarter or two."

Qwess nodded. "What about new artists?"

Doe shook his head slowly. "YouTube has changed the game, bro. A lot of the new artists are going straight to YouTube, releasing their music free and independently, then touring off one hit single."

Qwess was aware of this trend. YouTube was nothing new, of course, but had it grown large enough to shift the culture?

Doe shrugged, "I mean, with the 360 deals becoming the norm, how can you blame them? And we're not in a position not to offer a 360 deal. We tried it with Noshon and we lost a bag," he recalled.

Qwess remembered the experiment with the underground rapper from Connecticut. When 360s were all the rage, they tried to position ABP to be the anti-360 label, a place where artists could be in charge of their intellectual property. They didn't anticipate Noshon being as savvy as he was. He milked the internet for clout and only dropped an EP for ABP. He used the advance ABP gave him and built his YouTube page up. Then he went on the road and toured for months with new material.

Typically, the label made money off record sales, while the artists made money off touring and merch. However, with Noshon touring new material, focusing on his merch, and directing the fans to his YouTube page, ABP never recouped off the half-million dollar advance they gave him. In the end, Noshon blew up and ABP blew it.

"Yeah, I remember," Qwess said. "And then he had the nerve to make a diss track aimed at us. These niggas . . ."

"Yeah," Doe seconded. "And with us being blackballed, we're really not in position to offer these new artists anything that either they can't get themselves or that the other big boys can't do better than," he explained.

Liam scoffed again. "Big boys? They're all crooks. Trust me, I used to be one of them."

"Yeah, I know," Amin sniped.

"Okay, so who else we got up?" Qwess asked.

"We have some unreleased material from Flame, Niya, and even some old tracks from you," Doe answered. "I'm thinking we put together a compilation album and capitalize on some of this press."

Qwess stroked the thick beard he had grown in prison while he mulled over the proposal. "That might not be a bad idea," he said. "How long would it take to put it all together and put something out?"

Doe shrugged. "Three, four weeks, maybe."

Qwess looked to Liam. "Could we upload it to Wave and test the technology with it? I'm sure with this many hits, we could correct any faults within the system."

"Well, there are bigger problems with Wave, things you and I need to discuss."

Qwess opened his hands expansively. "Now is the time."

Liam was reluctant. "I don't think this is the place," he insisted.

Although Qwess understood there could have been better ways to handle things, he wanted to open the floor this way. He was making a statement that they were all on the same team and needed to be open and transparent with each other. He was under no illusion; he knew he was fighting for his life. There was always a chance for things to go left. If this was the case, he wanted his team to maintain his legacy and keep it intact. More importantly, he needed to know they were on his team.

"No," Qwess said. "This is exactly the place."

Liam was uncomfortable. He scanned the room and found all eyes on him, except Shabazz's. His were glued to his iPad.

"Well, it appears the initial system broke down and we need to acquire some new patents to make it more compatible with what we initially envisioned," Liam explained.

"So what exactly does that mean?" Doe inquired.

"It means more money," Amin interjected. "It's always about more money with these guys."

"Not exactly," Liam denied. "Well, yes, we need more money, but it's not what you're thinking."

"Of course not," Amin sniped.

Liam rattled off some more techno mumbo jumbo, but Qwess was deaf to it. This whole meeting was turning into a money grab.

After Liam finished his spiel, the meeting shifted to the legal side of things with Shabazz. He wasn't discussing the criminal case; he was discussing the civil aspect. Normally this would be a conversation that was held in confidence, but Qwess was insistent on proving his point that he was in charge of his team. True, each of the people in the room was formidable in their own right, but in this scenario, they were under the auspices of Qwess and the needs of ABP.

"Well, son," Shabazz said, staring at Qwess. "This thing isn't going anywhere. We rejected the settlement offer, so we need to begin preparing for trial. And that means . . ."

"More money," Amin interjected.

Shabazz nodded. "Afraid so."

"So what we talking here?" Qwess asked.

Without hesitation, Shabazz answered, "Could be a mil, could be two—or it could be five." He shrugged. "Who knows how this thing goes."

Qwess nodded. He figured as much, but he didn't figure *that* much. "What does the case look like, though? Is it winnable?"

Shabazz sat up straight and looked Qwess in his eyes. "It depends. If you're convicted on these criminal charges, there isn't a judge in the land that will rule in your favor on these civil claims. The criminal conviction will make you a monster and negate all of the positive that you've done. Of course, if you're convicted, I'm sure none of this will matter."

"My husband being convicted isn't even a part of the equation," Lisa Ivory snapped from her standing position against the wall. She was so discreet as she watched the meeting, most forgot she was still in the room, but she felt her voice had to be heard on that subject. "Never will we allow that to happen," she insisted.

Shabazz turned to Lisa. "Ma'am, I understand your concern, but we have to understand the gravity of this. Salim has serious evidence stacked against him. If we can't get that evidence thrown out, then chances are a jury is going to decide whether he lives or dies."

Qwess watched the exchange between his wife and attorney with a sense of detachment. Shabazz's words forced everything else to the back of the table. Neither Wave, ABP, nor anything else took precedence over his life. He was home, enjoying the luxuries his life had afforded, but he wasn't under any illusion. He was still at war, and if he couldn't find a way to either discredit or eliminate his former comrade, then he knew the Feds would happily jam a needle in his arm.

Qwess peered around the table at all the participants and suddenly had an epiphany. The most important person, the one person who possessed the power to help him the most, was absent. The only question was, with a war going on in the streets, how could he summon him?

Chapter 16

The blue light flashed in the rearview, and the man's heart skipped a beat. He was riding extra dirty with two kilos of cocaine and one kilo of heroin in the trunk, not to mention the fully loaded .40 cal tucked beneath the seat. He had a split second to make a decision that would affect the rest of his life—as if deciding to ride dirty hadn't done that already. He glanced in the rearview to confirm that the blue light was for him, and indeed it was. His breath nearly caught in his chest as he contemplated his next move. He told himself he would never return to prison, but that was before he joined his new team. He was rolling with a crew of money-getters now, so he could afford a bail or two. It was nothing like the old days when he was petty hustling. Weighing his options, he concluded he could live to see another day if he pulled over.

He flipped on his signal and pulled the Dodge Challenger to the side of the road. He rolled the windows down and placed his hands on the steering wheel as the officer approached the passenger window.

"Good day, officer, how's it going?" he asked in the most genial tone he could muster. "What seems to be the problem?"

The officer ducked his head in the window and quickly scanned the car. "License and registration, please. You got any drugs or weapons in the car?" he asked.

"No, sir!"

The officer narrowed his eyes. "You sure?"

The man shook his head vigorously and passed him his license. "No, sir!" He repeated.

The officer studied the license, then tapped the door suddenly. "I'ma need you to step out of the car."

The man sighed and smacked the wheel. He knew stepping out of the car would only extend the encounter. Extending the encounter would increase the chances of the cop finding the work and the gun. But he was in no position to resist at this point.

"Come on, you're not moving fast enough," the officer said. "Step out of the vehicle."

The officer came around the driver's side and helped him out of the vehicle.

"Turn around and place your hands on the vehicle," the officer instructed.

He patted him down from his head to his toe and didn't find anything.

"Place your hands behind your back," he instructed.

"Place my hands behind my back? For what? I don't have nothing!"

The officer popped him upside the head. "Put your damn hands behind your back. Now."

The man complied, and the officer slapped the bracelets on him. He led him to the back of the car and made him sit on the ground while he searched the vehicle. It took him less than a minute to discover the .40 caliber handgun.

He dangled the gun up in the air. "Ohhh, what we got here?"

The man looked at the gun with a straight face. "Shit, I don't know. You tell me, you the one holding it."

The officer walked to the back of the trunk and tapped it. "Hmm mmm, I wonder what we will find in here."

The man tried to keep his poker face. But it was obvious that his goose was cooked. The officer popped open the trunk and dug inside. A few seconds later, he found the drugs. He turned to the man and held up the package.

"I guess I have to tell you about this too, huh?" the officer mocked.

"Hell yeah."

"Yeah right."

The officer left the man sitting on the pavement while he walked to his police cruiser.

A weird feeling settled into the man's gut as he visualized the bars closing him inside a cell. He watched the officer turn the lights off on the cruiser and take pictures of the bricks of drugs. He kept swiveling his neck around, looking for the backup that he was sure was coming, but after a few minutes, backup never arrived. He shook his head, cussing himself for not making a run for the border.

The officer stepped out of the cruiser and walked over to the man with a sick smile. He scanned the highway, but there wasn't much traffic. Old Bunce Road was a back street, a virtual no man's land between busy Cliffdale Road and Raeford Road.

"So," the officer said as he held up one of the bricks, looking at the label. "It appears you chose the wrong side, young man." His pale skin was flushed with red undertones as he gloated.

"Huh?"

The officer repeated himself then added, "You'll see soon enough. Stand up."

The man did as he was instructed, hoping that if he complied the officer would go easy on him. As if heaven heard his pleas, he felt the officer remove his cuffs. He breathed a sigh of relief, but before he could totally relax, he felt the cuffs snap back around his wrist tighter than the first time.

"Yo, what are you doing? These fucking cuffs are too tight!"

"I know."

He pushed him to the rear passenger side of the patrol car, leaned him over the trunk, and frisked him more thoroughly this time. When he found nothing, he sat him down on the ground near the tire and looked at his watch.

"What's going on, man? Something doesn't feel right," the man said, peering around anxiously. He had been arrested before, so he knew the protocol. This didn't feel like the normal protocol. This officer's mannerisms were all wrong. He seemed too skittish, confused. He had a slam dunk in his hand—bricks of raw and heroin *and* a loaded pistol. Yet where was the backup?

Almost on cue, a black Dodge Charger with obsidian tinted windows roared past them, then bust a quick U-turn. The Charger pulled up and parked behind the police cruiser.

"Ahh, here we go," the officer said. "Get up, let's go."

The officer grabbed him by the arm and dragged him over to the Charger. He yanked the back door open and tossed him inside with his hands cuffed behind his back.

The man gathered himself and looked up at the front seat. He expected to see some type of detective. Instead, he looked right in the eyes of Bone.

★　★　★

Qwess sat inside his home studio, lost in thought. The lights were low and candles burned all around the room. There was an eerie glow that echoed his mood.

His meeting a few days ago had gone as well as expected, considering the circumstances. He at least knew where he stood now, and although his circumstances were dire, he felt relieved that he was aware of his position on the board.

Qwess couldn't have imagined that he would ever have a need to worry about money in this lifetime. He had amassed an astronomical amount of wealth in the music industry, and even inherited his comrade King Reece's funds as well. He had married well, a woman that brought her own money to the table. Yet it cost to live this lifestyle. It cost to be a boss. Living like a king required a king's ransom, and Qwess was learning this the hard way. He knew that the key to his financial resurrection was Wave.

As predicted, streaming was changing not only the music business, but the entertainment business as a whole. The possibilities were endless! Videos, music, movies . . . everything was up for grabs. Streaming was changing the world, and although Qwess and Liam were some of the first players at the table, the rest of the world had quickly caught on. Like most things, demand determined cost, so now what they were previously getting for the low was now going for the high.

This meant more money, which equaled more problems.

Qwess cued up a track on the computer and a slow melody poured through the speakers. The deep bass beat thumped through his body and whisked him away from his problems. Music had always been his escape, and since being confined to his home, he had found solace in producing beats.

Qwess moved a lever on the computer and his lovely wife's silky voice laid on top of the track. He closed his eyes and savored the sound.

Qwess still adored Lisa, and the way she held him down while he was away made him love her even more. He had thrust a heap of responsibility on her crown, and she handled it like a queen. Now all he wanted to do was reciprocate her efforts and get their life back to normal. Interestingly enough, the debacle had forced Lisa back into the studio to vent her frustrations.

Like most artists, Lisa turned life's pain turned into musical pleasure. While Qwess was away, Lisa recorded a ton of music in their studio. Her intent wasn't to release the music to the world. Rather, it was just a release from her stress. However, the tracks she recorded sounded better than anything she had released in years. All it needed was the right touch.

Qwess twisted the knob on the mixing board and Lisa's vocals overpowered the melody. He leaned back and fell into the words:

"A queen without a king is like a ring without the bling/ You know, just any ole thiiiiiing/ And we know that diamonds are a girl's best frieeeend/ So don't ask me about my day/ you know my skies are grey/ as long as my king is awayyyyyy."

Lisa's voice was as vibrant as ever, and her signature vibrato still cracked enough to be her acceptable trademark. The beat Qwess produced accompanied her vocals; it didn't fight with them like so many tracks produced by others in the past. It was as if they were the perfect match in life and music.

Qwess turned that song off and made a note on the mixing board. Then he queued up another track from Lisa. This track was a ballad. As soon as it began, Qwess became excited all over again. He loved to hear his wife showcase her vocal skills. He felt she had one of the best voices in the history of music, sort of like a Patti LaBelle and Whitney Houston combined—powerful and sultry.

When Lisa's voice poured through the speakers, Qwess fell in love all over again. She sang:

"Never could a love so strong, so true, keep me away from loving youuuuu/ You're more than my king, you're my God in the flesh/ With you away, my life is a mess/ So I'll hold my breath until you come home/ Cause they can never take away a real king's throne."

Qwess bobbed his head with pride. He was vibing to it. His wife was putting on for him, repping their love, and even though she had recorded it for therapy, it still felt good knowing that her multimillion-dollar mouthpiece dripped with love for him. Qwess thought about all the lost souls inside, men that longed for the type of love that Lisa held for him. He thought about the countless calls to visitation each week as women trekked down to the jail and endured harsh, inhumane conditions to see their men and offer them a glimpse of hope. He imagined these women felt like Lisa did when she sang these tracks.

Qwess searched his mental musical rolodex and concluded that there was no music with this type of theme, music directed toward the men inside—and the women who held them down. There were no songs about love on lockdown and the feelings that came with it. Not since Mary J. Blige and Method Man's classic did anyone rep that ride or die love. An idea slowly started forming in Qwess's head . . .

What if he could get his wife to release some of this music exclusively on Wave? The world hadn't heard new music from Lisa Ivory in years! What if she came back on his platform? Sure, she held obligations to her other label, but with streaming being a fairly new thing, he was sure there were some loopholes in there that could allow him to maneuver around standard industry contracts. Hell, and if there weren't any, he would be off laughing at the bank before her other label could gain any traction on a lawsuit. He was already being sued, what could one more lawsuit hurt? They couldn't get blood from a cactus. If he could put Lisa Ivory's new music on Wave, he was sure cash would pour in and grant him some financial relief. The only problem was Lisa didn't want to share her music with the world anymore.

But would she take one for the team?

Qwess turned off the music and pondered on a few moves. While he conjured up a master plan, he stared at the TV on the wall blankly. Then something suddenly caught his attention.

On the television was video of his old comrade from jail, Mahmoud. Mahmoud was being led into a federal police vehicle in handcuffs. His beard was long and unkempt, and his face was bruised. On the bottom of the screen, the caption read: *"Narcoterrorist Mahmoud Abdul Muhammad Kareem Trial Begins Next Week."*

Qwess adjusted the volume to hear more from the report:

"Narcoterrorist jihadist Mahmoud Abdul Muhammad Kareem is set to begin trial on international drug smuggling and terrorism charges next week. You may recall Kareem is accused of funding and managing a heroin distribution pipeline from the Middle East into Europe, South America, and the United States. The government alleges that Kareem then used the proceeds from his illegal smuggling operation to fund Islamic terrorists back in Pakistan. At the time of his arrest, sources allege he was plotting to overthrow the Pakistani government and install his own government with members from his clan. The federal government alleges that Kareem was responsible for sixty percent of the heroin supply in the United States, and that he masterminded an elab-

orate shipping method using underground tunnels, private aircraft, and even submarines to get his drugs into foreign countries . . ."

While the reporter spoke, photos of a seized submarine and private jet flashed across the screen, followed by photos of palatial mansions and bespoke Rolls Royces.

The reporter continued:

"Sources say that Kareem hid behind the guise of a jihadist while simultaneously living a lavish lifestyle of luxury homes in Dubai, London, and New York City, along with a fleet of exotic luxury vehicles for him and his four wives to enjoy. If convicted, Kareem could get the death penalty."

Qwess couldn't believe his eyes. Mahmoud, a narcoterrorist? The good Muslim brother was a drug dealer? Nah, that just didn't seem right. The brother whom Qwess met, his heart was pure. He never spoke of drug dealing, only Islam. However, this would explain the notoriety that Mahmoud possessed in the jail. *Damn, all this time Mahmoud was the plug,* Qwess thought.

The door to the studio opened, and in walked Lisa with King Reece's son Prince in tow.

"As-salamu alaykum, babe. Look who is here with us for a while," Lisa said.

"'Sup, Uncle Qwess!" Prince greeted him. At eight years old, he was a carbon copy of his father.

Qwess grabbed him in a tight embrace and noogied his locs. "'Sup, P, what's the deal? You staying with us awhile?"

"Yeah, I was staying with Uncle Doe, but I told him I wanted to stay here with you for a little and kick it with you since I missed you while you were away," Prince explained.

"Okay, that's what's up! Glad to have you here. I can use some company."

"No doubt!" Prince exclaimed, as if he were a grown man.

Lisa chuckled. "I'll leave you two men alone so you can bond," she said, heading toward the door.

"Hey babe, hold up," Qwess said.

Lisa turned to face him. "What's up?"

Qwess paused a bit, unsure of how to approach the subject. He walked to the door and left Prince sitting at the mixing board.

"So um, I've been thinking . . ."

"Yes?"

"We need you to come off the bench."

Chapter 17

Flame's right foot dragged on the ground while he braced his weight on his walker. He swung himself forward until his feet touched the ground, and a smile crept across his face. He couldn't feel his feet touching the ground, he just saw them. Or could he? Flame could've sworn he felt the floor tickle his big toe. He did not want to get excited, lest he would be disappointed, though it felt as real as his hands touching the walker.

Flame planted one foot on the ground while bracing his weight on his walker. He swung himself forward until his feet touched the ground. He couldn't *feel* his feet touching the ground—he just saw them, but in his head he could've sworn he felt the floor tickling his big toe. A bolt of excitement ripped through his body! He repeated the move, and when his foot touched the floor again, he just knew he felt the same sensation in his big toe. He wanted to tell Kim, but he didn't want her to think he was a fool or that he wasn't content with his fate, so he continued to drag himself on his walker into the other room to wait on the doorbell to ring.

Flame had been eagerly anticipating this visitor all morning. Butterflies the size of eagles rumbled in his stomach as he thought about what he was about to do. The butterflies weren't there because of doubt; he had never been so sure about a thing in his life. Rather, he was nervous about the whole act itself. This was new territory for Flame. He had lived most of his life a certain way. Now he was about to live life the complete opposite—just like his paralysis had forced him to.

The doorbell rang, and Flame looked at the cameras to confirm the guest. He saw that it was him and he quickly buzzed him in. A few minutes later, Johnny the Jeweler joined Flame in his living room.

"Flaaaaame! My man, how's it going?" Johnny greeted him as he sat on the sofa next to Flame. "It's been a long time, my brother. I'm glad to see you're doing well."

Johnny's diamond teeth gleamed when he spoke. A short Asian man with spiked hair, Johnny looked like the jeweler to the stars that he was. A huge diamond-encrusted chain adorned his neck, with an emblem the size of a dinner plate. Baggy jeans hung from his waist, and his white V-neck T-shirt was crisp and new.

"Aye, if you call this doing well," Flame returned, motioning toward his limp legs.

Flame was embarrassed at his predicament. Johnny was plugged into the industry, and over the years Johnny had done a lot of business with him. The last time Johnny had seen Flame was at a show in his native Houston, Texas. Flame was on top of the world at the time, and Johnny had paid homage to his greatness like everyone else in the world. Now he was a shell of that man, and although he had come to grips with his new life, it would take some time to get used to people in the industry seeing him like this.

Johnny frowned. He palmed Flame's shoulder and gave him a stern stare. "My buddy, you still have your life, and you have your faith." Johnny reminded him. The whole

world was witnessing the rebirth of Flame through the catalog of social media videos he had been posting about his re-
covery. "Not to mention, you have a beautiful woman by
your side. I'd count that as doing better than well."

Flame smiled. Johnny was correct. He had a lot to be
thankful for, and Kim was at the top of the list. She had done
right by him. Now it was time for him to do right by her.

Flame smiled. "You're right," he agreed. "Now, let's get
down to business."

Johnny smiled and placed a suede-covered briefcase onto
the ottoman. He slowly popped it open and slid it over to
Flame. A beautiful array of women's diamond rings of vary-
ing sizes lined the inside of the briefcase. Flame marveled at
the masterpieces before him, studying each ring carefully before selecting one with a large center stone accompanied
with a band of smaller diamonds.

"I like this," Flame announced.

"Ah, good choice. That one is a total of four carats. VVS
stones, of course. The center stone is three carats alone, and
the band adds the other stone. It's loud enough to say, 'I love
you,' yet elegant enough for a classy lady such as Miss Kim
Rawls," Johnny claimed.

Flame turned the ring around in his hands repeatedly, in-
specting it, visualizing himself popping the question. Was it
enough for her? Would she appreciate it? Would she agree to
marry him? A series of questions flooded his mind as the reality of what he was about to do set in.

"How much?" Flame asked.

"Well, this goes as a set," Johnny explained. He pointed
to another diamond ring, a simple band with a cluster of
stones. "That goes along with it, and adds another carat to it,
so now she has a whole garden," he joked. "Total price for
all . . . for you, I can do just above two."

Flame thought about it. *Two million dollars* . . . He knew

that wasn't a bad price and Johnny had always been fair in the past. Flame had purchased easily over four million in jewelry over the years in his heyday. But this wasn't his heyday, and the money wasn't flooding in as it once had. Still, Kim had been a bigger asset to him than any amount of money, so she was definitely worth it.

"I know things aren't what they used to be," Johnny said, seeming to read Flame's thoughts. "So I can do half up front, and we can work out a payment plan. Matter fact, I'll even knock off two points as a wedding gift as long as you invite me to the wedding."

The wedding . . . Flame smiled at the thought. He could visualize Kim walking down the aisle to meet him in a stunning dress. He saw her face light up when he presented the ring to her at the altar. (Of course, in his vision, he was standing tall instead of sitting in a wheelchair.)

Flame made his decision on the spot. "You got a deal!"

Johnny erupted in laughter. "Good choice, my buddy."

They shook on it, and the smile that spread on Flame's face was nearly brighter than all the diamonds in Johnny's arsenal.

Qwess pushed a button and the V12 engine whirred to life with a wailing rumble. As the car vibrated beneath him, he moved his hand over the superior craftsmanship of the bespoke interior. The shiny silver metal of the center console contrasted perfectly with the red leather bucket seats. He gripped the odd-shaped steering wheel and pushed the accelerator. A loud pop echoed, and a ball of fire shot from the center pipes at the back of the vehicle. The explosion simultaneously startled and excited Qwess. He could never get enough of the Pagani Huayra. This was what a million-dollar machine was made of.

He shut off the engine of the Huayra, then went to his

Ferrari Enzo. This was the star of his car collection. Although it was older compared to the other horses in his stable, the Enzo held special meaning for him. This was the first hypercar he had purchased, a testament to him reaching the next level in life. The Enzo had been his trophy of sorts back then. Most of his peers could afford Benzes and Bentleys, but the Enzo was rare. Enzo owners were an elite club, and when Qwess joined those ranks, it was all the way up from there.

Qwess settled in the seat of the Enzo, and it felt like the world was caving in on him. He was in his garage, not to marvel at his collection. Rather, he was appraising his collection to see which exotic car would fetch him the most money. He was in the process of performing economic triage on his life, so he had to begin purging some things that didn't make good business sense anymore. First on the list was his beloved car collection.

Qwess owned twenty vehicles in all. Some were here, and others were stored at his other homes. Just in this home alone were over ten million in cars. As much as he loved the Huayra, he reasoned that it would be the first to go. Someone had recently crashed another Huayra, so the incident would raise the value on this Huayra to just under two million.

Qwess's phone buzzed to life. He looked at the text then opened the garage door. As the door raised, he saw a black Dodge Challenger Hellcat idling outside the door. The car rolled into the garage, and Qwess quickly closed the door behind it. The engine shut off, and seconds later Bone emerged from the driver's side of the vehicle.

"As-salamu alaykum!" Bone greeted with excitement. This was his first time seeing Qwess since he had been home, and he was genuinely happy to see him.

"Wa alaykum as-salamu!" Qwess returned, embracing Bone with a tight hug.

Qwess released Bone, and the two giants stood in silence as they sized each other up. It had been a long time, and so much had changed.

The last time Qwess had seen Bone was when Bone had snuck into the bowels of the jail to meet Qwess. It was then that Qwess had confirmed to Bone that his big homie was sour and needed to be exterminated. That revelation had forced Bone to wrest control of the Crescent Crew from Samson. That act—and Samson's subsequent betrayal—had been the catalyst to the bloody war that now waged in the streets. Months later, and despite all that had been done, they were right back at square one. Samson was still alive, and Qwess was still facing the death penalty.

"I hear things are crazy out there," Qwess volunteered.

Bone shook his head. "Crazy ain't the word, OG. It's beyond crazy! You got this rat masquerading as a cat—he got nine lives."

"Yeah, and him and his bitchass brother got a *life* sentence hanging over my head," Qwess emphasized.

"No doubt."

"You know I took care of both them niggas?" Qwess recalled. "When they met me, they were some country bumpkins from the backwoods of Alabama. We served in the Army together."

"Yeah?"

"Yeah! You didn't know? I brought both of them niggas here to the Carolinas. Put some money in their pockets and made them men again," Qwess recalled. "Uncle Sam ain't do that for them. I did—the Black man. I took them in and made them a part of our family. Made them both rich beyond their wildest dreams . . . and this the thanks I get?" Qwess shook his head, and his voice dropped an octave. "They made me slaughter my own brothers, man. I killed some innocent Muslims behind these niggas in Muslim suits," Qwess recalled. "So not only are they trying to kill me off here; I may not even see *Jannah* because of them."

Qwess was referring to an order he issued for Bone to carry out. Bone was instructed to eliminate any remaining members from the "first fruit" of the Crescent Crew. Any members that could have tied Qwess to the allegations against him had to go. Bone carried out the order in a magnificent fashion. He orchestrated a meeting in the mountains for the Crew, and when the members showed up and gathered in the cabin, Bone blew the cabin up in an explosion so big that it made the national news. The incident had killed over a dozen innocent men in one swoop.

"Well, all of them weren't innocent," Bone corrected him. "I did find out later that one of the brothers was cooperating with the Feds."

Qwess shrugged. "Don't matter, Akhi. They were innocent of what I accused them of, though."

Bone nodded. He had seen a lot during his tenure in the streets, but this latest web of betrayal had taken the cake.

"And after all that, neither one of these niggas is dead yet," Qwess stated.

Qwess walked over to a cream-colored Lamborghini Aventador roadster with the top out. He plopped down into the emerald-green colored leather seat and fired it up. The V12 roared to life. Qwess tapped the accelerator and the engine wailed like a pterodactyl. A plume of dark smoke shot from the back, and the car sputtered to silence.

"Damn," Qwess said. "This one dying on me."

"It might be oil in the engine," Bone advised. "I had the same thing happen to the one I had."

"Nah, I just haven't cranked it up in a while. These cars are meant to be driven. When you don't drive them often, you have to fire them up every now and then to keep the parts fluid," Qwess explained. "Talk about champagne problems," he added.

Qwess fired the engine up again and let it run. Then he stepped out and stood close to Bone. "So tell me something good, Akhi. What's the word out there in them streets? Are we any closer to resolving things?"

Bone didn't miss the fact that Qwess left the engine running to drown out their conversation—just in case anyone was listening. Any other comrade would've been offended, but not Bone. He was true to the game. He probably would've done the same if his right-hand man had double-crossed him.

"We still can't get to him inside," Bone reported. "He took out a couple of our guys that we sent at him."

Qwess nodded. "And let me guess, he checked in to PC, right?" He said, referring to Protective Custody. In prison, inmates who fear for their lives have the option to "check in" or go to a special housing unit for protection against threats.

Bone shook his head. "Nah, the nigga turned up."

"Huh? What you mean?"

"Check this out."

Qwess switched off the Lamborghini and followed Bone to his Challenger. He watched as Bone popped the trunk and pulled out a duffle bag. He tossed the duffle bag onto the hood of the car and snatched it open. He dug in and pulled out two kilos. One was a kilo of heroin, and the other was a kilo of cocaine.

Qwess flinched. It had been so long since he'd been around drugs of any kind. Just seeing the packages made him nervous.

"Look at this," Bone said, pointing to the bricks. In the center of each brick was stamped a picture of Samson's face from the *Wanted* posters prior to his surgery. "This nigga done got his own stamp, bruh. He in the motherfucking joint and got the nerve to put his own face on the work."

This didn't make sense to Qwess. There was dumb, and then there was dumber. "How you know he behind the stamp?" Qwess asked. "You know these young dick riders these days. They might be trying to pay homage to some shit they know nothing about. They praise the villain, and Samson was on America's Most Wanted before."

Bone shook his head vehemently. "Nah, OG. I got ten of each of those inside that bag with identical stamps. Ain't nobody moving that type of weight except us. And one, we damn sho' ain't praising this nigga. Two, we ain't got weight like that right now."

The confusion was evident on Qwess's face, so Bone broke things down to him. He relayed to Qwess everything that went down from the day he left Qwess in the jail. He shared everything, from the meeting at his club where Twin was executed to the situation in Miami with El Jefe, up until his current situation of having no supplier, minimal work, and a ton of re-up money.

"Wait," Qwess said. "So you telling me this rat staged a coup from federal prison? He managed to work the Feds *and* the cartel?"

Bone nodded. "Yep. El Jefe cut us off and gave him the plug, so now he stronger than ever. He got his brother running shit out here, and he steady recruiting dudes from inside, former gang members and stuff."

Qwess couldn't believe what he was hearing. On the one hand, he abhorred the thought of a rat "bossing up." On the other hand, the man had pulled off a brilliant move. He had managed to turn the ultimate negative into an uber positive. He had the protection of the federal government and one of the most powerful Mexican cartels in the world, along with a pipeline of raw dope bearing his face. Qwess shook his head at the audacity. He couldn't make this shit up!

Qwess picked up the brick of cocaine and inspected it. The shiny flakes glistened beneath the bright lights in the garage. Qwess didn't need to be in the game to know this was straight drop. Once a hustler, always a hustler. He stared at the picture of Samson's face with open contempt. How could one man be responsible for so much trouble?

"So what's the plan?" Qwess asked, as he continued to inspect the drugs.

Bone was lost for words. He washed his hands over his face. "To be honest, OG, I don't even know," he admitted. "This is all new territory for me. I inherited this thing from King Reece. I knew how to maintain it, but being real, I never actually built a crew like this. I was a soldier that got promoted to a general; everything else was already in place. I had one job—not to fuck it up." Bone shrugged. "I mean, I understand money and violence. I thought that's what it took to keep this thing in line, but now I see it takes so much more. I was so glad you sent for me because I was drowning with no one to talk to. Like, how did y'all do it?"

Qwess understood the enormous amount of pressure Bone was under. It took a lot for a man of Bone's stature to break down in front of another man like this. Bone had risen to be a king in the streets. Yet the streets were different today from they were yesteryear.

In Qwess's day, to rise to the rank of general, you had to do more than be willing to bust your guns. You had to be a thinker, a visionary. Even the violence you inflicted had to be calculated. Contrary to common thought, for the lords of the game, the money was the reward, not the motivation. For men like Qwess, their motivation was being their own bosses and living life on their own terms, not answering to the demands of the "shit-stem."

Then there were the other types of men, men like King Reece. They were . . . different. For them, money allowed them the freedom to practice their savagery. They were sociopaths who were lured to the game by the lawlessness of it. Once they amassed enough wealth, their alter egos came out and they relished the opportunity to terrorize the streets. These men often crashed and burned before their stars were able to shine bright, unless they had a counterpart who balanced them out. This was what made the Crescent Crew such a force to be reckoned with in their day.

Reece was fire and Qwess was ice. Qwess was the thinker, the visionary, the voice of reason, the man that constantly held on to the *why* of their movements. He orchestrated calculated moves, and Reece was all too happy to carry them out. Together they rode their wave to the top.

Balance was what Bone was missing. Sure, he had an army of troops ready to ride, but they lacked the proper guidance from Bone. He was sworn in it, not born in it, so he lacked the leadership required to return them back to prominence. The current Crescent Crew was the V12 in the Lamborghini without the computer chip that programmed the horses on where to go. But Qwess was ready to be Mr. Ferruccio; he was ready to take it back to the basics.

"The game was different back then," Qwess replied. "It was about the money, not the fame. Plus, you didn't have all these snakes. We had honor, so it was different."

"Yeah," Bone agreed. "I got all these brothers depending on me. I got you depending on me. It's a lot. At times, man, I think about running off to the Middle East somewhere with all my money, just escaping, you know, but that's not in me. I just don't know how to proceed. I know I came here because you called me, but I was hoping you could help me out too."

While Bone spoke, all types of thoughts ran through Qwess's head. Both of their backs were against the wall, and the irony was they needed each other to come out on top. For Qwess, his only dilemma was whether he wanted to get involved in a lifestyle he swore years ago he would never partake in. When he turned his back on the drug game, he vowed to never look back—in any capacity.

But life has its own sense of humor.

Qwess's money was low, and his freedom was on the line. Helping Bone could resolve both of those issues, while simultaneously putting an army beneath his fingers. On the other side, his wealth and power could be restored.

"Tell me exactly what your problems are, in order of importance," Qwess said.

Bone ticked off the answers on his slender fingers. "For one, we need to end this war, because war scares away the money. Two, I need a new supplier. If I can't feed my people, then I can't lead my people. Three, I need soldiers; I'm taking huge losses."

"Okay," Qwess nodded, taking it all in, allowing his mastermind to calculate scenarios. The same mind he used to build one of the biggest independent record labels in history he was now directing toward the streets again. He mulled things over in silence for a few minutes until he came up with a solution.

"Okay," Qwess sighed, clasping his hands together. "So the number one thing *we* have to do is eliminate that rat. I'll help you devise a plan for that, and then you can carry that out. Remember—if you kill the head, the body will follow. In the meantime, I'm going to help you find a new plug. On that tip, I will only talk to you, and you better not ever even remotely mention my name to anybody outside this garage about it."

"Okay," Bone said, gratefully.

Qwess smiled triumphantly. "Now, I'm going to show you how to do Crew business."

Chapter 18

"Oooh baby . . . that shit feels so good!" the woman cried out.

Samson's huge hand clasped around her mouth to silence her pleasure. "Shut up, bitch, before somebody come in here," he grunted.

Samson slammed her face back onto the desk and pushed his erection deeper inside her womb. He wrapped his huge hands around her tiny waist and thrust his hips into her soft wide ass, nearly forcing the desk through the wall. Her wails only enticed him more, and he pumped his passion inside her furiously. Like a cow buckling beneath the pressure of a bull, the woman collapsed onto the desk helplessly. Samson wrapped his beefy arm around her neck and pulled her towards him while he continued to punish her. Just as he felt the familiar fizzle inside his balls, the intercom and radio crackled to life.

"First responders to the cafeteria! First responders to the cafeteria!"

"Shit!" Samson hissed as he pulled away and adjusted his pants. "I was about to bust."

The woman reached on the floor for her pants and snatched the walkie-talkie from the waistband. As soon as she picked it up, she heard her name being called over the loudspeaker.

"Lieutenant Adams, what's your 10-20?" It was the Captain of the shift, requesting her location.

Lieutenant Adams quickly gathered herself and responded, "I'm 10-16—cafeteria," she lied, insinuating that she was en route. The lie gave her more time to get herself together. She pulled her shirt down and stepped into her pants, breathing heavily.

"Samson, you and that country dick can do something to a woman. Whew! Got me feeling it all in my throat." Lieutenant Adams rubbed her neck and eyed Samson's twelve-inch cock, still slick with her juices, as he stuffed it back inside his pants.

Samson chuckled. "And I didn't even get a chance to put it there yet."

"Next time, next time," Lieutenant Adams promised. "This better not be one of yours cutting up in that cafeteria. You told me that you were going to keep my yard under control, but lately, it's been incidents every day."

Samson shrugged. "It's not mine. But when I find out who it is, I'm going to get them in line too. I got too much money out here."

Lieutenant Adams buckled her belt and turned back into an officer from the bombshell she was without her uniform. Lieutenant Adams was Carolina born and bred and had the body to prove it. She stood only 5'4", but she weighed a solid hundred and sixty pounds that she carried mostly in her hips and ass. Her stomach was as flat as the desk she was just laying across and her 36Ds stood firm, yet soft. Her skin was the color of peanut butter and just as smooth. Her silky black hair stretched down to the middle of her back, but she wore it pulled into a bun at work. The penitentiary graded women on a curve. For example, an adjustable "6" on the street would be a penitentiary "dime." Lieutenant Adams was a dime on the street, so she couldn't even be rated on the penitentiary scale, and since the second week Samson arrived at Butner, she had been his toy.

Lieutenant Adams craned her neck up and slid her tongue in Samson's mouth. "I gotta go, babe. But you better get my yard under control."

Samson smacked her on her ass. "I got you."

Lieutenant Adams left her office. A few minutes after she left, Samson slid out unnoticed. There was a First Responders called, so the yard was essentially locked down, but those rules didn't apply to Samson.

Samson not only ran Butner, he was law throughout the federal penal system.

Samson had finagled his way into a unique position in the underworld. With El Jefe's cartel backing him outside, along with his reputation in Mexico, he was untouchable in the Mexican criminal underworld. With his legendary exploits in the Crescent Crew and the new Crew he was building, he was at the top of the food chain in the Black underworld. With him working for the Feds, he was untouchable to law enforcement. Samson had managed to insulate himself on all sides, making him virtually invincible.

However, there was one faction that didn't give a fuck about Samson and his alliances.

Qwess dialed the number, and a few seconds later, a familiar voice was on the other line.

"As-salamu alaykum!" Mahmoud's voice was cheerful and strong, nothing like a man going to trial for his life.

"Wa alaykum as-salamu!" Qwess returned. "I pray that everything is well."

"Eh, you know how these things go. Man plans, but Allah is the best of planners," Mahmoud replied nonchalantly. Qwess could almost see him shrugging his shoulders.

"Indeed."

"I knew you would be reaching out to me sooner than later, so I wasn't surprised when I got your message," Mahmoud said. "Even though I'm back here, I'm still very aware of out there. Even when you were here, I knew who you were and what you were going to be facing upon your release. Allah has blessed me with sight beyond sight. That's why I gave you the info. I knew when you truly discovered who I am, the pieces would line up. And now here we are. So how may I serve you, Akhi?"

Qwess paused. Even though they both knew the nature of the call, Qwess still felt like a creep delving back into that space. He held so much respect for Mahmoud, even after it was revealed he dealt in narcotics. Qwess didn't want to lose the respect Mahmoud held for him, regardless of Mahmoud's dealings.

Mahmoud sensed Qwess was apprehensive about things. He knew where he was mentally because he had been there many moons ago.

"Akhi, let me tell you something. I used to think that what I was doing went against Islam because ultimately the materials left an indent on the community. However, in Islam we are judged by our *niyyat*—our intentions—first, and our actions second. So as long as what I was doing was *fisabilallah*, then it was okay," Mahmoud explained.

Qwess listened intently to Mahmoud's words. Mahmoud was considered a scholar in Islam, a *shayk*, so he was very learned. He was essentially telling Qwess that as long as what he was doing was "in the cause of Allah," then he need not worry. For Mahmoud, his cause was funding the tyrannical regimes that sought to oppress the Muslims in the region. There was no doubt what his *niyyat* was. But what was Qwess's *niyyat*?

"For you, your cause is different," Qwess admitted. "Mine isn't as noble."

"Sure it is! What can be more noble than helping Black people in the West? Who has experienced more oppression than the brothers in the West?" Mahmoud posed. "When you succeed in the industry, you give brothers jobs, a future, a way to feed their families. The more you succeed, the more people you help. That's your *jihad*," Mahmoud reasoned. "We all have our arsenals in this war. This is why I am extending my network to you, because I see the impact you have on the world. I see what you are on the other side of this *fitnah*."

Qwess mulled things over in silence, weighing the pros and cons of his next few words. Those words would set into motion an irreversible train of events. However, that train was needed.

"So tell me what you need from me, my brother?" Mahmoud asked. "Name your destiny."

Qwess hesitated a moment, then spoke his truth. "I need access to your pipeline."

Mahmoud chuckled. "Which pipeline? I control several."

"I need it all. Heroin, cocaine, weed—anything you can put your hands on, I need it."

"Ah, so the news of the Crescent Crew is not exaggerated? They're destitute?"

Qwess didn't confirm anything. Crew business was Crew business. "So can you help me?"

Mahmoud chuckled. "It's the least I can do, my brother. Do you need consignment?"

Qwess thought about his own funds and how drab his conditions were. Then he recalled the figures Bone discussed with him that the Crescent Crew were holding onto. He had learned that the number one rule in business was OPM, or "Other People's Money." In the drug game he had always played with his own money, but the game had changed, as had his circumstances.

"Yeah," Qwess answered. "I may need consignment on the first shipment."

"I'll tell you what," Mahmoud said. "You have something I want that can offset the cost a bit."

Qwess was all ears. "Oh really? And what's that?"

"I hear you have a Pagani Huayra in that collection of yours . . ."

Qwess chuckled. Mahmoud was going for his pride and joy. His penchant for exotic cars was well-known. "Yes, I do," he replied.

"Now, that sounds like a nice start, a perfect act of good faith."

Qwess didn't think twice. "Consider it done."

"Very well." Mahmoud agreed. "So for the particulars, I will put my buddy in contact with your buddy to handle everything. I'm assuming this will be the only discussion we will have about this?"

"Absolutely. How soon?"

"I can have the first shipment in your hands after this phone call if you'd like."

Qwess chuckled. He knew Mahmoud was the man, but he didn't realize he was the man. "Let me verify things on my end, then we can proceed," he said.

"Very well."

"So how are things looking with your case?" Qwess asked, switching the subject.

"Allah is the best of planners, Akhi. What he decrees, no one can prevent; what he prevents, no one can decree."

"Ameen," they said in unison.

Qwess heard Mahmoud speaking with someone. A second later he returned to the phone in a hushed tone. "I have to go now, Akhi. I will speak with you soon." Mahmoud ended the call.

Qwess sat in deep reflection. He was now back in the drug game, something he vowed to never do again. He didn't plan on making this his lifestyle, but without it, he would be facing death—literally and figuratively. So he had to make a move. He had given Bone his word and made good on his promise.

Now if only Bone could do his part . . .

Samson couldn't believe his eyes. He walked into the mess hall and saw one of his comrades on the ground, leaking and motionless. The stench of Mace lingered in the air, so he knew that the goon squad had not long left the area. Inmates were lined up against the wall, frantic about what had transpired. As soon as his big frame lumbered through the door they had cut a path for him to walk through, maybe so he could get a bird's eye view of the carnage. Before he could make it to his fallen soldier, one of the officers on his payroll pulled him aside.

"What the hell happened?" Samson demanded.

Officer Tibbs shrugged. "AB guys came in about five deep and just started jugging him. Time we got here it was too late."

"AB?" Samson repeated in a mixture of disbelief and disgust.

AB was short for the Aryan Brotherhood, the white supremacist gang. The AB (or Brand) were the only gang in the penal system strong enough to challenge the more popular Black and Mexican gangs. The AB controlled a sizeable portion of the drug market, particularly the methamphetamine and heroin markets. They were known to be racist, ruthless, and greedy. They didn't just pay lip service to their bigotry, they showed it in real time, never missing an opportunity to inflict harm on their non-white counterparts in GP. Add money into the equation, and they would perform acts that would shame Hitler himself with the level of violence they carried out.

"There is no way the AB is that stupid," Samson estimated.

Inside the penal system, drugs were sold at sometimes 100 times the street price. For example, an ounce of weed that would go for two hundred dollars on the streets would fetch two thousand or more inside. For heroin, the price quadrupled, so there were millions up for grabs behind the wall.

Previously, there had been an unspoken truce between the Nuevo Crew (the name of Samson's fledgling organization) and the AB. Samson had given the meth market to the AB, and he controlled everything else. With his sway over the brown and Black, he could've easily waged a war to eliminate them altogether, but he let them live to keep the balance. For a few months, things were running smooth . . . until now.

"Word on the yard is that their leader, Jimbo, is looking to take you guys down," Officer Tibbs shared.

"That's crazy. That's suicide," Samson said, thinking aloud as his eyes were glued to his fallen soldier. The man on the ground was a former Blood that Gangsta Black had flipped for the Nuevo Crew. Samson felt personally responsible for his welfare. "Where he at now?"

Tibbs shrugged. "He's still on the Hill from the last stabbing. Remember?"

Jimbo had recently stabbed a Puerto Rican prisoner named Sammy Stylez. He was a popular barber on the yard that refused to pay the AB tax for doing business on said yard, so Jimbo wet him up. Although Jimbo held an army of minions at his disposal, he preferred to do the dirty work himself. Part of his logic was to lead by example, the other part was just him being sadistic.

"Yeah, I remember. When does he come down?" Samson asked.

Just then, Lieutenant Adams emerged from the back of the mess hall. She noticed Samson right away. For a split second, their eyes locked, then hers dropped to the floor and upon the fallen man. She touched his neck and checked his pulse. Shocked, she looked up at the guards standing around. She checked his pulse again and shook her head. The results were obvious. He was dead.

Samson witnessed his prison girlfriend pronounce his comrade dead and lost his cool. He roared and stormed from the mess hall in a rage, headed straight to the dorm to rally the troops.

If the Brand wanted war with Nuevo Crew, then he would release his power on the whole FBOP!

Chapter 19

Flame stared at Kim as she moved through the positions of her morning yoga routine. She was alone on the back balcony, naked, sweating it out on her yoga mat. He was in awe of her beauty. Her toned body was a Wonderland.

Kim had always been in shape, but the yoga routine she adopted while she was in quarantine with him took her physique to another level. Her six-pack now resembled an eight-pack, and it snaked down to a perfect V leading to her other "V." Her shoulders and back were ripped, yet still feminine enough to be admired and adored. Her back tapered down to a perfectly round inverted heart with just the right amount of hang time. Even her thighs and calves were toned to perfection. In her down time, Kim Rawls had honed her body into a masterpiece. In their Kismet days, it was Sasha Beaufont who had the milkshake that brought all the boys to the yard, but this version of Kim would bring the whole city out. And each morning Flame had a bird's eye view.

Too bad all he could do was stare. Until now.

Flame flicked the joystick on his wheelchair and glided

onto the balcony. While Kim was holding steady in an *asana*, Flame heaved himself out of his chair onto the floor. Kim was about twenty feet away from him now, lost in her own world.

Flame crawled on the floor with his elbows, dragging his numb legs behind him. Although there was no feeling in his legs, the dead weight of them put an enormous strain on his elbows, but he pushed on to his destination. He reached Kim just as she came out of her position.

"Joey! Oh my God, what happened? How did you end up down there?" Kim rushed to help Flame up, but he stopped her.

"No, I'm good. Let me finish," Flame insisted.

Kim was confused, but the closer Flame slid to her, it all made sense. While Kim stood tall, Flame tugged at her waist to give himself leverage to pull up. He wrapped his arms around her waist and balanced himself on his knees. Kim looked away from him as to give him his dignity; surely he was embarrassed to have to pull himself up in this manner. As soon as Kim looked down, Flame smiled at her. Between his teeth he held the huge engagement ring he had purchased from Johnny the Jeweler.

Kim's hands flew to her face. "Joey, what is that?" She squealed. "Is that what I think it is?"

Flame nodded and took the ring from his mouth. "Kimberly Rawls," he said. His balance was wavering, but he refused to be denied. "You are the best thing to happen to me since birth, and I want to spend the rest of my life with you. Would you give me the honor and pleasure of being my wife?"

Kim was shocked. She couldn't believe her ears. Flame— a man that had a reputation with the ladies that would rival King Solomon—was asking her to be his one and only. He had even gone to great pains to give her the proper respect and propose to her on his knees. She knew they had grown super close over the past few months, but she had no idea she had penetrated his heart so heavy. Now, here he was putting it all on bended knee.

"Yes! Yes, I will marry you!"

With those words, Flame released his grip on her waist and dropped to the floor in tears. The ring tumbled from his mouth onto Kim's yoga mat. She bent down to pick it up, and Flame pulled her to the mat with him. He rolled over on his side and wrapped her into a tight embrace. The two stared in each other's eyes for what felt like an eternity. A ball of heat rushed up between them. They rode the fiery passion and locked lips in a deep, sensual kiss. Flame pulled Kim closer to him and her naked body pressed against his. He could've sworn he felt an erection poking from his center, but he just knew his mind was toying with him. However, Kim confirmed the erection when she looked down at him.

"Oooh Joey . . . is that what I think it is?" Kim gasped. "I haven't seen this happen in a long time."

Flame was so excited he struggled to breathe. "I think it is! And I think I can feel it! Is it . . ."

"Hard? Yes, baby, it is definitely hard!"

Kim was just as excited as Flame. Where she was shy and reluctant to engage in sex before, she was more than eager and willing to indulge him now. Before, there was apprehension because they were striving to walk a righteous path, and although they had developed a strong bond, there still wasn't the lifelong commitment necessary for their sex to be permissible under the covenant they were walking. Now that there was a proposal and acceptance, they were betrothed and thus able to act in the manner of husband and wife. Translation: She was with all the smoke Flame could give her.

Kim reached down and stroked Flame's erection. She gazed in his eyes while she pumped him to see if he could feel anything. Sure enough, each time she squeezed him,

Flame's eyes fluttered, and a smirk tugged at the corners of his mouth.

"That feels good, baby," Flame moaned. He felt as if he was dreaming, partly because he was with Kim and partly because he was *feeling* what Kim was doing.

Kim smiled at him. "Yes, it does feel good. It all feels good."

Kim continued to stroke Flame's erection. She felt him pulsating inside her palm like he was ready to explode. She rolled him over on his back and mounted him.

Flame's dick was sticking straight up like a flagpole. It was such a marvel that even he had to steal a glance at it. When he looked down he received a two-for-one. Not only did he see himself at attention, he saw Kim's waxed vagina seeping her arousal. He watched as she slowly lowered herself onto him. He received double stimulation—physical and mental—as he watched him spread her tight lips open. As soon as he slid inside her juicy, warm center, he exploded.

"Ahhhh!" he wailed out in agony.

"Ahhhh!" Kim squealed in pleasure.

Kim sank onto him and absorbed all of his essence. Then they showered each other with kisses.

It had been a long journey, but Flame was finally making his way back.

Bone leaned low in the passenger seat of the Dodge Charger. His eyes never left the building in front of him. He had been staked out outside the hair salon on Reilly Road for the past hour, and he wasn't leaving until his mission was accomplished.

Bone had discovered that a woman Gangsta Black was dating got her hair and nails done at the same shop every week at the same time. It took him no time at all to track the lady down and follow her to the salon. Clearly Gangsta Black was mesmerized by her banging body and not her brains, because she was as slow as traffic in the right lane. She never even saw them following her, and that would prove to be her folly as well as Gangsta Black's.

"Yo, go in there and see if she almost done," Bone instructed Maleek, who was in the driver's seat.

They had three other cars surrounding the building at various intervals, and any one of them could've handled this business, but it was imperative for the soldiers to see the generals in action as well.

"Okay, Ahki, but what if she recognize me? Or if they cameras record me or something?" Maleek asked.

Where Maleek was once young and reckless, he was wiser and more cautious now. He was getting real money and was in love; he had a lot to live for now. Keisha was doing better, and when this war was over, he had plans of taking her somewhere remote and hot to put some warm sand on her *cinnabunz*. Getting put on a *Wanted* poster wasn't in the equation.

"Don't worry about that shit," Bone said dismissively. "If need be, we will terminate everybody in there. We got big plans, and it starts with eliminating everybody who ain't crew."

Indeed, Bone had big plans. He had received confirmation from Qwess that their supply woes were over. There was a motherlode on the way from the Middle East, and it was better than anything they had previously been dealing with. According to Qwess, this was directly from the cartels without any cut. When this load came in, money would rain from the sky on their heads as if they were the headliner at a popular strip club. First, they had to clear the way for their plane to land.

Maleek checked the barrel on his Sig. "So, you saying we back good again? If we run these niggas out of town, they taking the work with them."

Bone smiled. "In the words of Khidr, surely I know that

which you do not know," he said. "Basically, since we can't track Hulk down and we can't get to the nigga inside, we gonna kill their whole body, from the smallest nigga to the biggest nigga. I got some heat on that rat nigga inside too. He feeling the heat too. It's only a matter of time."

"Ahh . . . so you saying—"

"I'm saying we gonna knock every nigga down until them niggas come down off their hill and beg us to stop. Then we gonna kill them too. Now go check shit out."

Just as Maleek was about to step from the car, a woman walked out the door of the salon, teasing her fresh leave-out with her hands. She was smiling hard as she strutted to her baby Benz.

"There she go right there," Maleek pointed out.

Bone nodded. "Yep. Let's let her pull out and the other brothers will get her from there." Bone was super excited. He had been down for long and now he saw the way up.

Bone waited for the Benz to leave the parking lot before he made his move. He saw the identical Charger follow the Benz as it made a left onto Cliffdale Road. He spoke into the walkie-talkie. "Don't make a move until I tell you."

Bone followed the convoy down Cliffdale Road at a distance. The four identical Chargers rolling down Cliffdale resembled an FBI raid in progress, but it only looked like it. This was Crew business—new and improved.

As luck would have it, as the convoy followed the woman, she pulled into a gas station near Bunce Road and stopped in front a pump. Seconds later, a triple black BMW turned off Bunce Road and rolled into the gas station. The BMW pulled up right behind the Benz and parked. The convoy slowed down and eased into the gas station on the other side of the building.

Gangsta Black honked the horn of the BMW and waited for Sherita to step from the Benz with his money. She'd called him right before he hit the road to Greenville and informed him that one of his amigos had dropped a bag of money off for him. Things were getting hot in the Ville, and he was going to disappear until the heat died down a bit. The more money he had, the better off he would be, so he was eager to pick up the bag. Since he was about to hit the road, he was rolling dolo. He felt as vulnerable as a newborn, knowing that a price was on his head.

Gangsta Black cracked the window and honked the horn again. "Come on, girl! I gotta go!"

He scanned the area to see if danger was lurking. That's when he saw them. Three black Dodge Chargers. Initially he thought it was the Feds, but he knew if it was them, they would have closed in on him by now. So if it wasn't the Feds, then that meant it could only be one group.

"Shit!" Gangsta Black hissed. He reached under his seat to grab his pistol while simultaneously slamming the car in reverse. To his shock, there was another Dodge Charger blocking his rear. Panicked, he peeped to see if there was room for him to slide between Sherita's Benz and the gas pump, but instead of a gap, there was a tall, hooded figure standing in front of his car, aiming a cannon at him. Before he could make a move, he saw an orange burst explode from the barrel. He never heard the sound, as the bullets had already crashed through the windshield and tore into his neck and shoulder.

Gangsta Black was gripped with excruciating pain. He dropped his Sig Sauer onto the floorboard and clutched his bleeding shoulder while ducking for cover. The pain was so intense he nearly passed out. Out of a fog, he felt his driver's door snatched open, and someone pulled him from the car and tossed him onto the pavement on his back. A boot slammed onto his chest and pinned him to the ground while he gasped for breath. The blood filling his lungs made it difficult for him to breathe, so he knew his time was short. He shook his head defiantly, as if he could fight back the reaper coming to claim his due. Through the hazy fog of his vision, he thought he saw the reaper walking toward him, and he was correct, as Bone advanced toward him slowly.

Gangsta Black's eyes stretched as wide as the charm dangling around his neck when he realized it was the head of the Crescent Crew standing over him with a big pistol clutched inside his palm aimed at his head. He knew he had been kicking up a lot of dust, but he didn't think he had made enough noise for the king to descend from his throne and pay a visit to the streets. Now he knew better, and now it was too late.

"You chose the wrong side," Bone said, looking down on him. "Your boss is a rat, and on this side, we exterminate rats and their whole line. We will track him down and get rid of him. The only thing is, you'll never know."

Gangsta Black felt cold metal press against his forehead. His eyes crossed trying to focus on the single barrel in the middle of his forehead, to no avail. As he came to grips with his fate, he saw his whole life flash before his eyes.

He saw the day his mother died when he was six years old. The day his father was sentenced to the death penalty when he was just eight years old. He saw the day his Blood homies "brought him home" at the tender age of ten. He saw the first time he killed a man at the age of fourteen. He saw the day he was sentenced to ten years in federal prison. He saw the day he met Samson in prison. This was the day his life changed, and that memory glowed brighter than the others. He saw the day he was released from prison. That memory made his heart skip a beat. He saw the day he had been delivered ten kilos. That was the day he really felt alive. And now, that day led to his death.

"It's a wrap for you, homie," Bone announced. Then he pulled the trigger.

Boom! Boom!

Chapter 20

Qwess lay on the massage table in ecstasy as the woman's expert hands kneaded him to another land far away. This was her specialty and just what Qwess needed.

Qwess had been stressed to capacity with all the things on his plate. He had a civil case looming, threatening to bankrupt him. Then there was the death penalty case he was fighting. Next it was his groundbreaking app, Wave, that was initially on the cutting edge of technology and slated to make him a billi, but was now sinking in a quagmire (along with the sixty million he invested) thanks to the rest of the industry catching up to the technology. Topping it all off was his decision to re-enter the dope game.

He was waiting to receive the call at any moment that the shipment had landed. Then his second reign as the head of the Crescent Crew would begin. The irony wasn't lost on him. He was under federal indictment for being the alleged leader of the Crescent Crew. At the time, he couldn't have been farther removed from the streets. Now, with the indictment open and him fighting for his life, he in effect made himself guilty as charged. His decision to return to the streets was akin to escaping a burning building that just caught fire, only to rush back inside when the flames were at their zenith. While foolish on every level to most, the decision was a no-brainer for Qwess. If he didn't become proactive, then chances were the reaction of his inaction would destroy him and his legacy.

"Turn over, bae," the woman said.

Qwess kept his eyes closed and rolled over on his back. The woman applied warm oil to his body and rubbed his chest soft and lovingly. He inhaled deeply, taking the essential oils wafting through the room deep into his lungs. He felt the woman's hands glide down his torso and draw circles around his torso. Then he felt her warm lips engulf his erection. *Ahhh . . . this was what he had been anticipating . . .*

The woman took all of him into her mouth slowly and hummed on him just as he liked. While she fellated him, she palmed his heavy balls and kneaded them like dough.

"Ahhh!" Qwess growled, tensing up and writhing in ecstasy.

The door to the room opened and in walked Lisa.

"Ruquiyah, you're supposed to be bringing him pleasure, not pain," Lisa scolded as she stepped into the room.

"Why don't you come join me and we please him together?" Ruquiyah suggested.

Qwess heard his wife enter the room and he grew excited, for he knew what awaited him.

Ruquiyah was Lisa's childhood friend who became her lover. For years it was rumored in the industry that Lisa Ivory was gay, and until Qwess swept her from her feet, she was. Ruquiyah had been her first female lover and remained her secret girlfriend for years until she fell in love with Qwess. When Lisa and Qwess were dating, Lisa flew Qwess out to Ruquiyah's homeland of Jamaica and introduced them to each other in a threesome that Lisa orchestrated. From that day forth, Ruquiyah had become *their* girlfriend, sharing both superstars at will and with their blessings. There were no awkward moments of confusion; their roles were clear. Lisa and Qwess were married, and Ruquiyah was the girl-friend. There was no jealousy because they all cared for each other the same and shared selflessly. For a reformed woman-izer like Qwess, the arrangement worked because it gave him the benefit of new sex without exposing himself to the streets. For Lisa, Ruquiyah remained her best friend and a constant lover in her life. For Ruquiyah, Lisa and Qwess were generous to her, funding her chain of massage parlors and spas. Their . . . *thing* worked for all of them.

Qwess felt Lisa join Ruquiyah in their quest to please him. While Ruquiyah sucked on his erection, Lisa licked his balls. Just as he was getting lost in his good fortune, his gate alarm shrilled to life, startling everyone.

"Who is that?" Qwess groused. He peered at the bank of security cameras on the wall and saw a black Bentley Ben-tayga idling outside the gate to his property.

Qwess racked his brain trying to determine who would just show up at his property unannounced. Shabazz came to mind, but he wasn't scheduled to see the high-powered at-torney for another few days. Bone came to mind, but he knew Bone was standing by for the call of a lifetime. Qwess's partner Lando was in New York with Liam trying to make Wave a success. So who would have the unmitigated gall to just drop by his home?

The intercom in the ceiling crackled to life with his an-swer.

"Sir, there is a Mr. Joey here to see you," his security in-formed him.

Qwess smiled. It was Flame. He had been anticipating this day for over a year now. Now it was time.

Samson ended the call and punched the concrete wall so hard it knocked a chip from it. He had just received word that they killed his number one soldier, Gangsta Black. Caught him slipping, did him dirty with two to the head and left him on the pavement. They left his girl alive, but only after they carved two Cs in her forehead. Then, to add insult to injury, they took his money but sprinkled two kilos of heroin out on the ground all around Gangsta Black's body.

Samson was livid. Bone was sending him a message, and he heard it loud and clear.

He looked at the calendar on the wall and struck off another day. His days behind the wall were getting shorter and shorter. His last conversation with the attorney general gave him hope. Qwess's trial was vastly approaching and once he performed his civic duty on the stand, he would be a free man. They had plans of relocating him into a witness protection program, or maybe even sending him back to Mexico, but Samson had plans of his own that involved him staying right in the good ol' U.S. of A.

Samson heard calls on the rock of "Fire in the Hole," which meant that an officer was walking around on the tier. A short time later there was a knock at his door. He glanced up and saw Lieutenant Adams coming inside his cell. Her usual cheerful smile toward him was now a somber expression.

"Hi, Love," Lieutenant Adams said. She closed the door and backed up against it to block off the window in the door. "I'm sure you heard the news about Flowers. How you holding up?"

Flowers was Gangsta Black's last name.

Samson shrugged his broad shoulders. "You know, the game is the game," he said cavalierly. Inside he was hurting, but he couldn't allow anyone to see his pain. He felt his power was in his invincibility.

Lieutenant Adams shook her head. "What. The. Fuck. Is. Going. On. Out. There? Dead bodies everywhere. Mutilations. Muslim gangbangers. And everywhere I turn, I hear your name. What are you involved in? I know you are a big shot here, but why are so many people around you getting killed?"

Samson walked over to the door, towering above her. He was so large that the small cell felt suffocating with both of them occupying the same cramped space.

"I can't tell you exactly what's going on, because I don't know," Samson lied. He had learned a valuable lesson from King Reece: Pillow talking was antithetical to the game. "That's why I need you to be my eyes and ears in here so I can stay one step ahead of everybody. Take care of me so I can take care of you," Samson reminded her. He clasped her chin inside his massive palm and gave her a stern look. "You feel me?"

Lieutenant Adams nodded as if she was under his spell. There was just something about Samson that did it for her. "I feel you," she agreed. "It's just that your name is ringing bells around here, so I had to come make sure you were good."

"Yeah, you know how it goes. Niggas gonna talk. I'm getting short now, so the haters starting to come out."

"Yeah? How long you got left?" Lieutenant Adams asked. Far as she knew, he still had close to ten years left on his sentence. The first thing she did when she arrived at work each morning was check his date in the computer.

"My attorney saying I should be home in a few months."

Lieutenant Adams had been in the system for twelve years. She had seen all the games and chicanery. She'd witnessed men with fresh forty-year sentences on plea deals lie and tell their women they were "short" (on the lower portion of their sentence) just to keep them hanging around. Yet she believed Samson when he spoke, despite what the computer read, because she had also seen the flip side of the coin. She had seen men whom the computer declared *deceased* walk up out of there in under five years. She figured if anyone could beat the odds, it was Samson.

"So, what you going to do when you get out?" Lieutenant Adams asked.

"Besides beat the brakes off that good pussy at will?"

Lieutenant Adams blushed and chuckled. "Yeah, besides that."

"I'm going to take care of you like I promised. Get you out of this damn prison, maybe have you as my VP in one of my businesses."

Lieutenant Adams crossed her arms. She wasn't convinced. "You sure? Because it doesn't seem like you have all the wild out of you, and I'm telling you, I'm not leaving my stability for a life of crime. Picture that!"

Now it was Samson's turn to chuckle. "Nah, I'm done with that life. I mean, I run things back here because I have to. It's eat or be eaten back here, and I'd rather be a dick than a swallower—know what I mean? But once I walk out those gates, I am done with this life."

Samson was lying so good, he almost believed himself. Truth was, he had plans all right. He had plans on being a crime lord, bigger than anything his mentor King Reece had ever been. He had amassed a considerable amount of power and stature on both sides of the border, and he was going to consolidate the two factions—the Black and brown—into a cartel the criminal world had never seen, with him at the top of the throne.

"I don't know," Lieutenant Adams insisted, shaking her head. "I've seen your kind before, and they never can seem to walk away from all that money and power."

"Yeah, well I'm not them, and they aren't me. I have businesses set up to keep me paid for a few lifetimes if I never make another dime. All I need is a Queen to help me spend it all. I hope that's you."

Samson wasn't lying, per se. He had set up a few businesses since he was down. He owned a car wash in Texas (thanks to Gangsta Black), and a club in Charlotte via a woman he was sleeping with prior to prison. Of course, there were the illegal snatch-and-grab operations he oversaw in Mexico (he had taken that operation to another level), but nothing as lucrative as the drugs his Nuevo Crew pushed. That was, and would always be, his bread and butter.

"I would love to be your Queen, but I'm not falling for the okie doke," Lieutenant Adams assured him. She would love to be his woman on the outside. Getting that good country dick on the regular and being spoiled rotten? What woman wouldn't want that? But it had to be right.

"Nah, I respect you too much to put you in harm's way," Samson said. "You held me down while I was back here, so I want to hold you down out there."

Samson wasn't exactly lying to her either. He could see himself being with her outside, but she would have to get in line. He had a whole family back in Mexico that he was eager to return to, not to mention the other Mexican women at his disposal. He was a major figure down there, and the rules were different for men like him. What he wanted, he got, and his fetish other than money was young Mexican women. The Lieutenant was fine, and the sex was good, but thirty-year-old pussy was a lot different than twenty-year-old pussy, and in Mexico he had his pick.

"I want to believe you," Lieutenant Adams said. "So, we'll see when you get out. In the meantime, I want you to—"

"*Lieutenant Adams?*" She was interrupted by the control room summoning her on her walkie-talkie.

She snatched it off her waist. "Yes, this is Lieutenant Adams. Go ahead . . ."

"*Are you still on the yard?*"

"Yes."

"*Can you escort Big Man to the Warden's office? There is a VIP here to see him.*"

Big Man was the code name that staff had adopted for Samson. He held so much influence in the BOP he earned a nickname.

"Okay. I'm 10-17 to his 20 right now. Standby," Lieutenant Adams replied.

She depressed the mic and looked dead at Samson. "What kind of shit are you into now?"

Qwess and Lisa stood in their foyer awaiting their guest to come inside. Anxiety ripped through Qwess's gut, as he had been anticipating this inevitable encounter for over a year. That's how long it had been since Qwess talked to Flame. He had so many unanswered questions. *How was his physical health? How was his mental health? Did he blame him for his misfortune?* He had so many questions, but they were soon to be answered.

Qwess watched as 8-Ball lifted Flame from the back of the car and gently placed him inside his motorized wheelchair. Kim Rawls stepped from the other side of the rear seat and joined Flame. Together they made their way up the marbled walkway and into the home.

"Long time no see, little brother!" Qwess greeted with enthusiasm. He turned to Kim. "And good seeing you again, sister."

"Hey Qwess, it's such a pleasure to see you as well. Congratulations on you being free. Give God the glory and He will see you all the way through this to the end. Amen?"

This was the Kim Qwess remembered, always the leader of the God Squad. "Amen," Qwess repeated, obliging her. After all, she was a guest in his home.

Kim turned to Lisa Ivory and offered her hand. "Thank you for having us in your home. I have been a fan of your work since I can remember, so it's truly an honor and a pleasure to grace your presence."

Lisa blushed. Adulation always made her shy. She had

been at the top of the entertainment game for years, broke records, garnered Grammys, and inspired a whole generation of minority pianists, yet she was still apprehensive about her celebrity status.

"Thank you, sister. I really appreciate that," Lisa said. "Come in, let me show you our home, and let these men talk."

Qwess smiled at his wife as she led Kim away. She always played her role to perfection. Despite being a superstar in her own right, she still deferred authority to her husband.

It was in moments like this where Qwess appreciated his wife the most. Outside the home she was a force of women's empowerment. At home, she was his wife and lady of the house. Once they were gone, Qwess turned his attention to Flame. In one glance, he analyzed Flame.

When the ladies disappeared from sight, the men sized each other up in silence. Qwess stared at Flame in the wheelchair, and he still couldn't believe it. How could a man once so vibrant and strong, so full of life and energy, be reduced to this man before him? Flame was dressed in a stylish track suit the color of a Carolina sky with the latest pair of Js on his feet. His high Caesar was lined to perfection with enough waves spinning to drown a whale, and his goatee was thick and crisp. At first glance, he looked as if he could be a model, but when Qwess looked deeper, he saw the scars on his face—his badges of shame. There was a light scar beside his mouth that was about two inches, and another on his forehead from where the stitches once were. The main badge of shame was the deep scar beside his eye. This scar was a reminder that his eye was nearly detached from its socket at one point, courtesy of his transgressions against Diamond.

"What's up, little brother?" Qwess asked. "How have you been?"

Flame smirked. "Clearly I've been better, but I am blessed."

"Yes, we are," Qwess agreed. "So, what are the doctors saying? Any word on your progress?"

Flame shrugged and frowned. "My health is in God's hands, bro. Those doctors don't have the final say on this."

Qwess nodded. He could relate. As was the saying in Islam: *Man plots, but God is the best of planners.*

Qwess jerked his hand in the direction of Kim and Lisa. "What's up with you and Kim?"

Flame smiled, and this time it reached his eyes. "Man, she is the reason why I'm still here," he said. "I was ready to off myself at one point. She helped me find me again by helping me find my way to God."

Qwess was shocked to hear Flame actually say this. He'd heard via social media that Flame was part of the God Squad now, but he thought it was just social media crap.

"Oh yeah?" Qwess asked.

"Yeah, man."

"It takes a strong woman to come back for you after all that happened between y'all," Qwess pointed out.

Just the mention of his and Kim's history brought the elephant into the room. Both men suddenly fell silent, thinking about the same person. It was Flame who spoke of her first.

"Have you heard anything from her yet?" Flame asked.

Qwess swallowed the lump in his throat. "No . . . not directly anyway."

Confusion etched onto Flame's face, so Qwess elaborated and told him about when the investigator came to see him. He left out the part about his and Sasha's daughter.

Flame stared at Qwess, gauging his mood. "You know I know, right? She came to see me when I came home. Told me everything."

"Who? Sasha Beaufont?"

"Yeah, your little girlfriend."

Qwess was speechless. *What did Flame know?*

"According to her, y'all had a uh . . . thing back in the day and she never got over you. She said y'all even have a secret surprise the world doesn't know about."

Flame was dropping blows on him, unearthing things that were long buried.

"What else she say?" Qwess whispered.

"A lot more. Basically, that Diamond hates you because of her, and that she hates Diamond because of you." Flame's voice cracked a bit. "She pretty much told me I was a pawn in your game. Then she disappeared."

Damn, Qwess thought. All this time he thought his secret was on the low, Sasha had aired him out. Is this why Flame hadn't come to see him yet since he'd been home? Did he blame him?

"For a long time, I blamed you," Flame revealed, as if he were reading Qwess's mind. "I felt like if it wasn't for you, then shorty wouldn't have came at me, and none of this would've happened.

"Then I had to be real with myself. You warned me not to pursue her, but the ego has its own advice to give, and I wasn't mature enough to listen." Flame looked away. "I was living like a savage out there, man. If it wasn't ol' boy, it would've been someone else to clean my clock, ya know?"

Qwess nodded. Flame was a wild boy in his day. Where some bathed in excess, Flame drowned in it. On one occasion, Qwess witnessed Flame have sex with six women at the same time, then pull an encore the next morning.

"But for the grace of God, I would still be living like that. So, in a weird way, I thank you for being involved in all this, because you brought me closer to my salvation. So I came here to thank you."

This was a lot coming at him at one time. Qwess didn't know what to say. It was clear Flame had a lot to unburden himself with, so Qwess let him speak.

"Since you helped me gain my salvation, I want to help you gain yours."

"What do you mean?"

Flame gave Qwess a crazed look. "Have you accepted Jesus Christ as your Lord and Savior?"

What? Qwess thought. *Flame was trying to proselytize to him?*

"Whoa, little brother," Qwess said. "No disrespect to your religion, but I have my own way of life. Now whatever worked for you, I'm proud of you for embracing it, but I'm cool."

"See, brother, you never—"

"Joey, I'm okay," Qwess insisted. "Two things friends shouldn't discuss: politics and religion," he schooled. "We're brothers, so it's deeper than that, but to you be your way and to me be mine."

Disappointment was evident on his face, but Flame took it in stride. "I know your way; I'm just trying to share the good news with you." He paused for a second before he dropped his next bomb. "And I'm also preparing you for my next album . . . it's a gospel album."

"A gospel album?"

"Yeah, my contract says I owe you two more albums. It didn't say what kind of album. I always wanted to make music that's from the heart and true to who I am. Right now, my heart is with the Lord."

"Your heart is with the Lord . . ."

"Yep. The Lord is my salvation, and I want to share that with the world. You may not be open to it, but I'm sure there are many others that are. If I can be the voice that brings a legion of people to the Lord, then I will have done what he asked of me."

Qwess stroked his chin in deep thought. This whole visit was getting more interesting by the second. His number one star, the lyrical lothario, was ready to return from the dead with a new album. Qwess had hoped Flame would be able to record again, because after all he'd been going through and all the press his incident was garnering, he predicted his sales would be massive. However, he hadn't anticipated a twist like this. ABP was home of the hottest hip-hop and R&B acts; he had no interest in gospel acts. He left this market alone for a reason.

"I understand your walk and all, but this is business. I don't even have the tools to create a gospel album—producers, videographers . . ." Qwess shrugged. "I don't know how to do this."

Flame nodded confidently. "I figured you would say as much," he said. "So I took the liberty of handling all of those details myself. I don't spend my money on the same frivolous things I used to engage in, so I can use it to fund my own project. That's how much I believe in this."

"I mean, why go through all this trouble if we already have systems in place for this? If it's not broke, don't fix it," Qwess reasoned.

Flame smirked. "From what I hear, it is broke. Word is, ABP is going broke."

Qwess scoffed. "You know you can't believe everything you read!"

In reality, the word on the street wasn't too far off from reality. The official coffers of ABP were stressed. With no real money coming in, and millions of dollars going out, his company was on the Donald Trump path of business—sliding toward bankruptcy. That's not to mention the lawsuit looming overhead. But Qwess always had a backup plan.

"Yeah, I know that. They practically labeled me dead when all this went down, but you can call me Lazarus, I guess," Flame joked. "Look, Big Homie, I always played fair with you—regardless of what we went through, right? Through it all, I stood by you. Now I know what I'm asking you for is a stretch, but I believe in this. Let me put my money where my mouth is. It's a win-win for you: If it flops, you can blame it all on me. If it blows, you'll look like a genius."

Qwess eyed Flame with skepticism. This was the most confidence he had exuded since he rolled in. What did he know? What was he hiding? As far as Qwess knew, Kirk Franklin's wave had come and gone.

"So you really serious about this, huh?"

"*So* serious!"

Qwess stuffed his hands inside the deep pockets of his Versace robe while he contemplated Flame's proposition. "Okay," Qwess said. He looked over his shoulder and sighed deeply. "I'll let you do it on one condition: You have to keep that little secret a secret until *I'm* ready to reveal it."

Flame smiled. "Deal."

Chapter 21

Bone opened the gate on the back of the trailer and had to adjust his sight to take it all in. There was so much white before him that it hurt his eyes. And tan . . . and green . . . There was so much product on the back of the semi that he instantly got nervous. His stomach rumbled from the anxiety of seeing so much work. A mélange of emotions washed over him. Excitement. Fear. Uncertainty.

Just a month ago, he thought he was done. He thought the game had finished him off, showed him he wasn't ready to play at the next level. What he was looking at now was redemption. In his mind, the God, King Reece, had smiled down on him and bestowed his blessings on him. There was no other way to describe it. And Bone was basking in the glory.

Bone removed his burner phone from his Dior thobe and shot a text to Qwess.

"It's here," he said.

Qwess returned a thumbs up through text.

Bone washed his hands over his face, still in disbelief. OG Qwess had come through. He turned the lights back on in the city with just a phone call. Bone had given Qwess nearly three million dollars cash. In return, Qwess had greenlit nearly sixteen million in drugs.

Bone had made sure to eliminate most of his rivals before the shipment came in. After disposing of Gangsta Black, the rest of the flock took for cover. Still, they were catching them from time to time. Bone had issued an edict that would rival Hitler in its racist audacity, but he felt it had to be done. He ordered his crew to murder every Mexican male in the city. He knew there would be collateral damage, but the end justified the means. In his mind, he reasoned that most Mexicans knew each other or had their own network. So once word spread that they were being hunted, the "legit" Mexican males would flee for greener pastures, because they were only here to make money and build their families. The Mexicans that remained would be of a tougher ilk and probably be affiliated with Samson's organization. Thus they were food.

Bone also was working another angle. With enough heat put on the Mexicans, he estimated that word would spread back in Mexico that they were being hunted in the Carolinas because of Samson. This would cause them to turn on their beloved *Monstruoso* and loosen his grip on their country. He had them thinking his reign was invincible, so they backed him. Once, they knew otherwise, would they still support him? That was the million-dollar question. Until that question was answered, Bone was applying pressure.

In the meantime, now that he had the work in his hand, he was ready to apply another type of pressure. He was ready to reclaim his position in the city.

Bone dialed a number in his phone. A second later Maleek Money was on the line.

"As-salamu alaykum!" Maleek Money greeted.

"Wa alaykum as-salamu! Where you at?"

"On one of these *amigos* ass."

"Oh yeah?"

"Yuuup. Took his ass from a construction site; now we about to get some answers out his ass to see what he know."

Bone thought for a brief moment. "Aye, I got another idea," he said. He pondered a moment to see if he wanted to really do what he was thinking. Then he said, "Let him go."

"Huh?"

"Let him go."

"Ah, Akhi, we kinda did him dirty already. He in a bad way," Maleek Money relayed.

Bone nodded. "Can he talk?"

"Yeah."

"Can he walk?"

"Yeah, barely."

"Okay then, that's good enough," Bone said. "Drop his ass off somewhere but tell him to tell all of his people that they have one week to leave town. Anybody we see after that, we gonna assume they with the other side, and it's on-site."

"Ah . . . okay."

"Then I need you to get over here ASAP."

"Okay, bet. Send me your location."

The army of men walked the yard in a perfect line. Black men and brown men of different hues and backgrounds, all walking to the beat of the same tune. There were no less than fifty men in total, but the sheer size and stature of the group made it seem even bigger. Front and center of the group was their leader.

Samson led his gang, the Nuevo Crew, across the yard to the cafeteria with his chest poked out. Inmates and officers looked at the gang walking the yard in a mixture of fear and awe. Tension had been thick on the yard since the murder in the cafeteria, so everyone knew it was only a matter of time before something occurred.

Nuevo Crew walked into the cafeteria where the AB were having dinner by themselves. The AB held so much sway on the yard that they were allowed to have chow by themselves. It wasn't always this way. Every time the administration forced them to eat with the rest of the population, they wreaked so much havoc shutting down the kitchen with violence that it was decided it would be best to allow them to eat alone.

This day, however, their unity would work against them.

As soon as Samson walked in, he laid eyes on Jimbo, who had just been released from the box. Jimbo was sitting at the back of the cafeteria feasting on a hearty meal that was specially prepared for him. He sat alone at the metal table while his minions surrounded him.

Jimbo saw Samson step inside the cafeteria and froze mid-bite. His sycophants caught his line of sight, and they all drew their breath in when they spotted the giant standing in the doorway with an army of men at his back.

Samson raised his hand and pointed his finger like he was E.T. In the next instant, the Nuevo Crew rushed the AB and a melee broke out in the cafeteria.

White bodies flung in the air, followed by brown and Black bodies. The blood that poured was red as two savage crews went to war while their respective leaders looked on in puffed up pride and arrogance.

As the crews went to war, the yard officer came and locked the door to the cafeteria from the outside, effectively sealing them inside until either they were all dead or they managed to burst through the door. A phalanx of guards waited at the door in riot gear, but their orders were clear that they were not to engage. They were to let them figure this out and pick up the pieces of the aftermath.

Samson stood in front of the door with his arms crossed, watching his soldiers go to war in his name. His eyes never left Jimbo's greasy face, and Jimbo's beady eyes never left

Samson. Grown men grunted and shrieked guttural sounds as if they were having sex. Blood poured from midsections like women on their first day of their menstrual cycles. However, this was the complete opposite. Where menstrual cycles prepared for life, this bloodshed precipitated death.

When the battle subsided just a little, Samson moved from the door and walked slowly toward the back in the direction of Jimbo, stepping over bloody bodies and dodging flailing arms like they were coming at him in slow motion.

Jimbo saw Samson advancing toward him and stood to greet the giant. He tore his shirt off as if he was impersonating his idol, Hulk Hogan, revealing the large tattoo on his torso that bore his allegiance to his gang. The brand was a beautiful work of art: a shield with a bright red swastika in the middle, topped by the letters *AB*. On the bottom of the shield, running underneath his dirty belly button was the word *Texas*, which meant this is where Jimbo hailed from. It was well known that Texas bred a different type of brotherhood, and Jimbo was ready to rep his set.

Samson walked through the sea of bodies with his eyes on his target. When Samson was ten feet away from Jimbo, Jimbo made his move. He flexed his wide back and whipped two long blades from his waistband.

"Ahhhh!" Jimbo stuck his tongue out and yelled as he charged Samson with both blades leading the way.

Samson deftly sidestepped Jimbo's attack and clotheslined him with a beefy arm. Jimbo somersaulted in the air. When he hit the ground, his body went one way, and his blades skidded the other.

Jimbo quickly hopped to his feet and regrouped. He threw his hands up to fight, but before he could plant his feet, Samson smacked spit and blood from his mouth. The blow was so devastating he nearly took Jimbo's head off, but before Jimbo could crumple to the ground, Samson held him up by his neck with one hand and pummeled his face with the other. The first blow broke Jimbo's nose, the other blows were overkill. Jimbo lost consciousness while still standing, and Samson hoisted him high into the air by his neck.

Samson squeezed his neck with all his strength, staring at him as he wrenched the life from him. Then he felt something crash into his back. He dropped Jimbo and turned to find an AB member holding a broken broom.

Fear registered on the man's face when he realized the blow didn't affect the giant. Before he realized it, Samson's hands were wrapped around his neck. He flung the man by his neck like a rag doll across the room. He crashed into a metal table and went limp. The only thing moving on his body was the blood that poured from the wound in his head.

Samson moved toward him to finish the job when he felt a stinging, burning sensation penetrate his arm. Then three more pings hit the same spot.

Samson turned and saw the source of his pain: The Rapid Response Team had bumrushed the mess hall and were using their pellet guns to defuse the situation. Everywhere he turned, he saw red uniforms and bursts of fire from the guns the team relentlessly discharged.

Samson smiled. He turned around, placed his hands on top of his head, and dropped to his knees, oblivious to the pellets peppering his body. This one was over. For now. He had proven his point. The Nuevo Crew was ready, willing, and able to get down and dirty with the best of them.

As he felt the officers wrestle him to the ground and clamp the cuffs on his wrist, he smirked, thinking about how he planned to assert his dominance in just a few months when he hit the street.

Chapter 22

Qwess lay in his huge bed staring at the stars in the sky through the glass ceiling of his bedroom. Lisa was asleep on his chest, snoring lightly while Ruquiyah lay on his other side with her thick thigh draped over his torso. Ruquiyah stirred a bit, and Qwess peeked down at her and found the Jamaican beauty staring up at him.

Ruquiyah had been staying with them for the past few weeks. She had flown in for a rendezvous, and discovered just how deep of a predicament their family was in. Lisa was in shambles, and Qwess was frontin' like he was holding it together. Ruquiyah's intuition was tuned to a million, so she sensed the disarray in their aura. They couldn't hide anything from her. She loved them both—in their own ways, respectively—so her heart wept for them both. There was little she could do for either of them. She wasn't rich enough to give Qwess millions of dollars to make his problems go away, and no matter how much she loved Lisa, she could not become Qwess. Although Ruquiyah had grown to love Qwess over the years, he wasn't the love of her life like he was to Lisa. Thus Ruquiyah couldn't fathom the prospect of losing her husband and the love of her life. That potential reality was what Lisa was faced with, and as the clock ticked, the day of reckoning was nearing closer.

"Wha 'ave you so vexed?" Ruquiyah whispered to Qwess.

Qwess smiled. "Nothing now," he replied. "Just seeing the future."

Ruquiyah smiled. "And what does that look like?"

Qwess nodded toward the stars twinkling in the sky. "Like that," he said.

Ruquiyah smiled, and Qwess returned to star gazing, thinking about his plate.

Now that Mahmoud had made good on his promise, and Bone was making moves, money was raining like someone had burst a piñata over his head. He had underestimated just how much money was still in those streets. As soon as he turned on the pipeline, he received an explosion of cash! Back in his heyday, it would have taken him a month to see the amount of money Bone had given him in just one week. Qwess had never understood the popularity of certain music that glamorized designer drug use that was forbidden in his day—until now. The pills and heroin moved faster than the coke, and his knowledge of the street told him that the users weren't the typical junkies of yore.

In just a matter of weeks, Qwess had raked in millions, and his war chest was growing with every call on his burner phone. That's how he referred to his new influx of cash—a war chest. He was under no illusion; every part of his life was under attack.

Qwess felt Ruquiyah grip his semi-flaccid dick beneath the silk sheets. He peeked down at her, and she grinned as she stroked him lightly.

"Let me help you relax," Ruquiyah whispered.

Qwess relaxed indeed, letting Ruquiyah please him while he continued to inventory his life. Now that his money was flowing in again, he had to direct the money in the right direction. He had two trial dates looming above his head, both with the ability to finish him.

AMG's attorneys in the civil case were going for the jugular since he declined yet another settlement offer, this time in the amount of thirty million. Since he snubbed his nose at them, they amended the suit amount, and now were seeking hundred and twenty-five million. The other fifty million added was deemed as additional compensatory damages, as well as increased value of the money lost from the incident. Qwess instructed his lead attorney, Shabazz, to decline the offer. As a result of his rejection, they were expediting the trial. That meant more money for Shabazz, and more pressure to the Aryan Brotherhood, whom Qwess had enlisted to take care of his problem behind the wall.

Qwess had established a tie to the Aryan Brotherhood in an unusual way. When he was locked up in Seg, there was a high-ranking member of the AB on line with him. He was facing the death penalty for a slew of murders in the Carolinas and was also accused of running a multi-state meth ring. On a whim one day, as both men took rec inside their cages adjacent to each other, Qwess struck up a conversation. On 23-and-1 lockdown, prisoners yearned for someone to talk to other than themselves, so it was no surprise that the AB member spoke to Qwess. The man knew who Qwess was, and he threw it out there that he didn't have effective representation. Qwess's altruism inside was well known, so the man hinted that if Qwess helped him out, he would have a friend for life.

After Qwess was released, he sent word back with Mahmoud inquiring about the man. He discovered that although the man was indigent, he held considerable rank in the AB. When Bone's attempt to take Samson out proved unsuccessful, it only made sense to Qwess to hire the AB to do the Crew's dirty work. According to the last word that Qwess received from inside, the AB was giving Samson's bootleg crew hell. At this rate, it would only be a matter of time before they took Samson out.

Ruquiyah slithered down Qwess's body and took his erection into her mouth. She slowly, quietly sucked him off so as not to disturb Lisa. Qwess was the first man that Ruquiyah ever felt something for, and she loved his sex. However, she masked her feelings because she didn't want to ever make Lisa feel uncomfortable.

Qwess palmed Ruquiyah's head and thrust his hips toward her warm mouth. While she hit all the spots he loved, he thought about anything except the pleasure he was experiencing so he could preserve his climax. His thoughts focused on the other issues at hand.

Most of his woes money could resolve, and now that he was liquid again, he had enough funds to throw at any problem, except the problem of a rat or two.

While the pressure was being applied on Samson, Hulk had yet to resurface. Qwess was confident that Shabazz could decimate Samson in a murder trial if he took the stand. After all, Samson had a record that would become admissible if he took the stand. Besides, being on America's Most Wanted list would ideally stifle his credibility. Qwess couldn't imagine the government using Samson in his murder trial, but in his civil trial Samson would be the star. Hulk was another matter altogether.

Hulk had never been in any trouble of any kind. He didn't have a record and had been an upstanding citizen. Plus, it was well-known that he had been Qwess's bodyguard for over a decade, which meant he knew where all the bones were buried. In Qwess's paperwork, Hulk's statements were the linchpin that would push the needle in his arm for sure. So while he rested assured that Samson would meet his fate well before his trial, he didn't have the same confidence as far as Hulk.

Qwess's eyes were closed as he pondered his plate while simultaneously enjoying Ruquiyah. Suddenly he felt a pair of soft lips press against his. He returned the kiss, and immediately knew it was Lisa kissing him. He knew the scent of his wife's breath anywhere. Lisa was the only woman he knew that didn't have night breath.

Lisa kissed him passionately and rubbed his chest. She eased her mouth beside his ear and whispered, "I love you, baby."

"I love you too," Qwess moaned.

"Is she doing it right? Is she making you feel like the king you are?" Lisa asked.

Qwess nodded.

"Good." Lisa sucked Qwess's neck while Ruquiyah continued to please him below. "Let us take your troubles away, my king. That's what we're here for . . ."

Moments like this were why Qwess loved his wife so much. She was never in competition with anyone, and she never made him feel guilty or uncomfortable about their mutual love for their sister-wife, Ruquiyah. Qwess was a Muslim, and thus permitted to have multiple wives; however, he never really imagined being able to exercise his right in peace. When he thought of polygamy, it was always in the context of a burka-wearing, garbed-down sister from the Middle East. Someone that lacked the sexual appeal that he had grown accustomed to in his fast life. Yet he was living his version of *Jannah* on earth, and although his lifestyle was polyamory rather than polygamy, he was still in paradise. His wife was one of the most desired women in the world, and their paramour had one of the best bodies on the planet. No way was Qwess trading this for a life in the box!

Suddenly Qwess's phone chimed to life with a text on the marble nightstand. Siri announced that the text was from Shabazz. Qwess instructed Siri to read the text, and he instantly regretted the decision as Siri said, "*Hey big man, I'll be out to see you first thing in the morning. They moved the date up on your trial.*"

Maleek Money cruised the streets of the Port City in his Porsche. The day was a comfortable eighty degrees—perfect to drop the top, which Maleek Money did as soon as he pushed the ignition on the left side of the steering wheel.

Maleek Money wore a tight wifebeater, not to show off his chiseled physique. Rather, he wore it because he wanted to make sure the world saw his newest piece of jewelry: a thick rope chain with enough diamonds to carve bricks out of a mountain. The huge pendant hanging from the chain was big enough to hold an apple pie, and the diamonds lining the chain were putting on a light show. Inside the pendant were the initials *M&M*, etched out in brilliant emeralds.

To Maleek Money's side was Keisha. She was riding shotgun, looking like the bossed-up diva she was. Designer shades covered half her face, and the long bone-straight wig she wore hid the long scar on her cheek from the bullet wound she endured. Keisha wore a blue, body-hugging shorts romper with Cinderella sleeves that clenched her soft curves in a vice grip and palmed her camel toe. She paired the romper with a pair of silver, red-bottom pumps. Diamonds danced on her wrist from the Audemars watch Maleek Money had gifted her with that morning.

Maleek Money hooked a left off 17th street onto Market Street, headed downtown. He was rolling right into the heart of the city in all his splendor. He wanted the city to know the Crescent Crew was back in power. He wanted his rivals to know that he wasn't running from them. He wanted the streets that were cackling about him being responsible for nearly getting Keisha killed to know what loyalty looked like.

Maleek Money stopped at the light at Market and 4th

street—right before downtown opened up—and checked his mirror. Sure enough, his security contingent was right behind him in identical black Range Rovers. Oh, he wasn't about to get caught slipping again. Maleek Money waved his jeweled hand and one of the Range Rovers zoomed around and got in front of the Porsche. The Range pulled slowly from the light, and Maleek Money followed closely behind it.

At the next intersection, Keisha saw one of her childhood friends walking on the sidewalk with her four-year-old daughter.

Keisha hung out the top of the Porsche and called her name. "Kina? Heyyyy girl!"

The young girl placed her palm over her brow to shield the sun and peered closer. "Wait, is that you, Keisha?" she said.

"In the flesh," Keisha returned.

"Girrrrrllll!" Kina ran over to the car and embraced Keisha through the open top. "I thought your ass was dead, gurl. They said them damn Mexicans killed you."

"Hmph, I wish they would. My baby ain't letting nothing happen to me," Keisha remarked, cutting her eyes at Maleek Money.

While the women spoke, Maleek Money scoped out his surroundings, taking note of everything and everyone around him. He wanted a waffle cone from his favorite ice cream spot in the world—Kilwin's—but he could see the long line stretching down the sidewalk. He was out to make a statement, but he wasn't trying to stand in anyone's line. The young boss hadn't stood on anyone's line for quite some time.

While he scanned the line, something caught Maleek Money's eye. He just knew his mind was playing tricks on him, for surely he wasn't seeing what he thought he was seeing.

"Yo, Keish, come on!" Maleek Money said. "We gotta go!"

"Huh?"

Maleek Money rolled his hands hurriedly. "Wrap that shit up, we gotta go."

Maleek Money pressed a button and the roof of the Porsche quickly eased up and covered them. No sooner than the top locked in place, Maleek Money pulled up beside the Range in front of him.

"Yo, you see this shit?" Maleek Money asked, nodding over toward Kilwin's. "Is that who I think it is?"

The brother driving the Range squinted his eyes. "I think so."

"Come on."

Maleek Money cruised down Market Street slowly, never taking his eyes off the woman standing in line waiting to get ice cream with her daughter. He bust a U-turn and ended up on the same side of the street as the woman and the little five-year-old girl. He slowed to a crawl and stopped right in front of the long line, contemplating his next move.

He dialed the brother behind him in the Range. "Yo, when I give you the word, grab both of they asses," Maleek Money instructed.

Maleek Money scanned his surroundings, noting all eyes were on his Porsche. His five-percent tint denied them access to the interior of the car, but he could see them well. Their gawking would work to his advantage.

He revved the engine and the turbocharged motor wailed to life, garnering the attention of the street. He locked the brakes and floored the pedal. The wheels broke free, spinning ridiculously, instantly creating a cloud of smoke billowing into the air. He kept the pedal pinned, and smoke surrounded his car and claimed the street.

Maleek Money barked, "Now!"

Maleek Money couldn't see behind him, but he could hear the commotion through the phone. The little girl screamed, as did the woman. He could hear a struggle ensuing, then shots were fired.

Suddenly, one of the Range Rovers zoomed past him. Maleek Money released the brake and peeled out in a cloud of rubber and smoke, following the Range Rover down Market Street. They hung a right onto 3rd Street and gunned it, flying down the narrow road. They barreled through an intersection and ran right into a Wilmington PD police cruiser.

"Shit!" Maleek Money hissed. Here he was trying to flex for his girl's city and now all hell had broken loose. He looked over to Keisha sitting all pretty in the passenger seat. He couldn't see her face behind the glasses and hair, but he could only imagine what she was thinking.

Keisha put her palm on the dash and looked at him. "Do what you gotta do, babe. I trust you."

"Bet!" That's all he needed to hear.

Maleek Money saw the cops bust a U-turn in his rearview mirror and turn on their blue lights. He quickly assessed the situation and made his move. He slowed down and rode the middle of the highway, the wide haunches of the Porsche hogging both lanes. Just as the police cruiser appeared to be gaining on them, he floored it and the Porsche rocketed forward. In seconds, the Dodge Charger grew smaller and smaller in the mirror. Maleek Money slowed down and let the Charger catch up. When the cop car got close, he gunned it again.

Up ahead, Maleek Money saw the Range Rover take a hard right turn, careening onto the highway leading to the bridge to leave town. He slowed down again and let the cop catch up, effectively blocking any cars from getting onto the highway to follow the Range Rover. As soon as the cop car got close, he gunned it again and kept going straight down 3rd street. Just as he planned, the cop followed behind him instead of the Range Rover.

Maleek Money zipped in and out of traffic on 3rd Street at breakneck speeds. The cop on his tail made every move with him. He hung the left where 3rd Street turned into Carolina Beach Road and the street opened into four lanes.

Maleek Money saw highway as far as his eyes could see. He smiled and clicked the left paddle behind the steering wheel twice. The Porsche squatted like a panther and wailed like a pterodactyl. The rush of power pinned Maleek Money and Keisha to the Recaro seats. It also instantly put about five cars' worth of distance between the Charger and the Porsche.

"Yeeeeah baby!" Maleek Money laughed as he felt the power surge of over 650 horses come through his feet. He stole a glance at the dash and saw he was doing a hundred and twenty miles per hour!

Maleek Money looked in the rearview and saw the first police cruiser had been reduced to the size of an ant, but before he could relax, another police cruiser drifted off Shipyard Boulevard and fell behind him with the siren blazing.

"Fuuuuuck!" Maleek Money exclaimed, slapping the steering wheel.

"Babe, you have to get off Carolina Beach Road," Keisha advised. "And don't take College; it's too much traffic."

Maleek Money held the Porsche in the road as he weighed his options. Suddenly he had a plan. "Hey Siri, call Akbar," he announced.

Before Akbar could answer the phone, Maleek Money saw the Range Rover pull up beside the police cruiser in his rearview. He saw fire extend from the side of the Range Rover toward the police cruiser, then the latter spun out of control.

"As-salamu alaykum!" Akbar's voice boomed through the car speakers. "I got you, Akhi. Now let's get the fuck out of here!"

Maleek Money smiled and hung a left on Independence Boulevard.

They were getting the hell out of the Port City!

Chapter 23

Flame rolled into the room and parked in the section they had cleared for him. He scanned the room and nodded at the familiar faces. The was the first time he had visited New York since he had left the hospital. He had lost a part of himself in the Rotten Apple, and the only way to reclaim it was to face his demons head on.

The last time Flame had visited this trio, he was on top of the world with the number one album in the country and the raunchy side of pop culture bowing at his feet. Gone was that man, replaced with a more somber, wiser version of a recording artist.

Flame placed the headphones on his ears, leaned back in his chair, and waited for the interview to start.

This was his first time in the media since his infamous beatdown and subsequent resurrection, and news had been swirling of his impending appearance on the highest-rated morning show in the country. Some believed he wouldn't show, others believed he would only appear virtually. Now here he was in the flesh.

"Flame, my Carolina bruddah, welcome back to the world," the lead host and obvious star of the trio, Charlie the Goat, said.

Flame raised his palm gently, "Joey," he said. "Call me Joey."

"Joey . . . okay."

"Yeah, you remember he doesn't want to be called Flame anymore," the female host chimed in. "He said that's the old version and now that he is following the path of the Lord, he wants the world to know who JOEY is."

"Correct," Flame said with a smile.

Charlie the Goat chuckled uncontrollably. "Shit, after what I saw online, I would've turned to the Lord too," he joked. "The Undertaker ain't got shit on Diamond."

Flame expected this interview to go left, he just didn't expect it to go left so soon. Flame glanced at him with a smirk. "Dang, so you just wake up in the morning and choose violence, huh?"

Charlie the Goat raised his palms in surrender. "My bad, my brother, I didn't mean any disrespect, but you have to know that's the last image everyone recalls seeing of you, so I'm just stating what's on everybody's mind."

Flame nodded. "I can understand," he said confidently. "So let's get to it and get through it. I'm ready. When we contacted your show, I could've put all types of stips on this, but I didn't. I'm a walking miracle, so I'm here to tell the good news of my Lord and Savior, Jesus Christ."

"Okay, I'm all for that, but first let's get this nigga shit out," Charlie the Goat returned.

The female host, Tangela Vee, reached over and patted Flame's shoulder. "Don't worry, Joey, I'll keep the civility here."

"No, God's in charge here. Carry on."

"Flame—I mean Joey—take us back to the moment when

you were on top of the world. I mean, you had sex with one of the baddest women on the planet—on video. What was that like?"

Flame glanced at his fiancée Kim standing in the corner. "Out of respect for my fiancée, I'll have to decline answering any questions about my sexual past."

"Fiancée? So, it's true?"

Flame nodded vigorously. "Yes, Kim and I are engaged to be married. For sure."

"Wow!"

"That's cool," Charlie the Goat nodded as he pecked away on his laptop for more information. "So, Diamond, can we talk about Diamond?" He didn't wait for Flame to agree before he continued. "After everything occurred, Diamond disappeared. Now *they* say he had Sasha Beaufont murdered and then went on the run in Africa some damn where. You spent a lot of time around him before you slept with his woman . . . Is Diamond as sinister as they say he is? You think he is capable of murdering his own woman like that? I mean, they were together for five years!"

With the mention of Diamond, a wave of emotions washed over Flame. The nightmares of him being driven through the pavement had ceased, but he still wasn't over the trauma of Diamond. He was born again in his spirit, but certain things were embedded in his psyche.

"I can't speak about the next man's intentions," Flame replied. "I just hope that wherever he is, he has atoned for all the wrong he has done to so many people, including myself."

"You? *He* wronged *you*? My brother, you recorded yourself sticking a baby leg inside his woman and released it to the world. No homo, but I don't think Diamond wanted to come behind that. You ruined his woman."

"First of all, I didn't release anything to the world. That was a private moment that shouldn't have happened."

Charlie the Goat shook his head and whispered, "This negro said he shouldn't have boned Sasha Beaufont. Hmm mm mmm. I never thought I'd see the day," he remarked. "Shit, I'm married, and I would fuck Sasha Beaufont. Well, not this Sasha Beaufont, but the one you fucked. Definitely!"

Flame shook his head in disgust. What so many people lauded praise on him for, he couldn't even remember. His memory of bedding Sasha Beaufont had been erased, either from the head injuries he sustained, or his brain purposely blocking it out to keep him from reliving it.

"But what was that like seeing how Diamond disfigured Sasha's face—

"Allegedly," Tangela Vee interjected.

"Ain't no damn 'allegedly,' we seen the girl's face on-line!" Charlie the Goat snapped. "So did you feel partly responsible for her misfortune?"

"Responsible? Naw, but if I did play a part in it, Jesus died for our sins, so I am forgiven for all that I've done before I accepted him as my personal Lord and Savior."

Charlie the Goat slapped his forehead, "*This* negro . . ."

The DJ of the trio finally spoke up. "So, Joey, tell us what it was like adjusting to your new life," he said. "Here you were on top of the world one minute, the hottest rapper in the game. Then the next minute, you're a paraplegic. I imagine it has to be tough."

"Tough is an understatement, but I give honor and praise to the good Lord for bringing me through."

"Yeah, I see you wearing the religious gear and all," the DJ noted, referring to Flame's snow-white tunic. "How serious are you about this? And how are you going to balance this new you out with the albums you still have due?"

"Well, fortunately, Qwess respects my faith, as he is a religious man himself. So, my next album will be a gospel album," he announced, getting to the real reason he arranged to come on the show. He wanted to test his star power and see just how strong it was. Would his fans follow him to a whole genre shift?

"You know, I'm not the one to deal in rumors, but it's rumored that Qwess and Sasha have a secret love child and that's the source of his beef with Diamond," Tangela Vee said.

This was the first time Flame had ever heard this uttered in public. He recalled his promise to Qwess and reminded himself not to betray the trust.

"I never heard anything about that," Flame lied.

"Aye, speaking of Qwess, what the hell them ninjas got going on down there in Carolina today?" Charlie the Goat asked. "Man, we just heard that they killed a police officer and kidnapped two people, including a little five-year-old girl. Said that they trying to intimidate any potential witnesses for Qwess's murder trial."

Flame shrugged his shoulders ignorantly. "Man look, I do music—gospel music—I don't know nothing about all that street stuff."

"Yeah, but the head of your record label is facing the death penalty for being the founder of the biggest Black crime cartel in the history of the country. This like a real-life trap-rap album. I'm sure you seen or heard something," Charlie the Goat persisted.

"So yeah, about my new album," Flame said, blatantly ignoring the host. "I'm almost done with it. We have eight songs completed and the only features on the album are my fiancée. It's the same fire tracks, melodies, and flow, it's just that the themes have changed for positive now."

"So how do you think that will be received?" DJ Ego asked. "You made a living being a ladies' man. Now you're engaged and making music about the Lord."

Flame cleared his throat. "To be clear this won't be your typical gospel album. I'm talking about my experiences, everything I've gone through since my last album. My pain, my joy, my revelations, and everything in between. It just won't have a bunch of profanity on it. This is the only interview I'm doing, so if the people want to know what I been through and my thoughts on it, they have to download the album."

"Wait, you said download," Tangela Vee pointed out. "So this will only be available via download?"

Flame nodded vigorously. "Yep, this will only be available on Wave," he confirmed. "In fact, we're officially launching Wave with the release of this album."

Charlie the Goat shook his head. "Wait, so you telling me that you about to base your career on a failed technology developed by a man who might be about to get a needle stuck in his arm?"

Flame had enough. "What's with you, *brother*? You always talk about Black empowerment and you for the culture this and that, yet I'm in here telling you how the biggest, Black independent label in the history of music is shifting the culture with new technology and all you want to talk about is nonsense," he pointed out. "I escaped death and lived to tell my story right here with you, and all you want to talk about is some gang stuff where Black people are getting slaughtered. What kind of media personality are you?"

Flame maneuvered his wheelchair to turn his back to Charlie the Goat and focused his attention on Tangela Vee and DJ Ego.

"Like I was saying, we're shifting the culture again with this one," Flame predicted. "You'll see."

Chapter 24

Qwess couldn't believe what he was hearing. He was anticipating that his civil trial would precede his criminal trial. According to Shabazz when he was initially released, his criminal trial wasn't supposed to begin for at least a year, maybe even eighteen months. Now he was telling him something different. Qwess estimated that he would have everything wrapped up in a year and that he would walk into the courtroom with a smile on his face, but with the timeframe accelerated, things weren't looking promising.

Qwess was heated! "Brother, with all due respect, what the fuck happened?" he demanded. He smacked the glass table in his home conference room. "How are we going to trial in three weeks? You told me I had at least a year to prepare!"

Shabazz recoiled from the loud smack on the table and the rage crowding the room. "Calm down, son."

"Don't tell me to calm down! I gave you over a million dollars to handle this and you come to me with this bullshit? I've been cooped up in this fucking house like an animal, waiting patiently, but I need some answers."

Shabazz sighed. "Brother, have you not seen what's going on out there? Your comrades are making it hot and the government is getting nervous," he explained. "They feel like the streets may be safer with you inside, quite honestly."

Qwess waved his hands dismissively. "That shit out there ain't got nothing to do with me!"

"They don't believe that. According to them, the level of violence has escalated since you've been free."

"What? That's nonsense! And who the fuck is *they*?"

"*They* are the government, son. They are saying your name in D.C. right now. The Crescent Crew is making national news. Have you not seen this?"

Shabazz slapped a copy of the *USA Today* on the table. On the front page were two pictures of Qwess—one in the courtroom in jail clothes and the other with him wearing a custom-tailored pinstripe suit with huge diamonds in his ear and his trademark Cartier frames. In big, bold words, the caption read: "*Hip-Hop's C.E.O. of Crime.*"

Qwess scooped the paper up. "What the hell?"

"Now you see what I'm saying? They're out for your blood. Right now, everything that happens in the underworld, they're attributing to you, and it doesn't help that one of their star witnesses' family has been abducted in broad daylight and their other witness is battling for his life in federal custody."

Qwess scanned the article and quickly realized their angle. They were tying him to King Reece as if they were one and the same.

The reporter recounted the exploits of King Reece and his connection with the FBI through Destiny, insinuating that because of that connection, the Crescent Crew's tentacles stretched to the halls of the DOJ. They mentioned that Qwess was raising King Reece and Destiny's child (although they didn't mention Prince by name). The article contained a photo of Qwess's first conviction well before the Crescent

Crew's rise to power. Then they mentioned Qwess's father and his connection to a life of crime, and how Qwess managed to spring him from a life sentence. Then they detailed the horrific murders of Dee and Scar, noting how the killings were professionally done, and how after their deaths Qwess rose to fame. There was incident after incident. The article was nearly six pages long, but Qwess couldn't stomach anymore.

Qwess slammed the paper onto the table. "Yo, this is bullshit! This shit isn't even about me."

Shabazz shrugged. "It doesn't matter. It's what the court of public opinion sees. All they know is there is a war going on outside that no one is safe from, and they put you as the face of the opposition. They want your head."

Qwess sighed. He turned and looked out the window over his expansive grounds as he contemplated what Shabazz was telling him. He couldn't believe they were trying to make him the face of King Reece's empire. The irony was that although he had stepped away from the game before Maurice became King Reece, now he was responsible for moving more work than King Reece ever had. Qwess had shipments from the Middle East on autopilot thanks to Mahmoud. That one phone call had rebirthed a new empire, a new Crescent Crew of sorts. With Mahmoud's trial stalled and him being in federal custody, and Qwess on house arrest awaiting trial, there was no way the federal government could tie him and Mahmoud to the elaborate distribution network they had arranged. Or could they?

"Son, are you sure there isn't anything else I need to know about?" Shabazz inquired. He shook his head. "I've been practicing law for a long time, and I've defended some of the most notorious criminals in the history of this country, including the infamous Justus Moore. I've never seen them go this hard; it's like they're on the verge of changing laws to get to you."

Qwess wondered if Shabazz was trying to pick him for information. At this point, he didn't know who he could trust. With his life closing in all around him, his paranoia was on tilt.

Qwess shrugged. "I've told you everything," he lied. "This shit isn't rocket science. A Black man found a way to beat them at their own game and they can't handle it. My new technology, Wave, is going to change the culture and pay them back for what they did to the Cold Crush."

Shabazz shook his head in frustration. "Even that, son. I've been looking over your paperwork with that again, and it seems that you let the Jew boy get over on you there."

"What the fuck you talking about?"

"Your partner, Liam, he put a clause in the contract that said if you were to receive any type of criminal conviction, then you forfeit your share of the company."

"What? How the fuck you let that happen, Shabazz! I trusted you to have my back on shit like this."

"It wasn't me. Your guy, Amin, drew up the contract; I just looked over it. I didn't anticipate you getting in any criminality. Even still, we have bigger fish to fry, son. We have to prepare to win a death penalty trial in a matter of weeks. If not, then none of that will matter."

Qwess spun around and stared Shabazz down. "Oh, we're going to win that trial, one way or another."

Bone walked into the palatial home filled with a mixture of trepidation and excitement. He was nervous because his Crew's name was on the lips of the world. But he was also excited. He knew they had snatched a pivotal piece in the chess game they were engaged in. He had not authorized such a brazen move, but he did agree with it. Now he had to see if the ends justified the means.

Bone opened the door to the master bedroom, and there was Maleek Money holding court in the middle of the room while three brothers surrounded him. A beautiful cinnamon-hued woman with curves popping out of her body dress cowered in the corner of the room. In front of her was a little girl with honey-hued skin, long, wavy hair, and bug eyes. The little girl held a baby doll while the woman clutched the little girl's neck for dear life.

"Hey, hey, hey, what's going on in here?" Bone said, scanning the room.

"As-salamu alaykum, Akhi!" Maleek Money greeted with pride. He was still reeling from all the press he had been receiving. The latest notoriety had given him a high. He was a local joker from a small town that had made the national news from his exploits. He was too young to realize his move had put him on a path of no return. "You see who we got here?" Maleek Money asked, pointing to the woman and the child.

Bone continued to stare at the woman. Even with mascara streaming down her face from her tears, she was still gorgeous.

Maleek Money said, "This is the rat bastard's girl and his daughter."

"I'm not his girl; we're not together!" the woman snapped.

Bone walked over to the woman and held out his hand. "I'm Bone, and you are . . ."

The woman covered her face with one hand and her daughter's eyes with the other. "We don't see you. And we don't know anything!"

Bone chuckled. "Calm down, sister. What's your name?"

The woman cracked her fingers and peeped through the slit at Bone. She didn't know what to make of the tall man in the white robe and red-and-black checkered kaftan. "I-I'm Celeste," she finally stammered, refusing to take his hand.

"Well, Celeste, I apologize for bringing you and your daughter into this mess. It seems that your man—"

"He's not my man!"

Bone smirked. "I agree; he's not a man," he quipped. "Whatever he is to you, he got you involved in some serious business—Crew business—and this can only end one of two ways: your life or his."

Shock registered on Celeste's face.

"Now," Bone said. "I'm going to go downstairs and talk to my brother while you think about what I said. When I return, I want you to have an answer."

Celeste slid to the ground with her back against the wall and began to sob.

Bone shook his head and summoned Maleek Money to follow him while the others remained in the bedroom. They walked all the way downstairs to the finished basement with the soundproof walls. The room resembled a man cave, with a pool table and huge TV screens on the walls. In actuality, it was a safe space to conduct their business. This home was one of the many safehouses the Crescent Crew owned in the Carolinas. This particular home was in an affluent community in Myrtle Beach, two hours away from their epicenter and just an hour away from the Port City. King Reece had purchased the home years ago as a duck-off spot. It wasn't long before he turned it into a torture chamber. If those walls could talk, they would speak of tales that would make a Stephen King novel look like a children's fable.

Bone plopped on the pool table and crossed his arms. "Tell me what happened out there."

"Well, we rode down to the Port to put an eye on things, and let Keisha see her family," Maleek Money explained. "We was downtown and who do I see but the dude Hulk babymama."

"How you know it was her?"

"I remember seeing her on Instagram. She post all the time. I couldn't believe she was out like this."

"So then what happened?"

"I made an OG call to snatch them so they can bring the

rat to us. We rolled up and I created a diversion so the brothers can snatch them. A Samaritan tried to play hero, so Akhi had to cap him in the leg, then we dipped off."

"And the cop?"

Maleek Money shrugged. "I mean . . . you know how it go; it was him or us."

Bone nodded and went silent for a moment. "You know this is all over social media, right? They have video of your Porsche burning rubber all in the street. Fortunately, there are no videos of the actual abduction—yet—but everybody saying we responsible for it, so the boys are headed down to set up shop."

"What boys?"

"You know, the Feds. Say that got a special Presidential task force created specifically to take us down."

"Whoa! Are you serious?"

"Yeah. They got the Big Homie on the *USA Today* front page. You know what that means? That's them white folks' newspaper. That's the people that vote, so when they get scared, Washington has to listen."

Maleek Money listened in silence as he visualized all the money he had begun to see in just a short time. It seemed that every time the faucet was turned on, something threatened to clog it up.

"So I fucked up, huh?" Maleek Money asked.

"Nah, Akhi, I would've done the same thing if I were you. We in it now, so we have to see it through."

"So, like, is this all for the Big Homie? Why we going all out for him if he not even in the life no more?" Maleek Money proposed, referring to Qwess. "It sounds like we gonna have to shut our shit down. Meanwhile, he rolling around in millions on the hill."

Bone hopped off the pool table and stood in his protégé's face. "Don't ever talk like that about anybody in the Crew.

You have no idea the sacrifices he has made for this family to eat," he said. "And you have to understand, he is riding this out for all of us. Got it?"

Maleek Money dropped his head in embarrassment. "I understand."

"Plus, you have to understand that if he gets hit on this, then it's an indictment on all of us," Bone explained.

"So what's the plan? We have to shut shit down?"

Bone sighed. "Nah, we can't shut it down now. We have to see this through with these two snitching ass brothers. Shit going too good to turn back now. We eliminate the head, and the body will fall. Now let's go see just how much this nigga love his family."

Bone and Maleek Money returned upstairs to find Celeste holding onto her daughter for dear life. When Celeste saw Bone walk in, she cringed and cowered down into her shell even more, turning her head toward the wall.

"Please, sir, I don't know anything," Celeste cried, speaking over her shoulder. "If you let us go, we will forget this ever happened."

Bone stood over her and thrust out his palm for her. "Get up," he instructed. "We're not going to hurt you. We're gentlemen here."

Celeste slowly turned around and looked up at him. Her hand shivered as she slowly eased it out toward Bone, her eyes never leaving his.

Bone stared down at the woman into her hazel eyes with pity. This was the part of the game he didn't enjoy, but it was a necessary evil. "Did anyone harm you since you've been in our custody?"

Celeste shook her head.

"Ok, there is a game room downstairs with all types of games, candy, ice cream . . . the works. Why don't you let . . . ?"

"Lateefah."

"Yes, why don't you let Lateefah go play in there so we can discuss grownup business."

Celeste shook her head vehemently. "No, I'm not letting her leave my side."

"Relax," Bone advised. "If we were going to do something to you, it would be done already. This has nothing to do with you. We can make a few calls and then you can be on your way."

Celeste wasn't buying the nice guy routine. She'd seen the man in the corner shoot a police officer in broad daylight.

Bone reached down and grabbed Lateefah's hand. Surprisingly, she didn't resist him. "Come on, baby girl, let's go get you some cake and ice cream and you can play video games."

Lateefah perked up. "Can I, Mommy? It's so scary in here!"

Bone locked eyes with Celeste, telepathically telling her that it was okay. Slowly, Celeste nodded for her daughter to go with Akbar.

When the child left the room, Bone turned serious. He gave Celeste the iPhone they had confiscated from her. They had deselected the *locations* tab the moment they retrieved the phone.

"FaceTime your baby daddy," Bone instructed. "And if that phone leaves your face for a second, you can say goodbye to Lateefah."

Celeste gasped in fear and nodded vehemently. She dialed the number and seconds later, Hulk's face was on the screen.

"'Lest, where are you? Are you and Lateefah okay?" Hulk asked immediately. His voice boomed through the speaker. "Talk to me!"

Celeste looked at Bone for confirmation that she could speak. Bone shook his head lightly and spoke instead.

"As-salamu alaykum, Akhi. You've been a bad boy . . ."

"Bone, is that you?" Hulk asked. "Is that my little flunkie? You little nigga, you. I know that's not you."

Bone snatched the phone from Celeste and stared right into Hulk's face. "It's funny how you talking like this but you running harder than a Greyhound on race day from your *flunkie*."

Hulk laughed. He looked as if he was inside an abandoned building, which amplified Bone's ridicule. "I'm not running from you; I'm running *to* you. You'll see."

"Well, I escalated the race now," Bone said. "And you have a choice to make. You used to be Crew, so you know what this is. Death before Dishonor is still the motto. So, you got a choice to make: your family's life for your bitchass life."

Hulk's eyes stretched wide. "Are you crazy, little nigga? You know who I am?"

Bone nodded vehemently. "Yes, I do. You and your brother are some rats, and you gonna pay for it."

Hulk laughed. "Yeah, right!"

"We have the paperwork; you can't hide from this. You made your bed and now you must lay in. You have twelve hours to surrender your life, or we will make the decision for you."

Hulk attempted to respond but Bone abruptly ended the call.

Bone clutched the phone in his hand and stared out the window in silence. In the distance he saw the ninth hole of the golf course. His eyes settled on a man putting on the green, while his mind's eye pondered solutions. He was so lost in his thoughts that he nearly forgot about Celeste in the room until he heard her sniffle.

"Are you going to kill us?" Celeste asked. "My daughter and I have nothing to do with this. He is living the life of crime, not us."

Bone glanced down at her and offered a crooked smirk. "You know, the last thing I want to do is harm you, but rules are rules. Your man—"

"He's not my man!"

"Well, yo nigga broke the rules of the game, so I have to enforce him."

Celeste shook her head. "It's people like you that give our people a bad name," she scoffed.

"Our people?" It was obvious that Bone was taking a shot at her fair skin.

"Yes, our people! I am mixed. My mother is Egyptian, and my father is an American Black man, so I'm a real African-American, and it's people like you that give us a bad name."

Bone gave Celeste his full attention. He narrowed his eyes at her. "People like me?"

"Yes!"

"Do you even know why you're here? Do you know what that nigga of yours did?"

Celeste crossed her arms in defiance. "No, I don't."

"Exactly! So let me tell you. After a great man pulled him and his country ass brother up from their bootstraps, put some money in their pockets, and made them men again, they turned on him. He didn't just give them money, he introduced them to a righteous way of life. Taught them the *deen* of Islam and made them rich beyond their wildest dreams. And this the thanks they give?" Bone shook his head.

"Death and destruction, that's what he gave them," Celeste scoffed. "Talking about Islam . . . I know real Muslims, ones who don't rob, steal, or kill for their money."

"We don't rob and steal from no one. We never made anyone use anything we sell. If we were Pfizer, or Hennessey, then you wouldn't be saying this," Bone pointed out. "You know how many people die every year from prescription overdoses, or from alcoholism? And let's not even talk about tobacco. Trust me, I've done the research, so my conscience is clear. Now let's get back to this rat."

Celeste shook her head. "You still don't get it," she insisted. "What I'm saying is, it's clear you have a talent. I mean, you have grown men willing to kill for you, so obviously there is something great inside you that if you applied it to something else you could be just as successful."

Bone laughed. "What a two-time felon with a GED gonna be besides what I am?"

Celeste frowned. "Men like you, they treat like animals and lock in cages, the same men that are stars when you put them on stages. I'm saying, if you applied yourself, you could be anything else you wanted to be."

"I am who I always wanted to be, though. I'm a rich, Muslim man with my integrity and respect intact, which is more than Hulk can say."

Celeste sighed. "I don't understand you guys."

Bone had enough. Who was she to be questioning him about his decisions? "Understand this," he said. "If Hulk doesn't come through for you, I'm going to make the decision that is true to who I am."

Chapter 25

Samson paced his cell like the caged beast he was. He had been in the hole for a week now.

It had been one week since he had to demonstrate the power of the Nuevo Crew. At the time, his adrenaline was high, and he was proud to be planting his flag of sorts. He had been dragged from the mess hall with his chest poked out as he put on for his comrades. Now, a week after the adrenaline had tapered down and the monotony of the SHU settled in around him, reality set in. He just wasn't cut out for 23-and-1 in the box. He had adjusted to being incarcerated and actually powered up, amassing considerable influence throughout the Bureau. And yet, isolated from his power source, he was just a regular prisoner, and he couldn't handle it.

"Aye . . . aye, man!" Samson yelled to the guard inside the booth at the end of the corridor. "Where the fucking book cart at, man?"

No one answered quick enough, so Samson pounded the wall.

Boom! Boom! Boom!

"Aye, mothafucka! You hear me? I need some books to read!"

Samson was serious about his book cart. Reading was the only way to pass the time in the hole. Rather than read psychology or leadership books like most incarcerated Scarfaces, Samson preferred to read erotic tales. He especially enjoyed reading the Gangsterotica tales by a popular author that rediscovered his pen while incarcerated as well. Samson loved the balance of the gangsta content and the erotic content. Plus, the author used his real-life experiences to make his stories pop with authenticity. It was evident by the way he described being incarcerated.

Samson started to bang on the walls again until he heard keys rattling outside his door. He quickly placed his back against the wall, just in case they were coming in with their shields, tear gas, and batons to try to rough him up for being unruly. With just his government-issued boxers on, he crouched down in a fighting stance as the locks turned on the door. The heavy metal door slowly swung open, and Lieutenant Adams peeked her head inside the cell.

"You all right in there?" She asked.

Samson's eyes had grown so accustomed to the drab conditions of his cell that he struggled to see clearly. "L.T., is that you?" he asked. He was being formal just in case it was her and she wasn't alone.

Lieutenant Adams walked into the cell with her keys jangling on her hip. Her white shirt was so bright it nearly blinded Samson. "Yeah, it's me, and why you banging on my damn walls like a lunatic?"

Samson relaxed just a little. Lieutenant Adams left the cell door open, so he wasn't sure who was outside. "I need the book cart," Samson demanded. He pointed to the worn books on his bunk. "I finished all those already."

Lieutenant Adams smirked at him. "And that's how you ask for things to get done around here?" She shook her head and walked closer to him. She lowered her voice to a whisper. "You need to calm down."

Samson's eyes turned to slits. "Who you wit?"

"I'm by myself. I took the keys from the officer and sent him on a break."

"So who all on this wing?" Samson asked.

"Just your guys. I had to pull some strings to get it done, but I told them it would be a security threat if we mixed you all with anyone else."

Samson nodded. "Good."

Lieutenant Adams moved closer to Samson and fell into his barrel chest. "I miss you so much! Why couldn't you just behave down there? You tell me you ready to go home and do right, but how are you going to do that if you can't even do right in here?"

Samson pushed her away slightly. "Come on with that, you know who I am."

"Yeah, babe, and look where that has gotten you." Lieutenant Adams palmed Samson's erection through his boxers, hanging down his leg. "You took all this away from me with all your bullshit."

Samson smiled. "It's still right here for you, wanting you too." Samson eyed the door and tilted his head. "My people the only ones on the wing, right?"

Lieutenant Adams nodded. She closed the door and turned to face Samson. His boxers were already on the floor.

Lieutenant Adams walked over to him slowly, licking her lips as she eyed the monster poking out toward her. She gripped him inside her palms and stroked him gently. Samson pushed the top of her head and she dropped to her knees and took him into her mouth.

Lieutenant Adams slid her lips down him and quickly spit him out. "Damn, babe, when the last time you had a shower?"

Samson shrugged and grinned with embarrassment. "They didn't let us take any this week. You know how it is."

"No, I don't."

Samson tried to pull her up by her arms. "Get up. All that's cool, but I'm trying to fuck something. Come on."

Lieutenant Adams shook her head. "Uh-uh, we don't have time for all that. The officer come back soon, and I came to tell you something too."

"So tell me after you finish this, then."

Lieutenant Adams returned to giving Samson expert fellatio from her knees. His balls were sweaty and dank, and he was dirty, but she didn't care. This was the man that she loved, and she was trying to give him a small slice of heaven while he resided in hell.

Samson peered down at Lieutenant Adams while she handled her business. He had been feeling like a shell of himself in the box, but now he felt omnipotent again. How could he not feel powerful when the top officer on the shift came to the hole to suck his dick?

"Shit!" Samson hissed as a wave of pleasure gripped him.

"You better not cum in my mouth!"

"Keep going!"

Lieutenant Adams kept going, sucking and pulling on his large dick. She felt the drops of his precum pepper her lips as she kept going. She sucked, pulled, and twisted until . . . voila!

"Ahhhh!" Samson moaned and shuddered as he emptied his seed all inside her mouth.

Lieutenant Adams stood with her cheeks bubbled. She ran to the toilet and spit the semen inside. "I told you not to cum in my mouth."

"Aye, I couldn't help it," Samson said with a giggle as he pulled his boxers on. "But what else you got to tell me?"

Lieutenant Adams fixed her clothes while she looked into the dull piece of mirror hanging over the sink/toilet that was supposed to be a mirror. "Well, it's not good, my love."

"Come on out with it."

"It's about your brother."

Before Lieutenant Adams could elaborate, keys jangled outside the door. Both Samson and Lieutenant Adams whipped their heads toward the door just in time to see the warden walk into the cell, followed by two huge men in black suits.

"Ah, Warden Harrison, what are you doing down here?"

"Lieutenant Adams, I'm wondering the same thing about you."

"Ahhh . . . I was coming to give Officer Jenkins a break, and to check on Big Man."

Warden Harrison gave a look that made it clear what he thought about her explanation, but he couldn't address it. There were bigger fish to fry.

"Big Man," Warden Harrison announced, turning to Samson. "These two gentlemen are from the FBI; I'm sure you know of them already. It seems that it's time for you to go to work sooner than expected."

If Samson was a block of ice, he would've melted into the floor. Here he was, busted in front of his babe. "What you talking about?" he asked, trying to save face.

The black agent stepped up. "Mr. Salim goes to trial in less than two weeks, and we've been informed that he has placed another threat on your life through the Aryan Brotherhood."

The white agent stepped up and added, "Also, your niece and her mother have been abducted, we believe by the Crescent Crew."

"What?" Samson was flabbergasted. The initial shock was followed by another bomb.

"So, it's imperative that we move you to a pre-trial safehouse until you can deliver your testimony at trial. From there, it's on to the witness protection program to start your new life."

Warden Harrison spoke. "Lieutenant Adams here will be

responsible for gathering your things from property. I'm sure she will do a great job of taking care of everything."

His jab wasn't missed by Lieutenant Adams, but it was small in relation to what the agents had just revealed.

Lieutenant Adams's whole face cracked. She thought her ears were playing tricks on her. Surely the agents had the wrong man. No way was Samson—her knight in shining armor—cooperating with the government. Not the man who had the whole yard under his thumb.

Lieutenant Adams nodded. "Yessir."

"So we will be taking him from here directly to custody, correct?" Agent Black asked.

"Yes, we're going to bring the transport van around back and load him up from here," Agent White said.

They were talking as if Samson wasn't even there. In a way, he wasn't. Samson was having an out-of-body experience. His soul had left the room the moment the agents entered the room and said he was being transferred. Not only was he busted for being a rat, but he had a war to run on the yard. Not to mention, he had his tentacles in other prisons throughout the BOP. He figured he would do a few weeks in the box, and then return to run the yard ready to rule with an iron fist. He still had thousands of dollars out on the yard.

Now they were telling him that he was leaving. Today?

Warden Harrison turned to Lieutenant Adams, "Hey Lieutenant, I'm going to put you in charge of this assignment personally. Nothing that has gone on in this room leaves this room. Got it?"

Lieutenant Adams nodded. "Yes, sir."

He didn't have to tell her twice. After all, who would she tell that the man she had fallen in love with and held so much respect for was a rat? She tried to hide the anguish and surprise that rumbled inside her gut, but she wasn't that good of a poker player. She stared at Samson, unable to hide her contempt.

Samson lowered his eyes to the dirty floor. He was a giant in appearance, but right now, he felt as small as a child.

"Let's go, Big Guy, time to saddle up," Warden Harrison said, patting Samson on the back. "Time to work those years off."

That was all Lieutenant Adams needed to hear. It was official: Her paramour, the man who held the pulse of an institution under his thumb, the man who had a legion of men ready to kill and die for him, the man whose children she had just babysat in her jaws, was nothing more than a glorified rat. The pressure was too intense for her. She couldn't take it anymore.

Lieutenant Adams collapsed onto the cold, dirty floor.

Chapter 26

Bone sat in the back of the G-Wagon in deep thought. Maleek Money was in the driver's seat. To Bone's left sat Celeste. In the front and back of the G-Wagon were two black Range Rovers. Lateefah was inside one of those vehicles with the brothers.

"You think this negro will show?" Maleek Money asked.

Bone shrugged. "I don't know. I don't know what a snitch will do. They have no loyalty."

Celeste shook her head and peered up at the moon in disgust. "I don't understand you guys," she said. "So much bravado, so much machismo, so many principles, yet you will manipulate and move people around like chess pieces to suit your goals."

Bone glanced at Celeste. They had been tied to the hip for the past twenty-four hours while they awaited Hulk to make his decision. Celeste wasn't a hostage, per se, and she didn't behave as such. At every chance she could get, she questioned Bone's thoughts and actions, reminding him that he wasn't as thorough as he thought he was. She wasn't mouthy; she was cerebral. At times, Bone enjoyed the banter; at others, she was worrisome. Either way, he was ready to get this whole charade over.

The call came in earlier that morning that Hulk was ready to make his decision. He was ready to sacrifice his life for that of his family. They agreed to make the switch on a neutral ground since Hulk couldn't be trusted. Bone saddled up the troops and prepared to make the switch for later that night. After calling and rearranging the site locations numerous times, Bone was finally at a location where he felt secure.

Bone glanced at Celeste. "All that sound good, but this real business right here. If your lil baby daddy don't show, then this show will be over before it even start."

They were meeting in the country in an open field in an area called Wampee, just on the outskirts of North Myrtle Beach. It was about an hour away from Wilmington, North Carolina, far enough away from civilization to control all the options. From where they waited, they could see everything that came and went.

A pair of headlights turned down the road and everyone tensed up.

"Showtime," Maleek Money sang. He clutched the HK assault rifle in his lap and wrapped his finger around the trigger.

"Be easy," Bone coached as his eyes zoned in on the headlights creeping their way. "This nigga been real slippery. We told him to come alone, so if we see any other car come down this way, light that shit up. I'm tired of playing with this rat. It's time to get back to the money."

Celeste sucked her teeth. "Money, money, money, that's all you care about."

"Hey, zip it, Toots," Bone snapped.

The car crept down the road slowly. All eyes were on the blueish lights as it crept down the road. The car came to a halt right in front of the first Range Rover and materialized to be an S-Class Mercedes. The limo tint prevented anyone from seeing inside, so they were forced to wait this one out.

Bone picked up his phone to call Abdul and put things in motion. He wanted to use this opportunity to teach a lesson to any would-be defectors that the penalty for treason was always death. He wanted everyone to see Hulk bow down and accept the bullet to the back of the head as his fate. Hulk had killed Khalil, so he was already guaranteed *Qisas*. Hulk had broken every covenant that he had ever sworn to, and dipped on the piper before he paid his dues. Until now.

Bone didn't wish to traumatize Celeste and Lateefah, so his plan was to subdue Hulk with chains, then allow Celeste and Lateefah to leave in Hulk's car.

Bone cut his eyes at Celeste. "I really hope you don't make us do you and the rest of your family dirty," he said. "We're gonna keep tabs on you for the rest of your life, and if you even remotely go to the authorities, we're gonna rain blood on 1759 Pepperwood Way . . . and 6539 Portsmouth Drive, and we might even go to Miami and see them too."

Bone had called out Celeste's mother's address, and her sister's, and her grandmother's.

Celeste had been keeping it together during the whole ordeal until now. The mention of her family being dragged into this was too much. "What's wrong with you people? I have nothing to do with this!" Celeste cried. "I didn't know he sold drugs. I didn't know anything about any of this!"

"You're not in any trouble as long as you do as we say. Apparently, this rat bastard loves you so much that he is trading his life for yours, so you're good unless you go to the authorities."

Bone was only telling half of the truth. The truth was he knew he couldn't allow Celeste to live. She had seen too much and knew too much. The baby he could spare; she was young, she would eventually forget. Besides, the trauma of losing both of her parents would descend bigger problems on her life. However, Celeste would never make it off the dirt road after Hulk surrendered. Too bad—Bone actually liked Celeste.

Bone picked up his phone to call Abdul to put the final part of the plan in motion. Before he could put the call through, his phone flashed to life with a text.

"DON'T DO IT. LEAVE NOW!"

Bone looked at the number the text came from. Restricted.

Another text came through. *"LEAVE NOW. CALL ME WHEN YOU ARE AWAY FROM THERE. Q."*

Bone knew who the text was from now.

He tapped Maleek Money on the shoulder. "Drive, now."

"Huh?"

"Pull off NOW!"

Qwess clenched the phone and closed his eyes, awaiting Bone's call. He was in his massive garage, the only place he felt safe amid the chaos. His garage had become his personal bunker and safe space. The only thing he loved more than music was cars, and although he had given the pride of his fleet to Mahmoud, he still maintained a mean collection.

The day was nearing for the rubber to meet the road. His trial was scheduled to begin in just a week, and he was stressed to the limits. Bone had done well by finally tracking Hulk down. When he told Qwess of his plan to lure Hulk in to kill him so he couldn't testify, Qwess thought it was genius. However, the brazen way Hulk's family was snatched, and the subsequent murder of the police officer had garnered national headlines. The abduction and murder had been dominating the news cycle, and the media were juxtaposing the abduction with Qwess's upcoming trial.

A hip-hop mogul that had made good was facing the death penalty. All the networks were running specials on Qwess and the Crescent Crew, and each network had their own angle. Some were painting Qwess as evil incarnate. Others were sympathizing with him. Black Twitter had him trending every day. The boom was the King Reece documentary that Netflix had released in conjunction with Don Diva Global. The documentary had been number one on the platform since its release. There was no one in the world that wasn't talking about Qwess, and general consensus was that Qwess was responsible for the abduction. He couldn't afford to have Hulk and his family murdered if he could prevent it. This would guarantee him a death sentence.

Qwess stared at his phone, willing it to ring. Finally, the call came through. "Yo!"

"Hey, OG, what's going on?"

Qwess sighed. "You good?"

"Yeah, we gone from there. What's up?"

"We're going a different route on this. You still got those people with you, right?"

"Yeah. The rat is still back there though. The other brothers are still back there watching him."

"Well, we going to a Plan B with them. Too much sun shining right now to execute that move, so we going to Plan B."

Bone was confused. "What's that?"

Qwess smiled as the other plan finally materialized inside his mind. "You'll see."

Chapter 27

Flame was in his studio putting the finishing touches on a song he planned to debut at his benefit concert he was having in a just a week at the Mercedes Benz stadium in Atlanta. Ironically, the concert was scheduled during the time of Qwess's trial, so he wouldn't be attending the latter. However, he was debuting a song about redemption that borrowed the melody from Bob Marley's "Redemption Song." He was excited because he was eager to showcase the blend of his old style of raunchy hip-hop and his new style of gospel rap/singing.

He was alone in the studio this night. There was nothing on except the TV on the wall and the speakers playing the lead track on repeat. He was sitting in his motorized wheelchair, visualizing his upcoming performance. Visualizing was an important part of any successful performance, and although he had not performed in years, the basics never eluded him.

In this vision, Flame was commanding the crowd, pulling them into the palm of his hand with his syrupy vocals and inspiring lyrics. He locked his eyes on a woman in the front row. She was chocolate with low-cut hair, and huge hoop earrings dangling from her ears. Her eyes locked on him, and lust poured from them. In his heyday, she would've been on his list to take backstage when he was done performing, and even in his vision, the beast still haunted him. He worked hard to put his mind under the same rehabilitation methods as his body, but it was a constant work in progress.

In his vision, Flame continued to woo the crowd. They were loving his second coming. On stage, of course, he wasn't in a wheelchair. He was walking around on his legs—strutting really—and he felt free. The vision was so powerful that he was actually moving in his wheelchair, rocking back and forth to the beat thumping through the speakers. In his mind he wasn't confined to the physics of reality. In his mind he was completely free of physical restraints like paralysis. This is why this was his favorite place to be.

Flame continued to mentally rock the crowd, rocking back and forth in his chair as the show in his head climaxed.

Suddenly he felt motion in his feet, then his thighs. Ripples of energy he hadn't felt in years. He had been getting these feelings for the past weeks, but he dismissed them. He thought he was feeling them but didn't want to hype himself up. Now they were back and stronger than the last time.

Flame came out of his trance and touched his legs. He felt like he could feel his legs, and he almost freaked out. He began to touch them again, but something on the TV caught his eye. There was a breaking news report flashing across the screen. In big red letters it read:

"Sasha Beaufont Returns From the Grave."

Flame quickly raised the volume, and the news poured from the studio speakers.

"Legendary R&B artist Sasha Beaufont walked into her parents' home in Houston, Texas, today from what seemed like beyond the grave. You may recall, Sasha went missing

some while ago after an explicit video surfaced with her and rapper-turned-gospel artist, Flame. At the time of her disappearance, Sasha Beaufont was dating music mogul Tyshawn 'Diamond' Barker who was embroiled in a bitter feud with his music rival, Salim 'Qwess' Wahid, who is scheduled to begin federal trial next week on murder, narcotics, and racketeering charges . . ."

While the reporter continued to speak, photos flashed across the screen of Flame with Qwess, Diamond with Flame, Diamond with Sasha, Sasha with her group Kismet, and the last photo of Sasha with her disfigured face just before she went missing.

The reporter said that Sasha wasn't doing any press at the moment, but she released a statement to her fans that read, *"Your prayers brought me home. I am thankful and grateful. Stay tuned."*

The reporter went on and on about Sasha's impact on the music industry, and the impact the sex tape had on her career, but Flame had tuned all of that out. He recalled the last time he had seen Sasha, and their conversation. He recalled the impact Sasha's presence had on his fiancée. He recalled the pact he had made with Qwess regarding their love child.

He noted there was no mention of Diamond either.

So many things were coming at Flame at once, so fast that he couldn't wrap his mind around any of it. But there was one thing he could wrap his mind around, for sure.

The tingling in his legs.

Chapter 28

The day of reckoning had finally come. All the legal haranguing and filibustering had proven inefficient. There was a war going on in the streets of America and those in the highest halls of justice wanted answers. Translation: Someone had to pay for the uneasiness of America's citizens at night. Bodies were dropping all over the country, people were overdosing from the potent drugs that hit the streets recently, and the brazen murder of a police officer had absolutely no leads, except the name of the Crescent Crew attached to it. Someone had to pay, and the scapegoat they were fingering was Qwess.

The case of *The United States of America v. Salim "Qwess" Wahid* was being heard in the federal courthouse in Columbia, South Carolina, rather than Florence, South Carolina to accommodate the huge influx of people pouring in to attend the trial. Qwess's trial was so polarizing he had divided a nation. To some, he was rap royalty, a philanthropist who embodied the American Dream. To others, he was nothing more than a drug dealing, murdering criminal who hid his criminal activity and black heart behind his music industry façade. Both sides had descended upon Columbia, South Carolina to see him have his day in court.

Qwess sat behind the dark tint of his Rolls Royce Cullinan gazing out the window in deep thought as they pulled up to the courthouse. The mandarin orange leather seats were among the most comfortable in the automotive industry, but they might as well have been as hard as toilet seats, because Qwess couldn't find comfort at all.

"Calm down, my King," Lisa said as she stroked his arm lovingly. "Allah has the final say in this matter. Surely, he is the Oft-Forgiving, Most Merciful," she reminded him.

Qwess looked to his left and gave his wife a weak smile. "I know, my Queen, I'm just going through the motions, you know. Reflecting. These people never played fair, and I don't feel too confident with Shabazz."

Shabazz was riding in the identical Cullinan in front of them with his legal dream team. Directly behind Qwess's truck were Doe and Niya, along with Prince, King Reece's son, in an identical Rolls Royce truck as well. Behind them was Qwess's mother, father, and sister riding in a new Maybach. Ironically, considering Qwess was facing the death penalty, the convoy of luxury vehicles that carried the bulk of Qwess's team resembled a funeral procession, but this was far from that. This was a procession that brought him life support.

"I mean, I did everything I can do on my end. Now he has to do his part."

Indeed, Qwess didn't leave much to chance. He crossed his Ts and dotted his Is on the back end. So while Shabazz was in control of things in the courtroom, Qwess had taken out a little insurance policy the best way he knew how.

"Babe, regardless of what happens in there, our love will see you through it all," Ruquiyah assured him from where she sat on Lisa's left. Typically, Ruquiyah was rumored in the public, never seen, but this time all bets were off. Qwess's

life was on the line, and he needed all the positive energy he
could muster in his corner.

The Rolls bent the corner and the front steps of the courthouse came into view on Assembly Street. There was already
a traffic jam on the street, but when the spectators spotted
the Rolls Royces, all hell broke loose. Media rushed the cars,
trying to be the first to get the coveted money shot. Fans carrying vintage posters and CD covers of Qwess screamed his
name. Protestors carried picket signs decrying the violence in
hip-hop.

Shabazz's Cullinan stopped, and his driver and bodyguard
came around to let him out. Shabazz exited the Cullinan
looking like Johnnie Cochran incarnate in his bespoke suit.
His bald head glistened beneath the sun as he stopped to give
a statement to reporters.

"Pull up and let us out," Qwess instructed his driver.

The driver eased the truck up directly behind Shabazz's
truck and let Qwess and his family out. Immediately, Federal
Marshals swarmed the truck and led Qwess inside past the
frenzy outside.

The Marshals led them through the back entrance on a
private elevator into a conference room. There they saw the
other members of the legal team, the legal assistants and in-
terns hovering over computers dissecting the last portions of
the case. Qwess took a seat near the door with his back to
the wall so he could see everything around him.

Suddenly there was a commotion in the hallway. Qwess
peeked out and saw the Federal Marshals leading a group of
men inside the other conference room. There were four in
all, but one was unmistakable. At the back of the line, he
towered above the others. He was so tall that his head nearly
touched the ceiling even though his head was bowed. The
man raised his head and looked directly at Qwess.

Qwess smirked and nodded at him.

"You motherfucker! Where is my family?" Hulk roared.

His voice echoed off the narrow walls and garnered everyone's attention. Hulk tried to rush Qwess, but four marshals
intervened and restrained him. "I'M GOING TO KILL
YOU!" Hulk raged.

Qwess was unmoved by the antics. He smiled. Hulk had
just let him know that his backup plan was being effective.

Bone's eyes were riveted on the television as CNN reported on the spectacle unfolding in Columbia, South Carolina. If there was any doubt that the Crescent Crew had
reached legendary status, it was quelled now. CNN's reporters
were recounting their exploits like a YouTube documentary,
complete with video footage from days of yesteryear.

There was video of Qwess speaking at King Reece's
memorial service, extolling the virtues of the biggest dope
dealer in the history of the United States. CNN made it a
point to drive home the fact the Qwess praised King Reece.

Next there was never-before-seen footage of the brazen
abduction of Celeste and Lateefah. The images of the actual
abduction were grainy, but Maleek Money's Porsche was
live and in color. They ran the video back a few times and
zoomed in on the little girl being thrown into the Range
Rover. The frame wasn't clear, but they narrated it enough
to fill in the blanks of what they were showing.

The next video was the video dash cam of the police car
pursuing Maleek Money in the Porsche. On the video, the
Porsche was seen zooming through traffic way ahead of the
police cruiser. As soon as the cruiser closed the gap, an explosion was heard, followed by a series of gunshots. The officer was heard screaming before a burst of blood splashed
onto the windshield. Then the screen went dark.

"Ladies and gentlemen, we understand the images that
you just witnessed were very graphic, however, we had to
show you the gravity of this whole situation unfolding in
federal court today," the reporter said.

"How can you even watch this? Do you get off on watching this?" Celeste asked in obvious disgust.

Bone glanced back over his shoulder at Celeste, "What are you saying?"

Celeste sighed. "I mean, it's bad enough you have me here against my will, but then you are actually watching our abduction."

Bone spun around and faced her. "First of all, I didn't know this was going to be on there. I was watching my Big Homie trial, and they put this on there," he corrected her. "Secondly, *here* ain't a bad place. People would pay money to be treated like you've been treated the last week or so. You've had the best food money could buy, pool, jacuzzi, tennis courts at your disposal . . . you practically living in a resort."

"Yeah, but it's against my will."

Bone shrugged. "I have my orders and I carried them out well."

Celeste recoiled her neck. "Orders? Hmph, I thought you were the boss."

"Yeah, but everyone has someone to answer to."

"So stop walking around here like you're the boss, then."

Bone spun around and returned his attention to CNN so he wouldn't blow his assignment.

Rather than kill Hulk and bring even more nefarious attention to his trial, Qwess had concluded it would be better for Bone to hold Hulk's family hostage until after the trial so Hulk would do exactly as they wanted him to do. Qwess had been around Hulk long enough to know how much he loved family. He knew that as long as Hulk's little girl's life was in the balance, there was no way he would testify against Qwess at trial. This was the leverage Qwess needed to ensure he would walk out the courtroom a free man. Qwess didn't trust anyone in the Crew other than Bone to carry out this mission. With indictments being passed out like government cheese, there was no way to tell who would hold strong under pressure. So he requested Bone carry this mission out himself.

Bone had moved Lateefah and Celeste to another one of his homes that no one knew about. This home was in a gated community that he sometimes used as a stash house for the Crew's drugs. It was situated on eight acres of land, complete with a fishing pond in the back. His closest neighbor was a half mile away behind gates of their own. This was the perfect place to lay low, away from society.

"You know, considering how bad this thing could've been, a normal person would be thanking me instead of talking shit," Bone noted.

For the past week, Celeste had been giving Bone hell every chance she got, questioning his logic, and even challenging his contradictions. This was new for Bone. Most people, especially women, bowed down to him these days, and they definitely didn't oppose him. Celeste was either oblivious to his power, or too stubborn to care. Either way, Bone came to enjoy the banter with her. Sometimes . . .

"Well, there is nothing normal about this, so we can remove that word from this conversation."

"Yeah, so what's normal, then, Ms. Saddity, huh? Tell me what's normal? You don't know anything about us and the life we live. If you did, then you wouldn't have bred with a rat."

"Look, I don't know anything about that. The man I met was a good man. He spoiled me and made me feel like a queen. He was a gentleman. I had no clue he was linked to all of . . . this foolishness."

Bone pointed to the television. "Well, here it is, live and in color. We about to watch big bird sing, and if he hum the wrong tune, it's going to be a lullaby for you and Lateefah."

Chapter 29

After a strenuous *voir dire* process, the jury empaneled for *The United States of America v. Sailm "Qwess" Wahid* consisted of six women and six men: three Black women, two white women, and one Asian. The men were four white men, one Black man, and a Latino. Shabazz had studied the prospective jurors extensively, attempting to see if they held bias or if they could be fair. Questioning them about their preference in music as well. All of this was important. This is why Shabazz was paid the big bucks.

Selecting jurors was a skill that won trials or lost them, and Shabazz took this as seriously as the actual trials themselves. He had utilized all his strikes before being forced to settle on the jury in the box. Trial was war, and he knew his adversary would spare no tactic to get the W. Outside the courtroom, people were people, and their lives mattered. Inside the courtroom, people were pawns in a bigger game.

The federal prosecutor on the case was very familiar with the Crescent Crew. U.S. Attorney Long had handled King Reece's case that sent him to prison for five years on a conspiracy conviction. Long had put on a splendid case, crossing his Ts and dotting his Is, and he had King Reece lined up on twenty-five to life, sure as shit. Then Crew business had intervened and taken that away from him. In the end, after he had Qwess and Doe arrested, he grudgingly conceded to allow King Reece to plea to five years. Somehow he always knew he would have a second crack at bat on the Crescent Crew, and although Qwess had made significant changes and impacted the culture, the only thing U.S. Attorney Long saw in Qwess was the Crescent Crew. He was determined not to botch this opportunity.

Judge Poston called court into session. After the spectacle that Judge Thomas had caused that resulted in Qwess being granted a bond, he knew all eyes were on him (as if the Defendant himself wasn't enough to have him under a microscope). He addressed the court and explained to them exactly what their roles were and what his role was. He advised them that the Defendant had to be found guilty *beyond a reasonable doubt*. He stressed the last part, then opened the floor for U.S. Attorney Long to open his case.

U.S. Attorney Long stood, adjusted his maroon tie, and cleaned his signature Cartier glasses with his handkerchief. He took his time, knowing that the eyes of not just the jury, but America, were on him. He placed the now clean spectacles on his face and addressed the jury directly.

"Ladies and gentlemen of the jury, I hope you are all as excited to be here as I am today. See, I know a lot of you would like to be somewhere else . . . maybe with your family or at work. Okay, scratch that—not work, but anywhere else but here. However, justice demands you be here, so my job is to serve justice, yet I added another job to my list of duties. That is to make your job as easy as possible, and ladies and gentlemen, let me tell you, he has made that job easier than ever because I have been following him for years, waiting on him to slip up like I knew he would. And he did!"

U.S. Attorney Long turned and jabbed a finger at Qwess

siting at the defense table as calm as snow falling in the winter.

"That man right there has fooled the whole world into thinking he is a legitimate businessman for the past decade. He used his illegal dope money to craft him a new persona. Entertainment mogul, they call him. Hip-hop star, they say. Philanthropist, they say." He paused for effect, then he dropped his voice to a whisper. "But I know the truth. I have always known the truth, and now I am excited to bring his truth to light inside this very courtroom. The truth is, he killed two innocent men before he escaped inside the music industry and sold tales to our children. The truth is, he used murder over and over and over again to maintain that lofty position at the top of the music industry. The truth is, as the head of the Crescent Crew, he funneled tons of drugs into the streets of America, killing men, women, and children. Then he taunted us from the covers of magazines and music videos, hiding behind the façade of lavish homes, luxury cars, and schools he constructed in the hood. He hid his black heart behind his green dollars! But not anymore. Today, he has to answer for his crimes."

U.S. Attorney Long stalked in front of the jury box in silence, gauging the reaction of the jury, seeing if his words had taken root before he drove the dagger home.

"Now, I know I just made a lot of claims, and you are probably thinking, 'How can he prove this,' right? Well, I'm going to prove it to you by bringing you the source to explain everything to you. See, at some point, some men of honor will have an attack of the conscience and want to do what's right. That's exactly what his former partners in crime did. They knew they were better than the life he had resigned them to, and they fought to get as far away from him as possible. Men who were with him every day. Men who killed with him *and* for him."

An audible gasp crescendoed through the courtroom. U.S. Attorney Long pumped his hands to silence the jury.

"That's right. This . . . *guy* . . . is about to be brought to justice by the very men whom he helped to corrupt. Stay tuned, you don't want to miss this."

If this were a theater, then Long would have just received a standing ovation, but in the courtroom they had to hold back their applause. The attorney knew he had exercised a powerful opening though. He strutted back to his table and shot a smirk at Qwess and Shabazz.

Shabazz appeared unfazed by any of it. He scrolled away on his iPad as if he were in a local coffee shop and not in a courtroom fighting for a man's life.

"Is it my turn yet?" Shabazz asked Qwess.

Qwess nodded. "I think so."

"Good, 'cause he bored me right to sleep. Be right back."

Shabazz stood tall in his blue, bespoke pinstriped suit and adjusted the bowtie crammed beneath his neck. He walked around the table and stood in the middle of the floor in silence. He eyed each juror with his steel gaze as he removed his topcoat to reveal a snazzy silk vest. A junior legal aide rushed from behind the table to take his jacket.

"Hello, my name is Malik Shabazz, and I am representing Mr. Wahid today. I'm also representing you too. Let us take a moment." He mock bowed his head in prayer. "Ladies and gentlemen of the jury . . . this illustrious court," Shabazz said. "I'm praying for protection for all of us from the danger we just heard, for surely if such a man exists as my good friend here just described, we all need divine protection against this character."

Shabazz raised his head and spun to face the jury directly. "Notice I said character, because that's exactly what Mr. Long has drawn up—a character! Mr. Wahid is none of those things that he just alleged. In fact, he is the total opposite, and I don't even have to work hard to show you, because

I'm sure you understand physics, right? Well, let's open with a physics lesson."

Shabazz walked over to the defense table and retrieved two mason jars. One jar was filled halfway with clear alkaline water, while the other was also half-filled with water, but clear sand rested at the bottom.

Shabazz held them up. "You see these jars? Well, if I gave them both to you, I'm sure I wouldn't have to tell you which jar to drink from, because it's evident which one is clean."

He paused to allow his words to sink in. Every eye in the courtroom was locked in on those jars.

"Well, that's this case. My good friend, Mr. Long, alleges that he has former friends—men of honor, he says—of Mr. Wahid who participated in these acts along with him. Well, when these 'men of honor' take that stand, I want you to remember these mason jars."

Shabazz placed the jars on the railing of the jury box and slowly walked back to the defense table.

Once Shabazz was seated, Judge Poston called a brief recess so the players could reset their boards. Qwess took the time to scan the courtroom and show his supporters that he was fine. Of course, his immediate family was in the front row: his wife, Ruquiyah, his mom and dad. His father was taking notes in his notepad while his mother's face was stoic. Doe and Niya were seated beside his parents, along with Prince. Qwess continued to scan the room looking for one person in particular, but he didn't see him. The courtroom *was* packed with spectators and media alike, but this person should've been at the front of the room with the others, so it's obvious he wasn't there. Yet. Qwess took a mental note to keep an eye out for him.

Although Qwess didn't see who he was looking for, he did note AMG's reps front and center, waiting for him. He wasn't surprised. Of course they would be there watching to see if the federal government could take chunks out of his ass and leave some of his remains for them to pick over. Qwess made eye contact with the rep, then shot him a silent salute before turning back around in his chair.

Qwess returned his attention to the front just in time for the recess to end. U.S. Attorney Long stood proudly and began presenting his case.

"I call to the stand Agent Wilfred Black of the Drug Enforcement Agency," Long announced.

The side doors of the courtroom opened and a Black man in a dark suit and tie approached the stand. He was sworn in and took a seat on the stand.

"Agent Black, will you please tell the court a little about yourself and how you're related to this case?"

Agent Black cleared his throat and spoke. "I am Agent Black, and I've been head of the special Crescent Crew task force for the past five years."

"Okay, so what is this task force?"

"Well, we have been investigating them for years, first locally, then as they grew, nationally. As their network expanded, so did the different factions they interacted with. They had dealings with the Mexican Mafia, then eventually buying arms from some Russians, which triggered the bureau of Alcohol, Tobacco, and Firearms. Then, more crimes brought more agencies into play, to where we eventually were forced to create an interagency task force to address all the crimes."

U.S. Attorney Long nodded. "Mmm hmm, I see. Go on."

"Well, once the task force was in place, we were able to gather a snapshot of their organization."

"Okay, and tell us a little more about this," U.S. Attorney Long said. "Ladies and gentlemen, if you direct your attention to the screens here, I will make this as easy as possible, as easy as the defendant has made it for us."

The attorney pulled up two headshot photos on all the

screens situated throughout the courtroom. The photos were of Qwess and King Reece. The photo on the left was a picture of young Qwess, with the goatee and ghost Cartier frames. It was obvious he was in the game in this pic; "the streets" were practically leaping off the screen. He was smiling in the pic, and his diamond-encrusted bottom grill gave him a look of hood chic. It was obvious they had chosen this pic to fit their narrative of him being a hoodlum. If this pic was to paint a picture contrary to the polished businessman he was now, then the pic of King Reece on the chart beside him was a Picasso.

In King Reece's pic, his locs were long and unkempt, and a huge Versace chain draped around his neck with a diamond-encrusted Universal Flag. Huge aviator shades covered his smooth baby face, and a wicked smirk tugged at his mouth.

U.S. Attorney Long pointed to the huge seventy-inch screen in front of the witness stand. "Can you tell us about these photos here?"

Agent Black nodded eagerly. "Sure. These are the founding members of the Crescent Crew, Qwess and King Reece. These photos were taken in the early days during their inception. Mr. Salim here was fresh out of the military in this pic, where he used Uncle Sam's ranks as his training and recruiting ground. See, he used the lethal tactics the Army taught him as an infantryman to instill fear in the hearts and minds of their would-be enemies."

"Objection," Shabazz stated, nonchalantly. He didn't even bother to get up or get excited. "He is testifying hearsay. There is no way he could prove this."

"Your Honor, our CI can corroborate all of this," U.S. Attorney Long interjected.

Judge Poston sighed. "I'll allow it for now, but tread lightly."

Agent Black continued, "It was while in the military that

Mr. Wahid met his Mexican distributor that would supply his gang with highly potent drugs. Once his connect was secured, he returned home and established a vast narcotics network that expanded throughout the Southeast." He pointed at the screen and more photos popped up, brackets of men leading from Qwess and Reece. "Alabama, Florida, Georgia, South Carolina, and Virginia, initially. Then they expanded their network as far as Texas with these men you see on those screens there. They employed a very sophisticated method of moving their narcotics and money in the early days, utilizing King Reece's car dealerships and funeral home. They hid the drugs and money in secret compartments built into the new cars and then shipped them to the dealerships in Fayetteville and Charlotte, North Carolina. Then they used the hearses from his funeral homes to move the money. Death is a very lucrative business, so there were hearses coming and going every day."

Qwess listened to the agent testify in disbelief. His face was poker, but his mind was reeling at these revelations. They had their whole operation figured out, but during the time the agent was referencing, Qwess had already left the Crew.

U.S. Attorney Long pulled up photos of Black Vic, a one-time adversary of the Crescent Crew. Black Vic had been a thorn in their side in the early days. He met his fate one day while driving his drop-top coupe in downtown Fayetteville in a horrific explosion caused by a grenade that was tossed in his car.

"Do you recognize this man?" U.S. Attorney Long asked.

"Yes, this is Victor, also known as Black Vic; he was an early opponent of the Crescent Crew who was murdered viciously. His murder is significant because this was their first attack in open air where they used military style weapons to eliminate a rival."

"What type of weapons were used?"

"A hand grenade was tossed into his vehicle." Low murmurs and gasps eased through the courtroom. "This was the first, but it wouldn't be the last time they used these style weapons. Black Vic is also important because he is directly related to the murders of Dee and Scar. See, Dee and Scar supplied Black Vic, and when Black Vic couldn't eliminate his competitors, his OGs devised a plan to do it for him, but they messed up."

"What do you mean they messed up?"

"Well, they were supposed to kill King Reece, but they murdered Qwess's fiancée, Shauntay. We believe this is what set Mr. Wahid off on an irreversible journey."

Qwess didn't expect them to bring this memory to court. Shauntay, his lovely Shauntay . . .

Shauntay was the love of his life, he realized, although he never even received the chance to tell her he loved her at all. Qwess was a super thug and playboy back then that abided by the code of the silly game. To gift a woman the L word constituted an L in the playa handbook. So, she died, never hearing those words while carrying their love child. The irony was never lost on Qwess, and he learned from that lesson. Shauntay was the reason Qwess married Lisa so quickly. She was also the reason he never had any other children— not intentionally anyway.

There was a little girl watching his trial unfold who bore an uncanny resemblance to him.

Chapter 30

Bone was having a hard time keeping his composure. After watching the trial all morning with Celeste, he finally gave in to her request to hit the pool with Lateefah.

Lateefah had been begging her mother all morning to swim. She had no clue that they were actually prisoners of war, and this is how Bone intended it to be. He didn't want to traumatize the young girl any more than he probably would have to if her father didn't do the right thing. So, he wanted their time to be more of a vacation than punishment. He didn't realize he would end up punishing himself in the process.

While Lateefah played in the pool, Celeste was lying poolside in a two-piece bikini that she found in the guest bath house. It was supposed to be a bikini, but the way she wore it, she might as well have been wearing Victoria's Secret. Bone was staring at Celeste so hard behind his dark shades, poor Lateefah could've been drowning, and he wouldn't have known. Celeste was already in his head from the dope convos they had been having, but he never would've guessed she looked like *this* beneath her clothing.

No wonder Hulk was willing to risk his life so many times to come see her. She had jaded-ass Bone ready to risk it all.

"Hey!" Celeste called to Bone, waving her hand. "Do you think you can help me please?"

Bone walked over to the chair where Celeste was lying on her stomach. The bikini bottom was cutting deep into the soft flesh of her skin, giving her a wedgie (or the perfect Apple bottom). Bone tried to look away, but he wasn't that strong.

"What you need?" Bone asked.

Celeste passed a bottle of sunscreen over her left shoulder. "Can you oil me up, please?"

Bone was speechless. Surely she wasn't asking him to touch her soft, smooth skin? In Islam, it was forbidden for a man to touch a woman that wasn't his wife.

"I would ask 'Teefah to do it, but I don't want to disturb her time. You said you wanted her to not feel as if she was being imprisoned, right?"

Bone sighed. She had a point. He grudgingly took the bottle of sunscreen and sat beside her on the chair. He lathered his hands and began to apply the sunscreen starting at her ankles. He rubbed the oil around her ankles and moved up to her strong calves.

"Hmmm . . ." Celeste moaned. "That feels good."

Bone's breath caught in his throat. He held his breath and continued to rub her legs. He eased up her knees and touched her thighs and it felt as if his hands were on fire. He didn't know if it was from the sun on the back of his hand or the heat inside his palms. His breathing became labored as he attempted to maintain his cool. His Islamic beliefs had him conflicted and his nature had him reeling.

"Make sure you get the inside of my thighs too," Celeste moaned. "Don't be scurred."

Bone gulped down the lump in his throat. He rubbed her inner thigh and Celeste gasped a bit. She shifted her body, and Bone's finger slid right between the crevices of her crack. Warm liquid immediately soaked his finger.

Bone jumped back. "Oh shit!"

Celeste pushed her rear back into him, and his finger eased inside the wet spot again. This time she looked over her shoulder at him as she did it. They locked eyes, and an electric current sparked between them.

Bone snatched his hand back and the bottle of sunscreen skidded across the concrete. He stood quickly and excused himself—ran really, back into the house, leaving Celeste on the chair.

Qwess sat at the table watching Agent Black weave the masterful tale of the Crescent Crew. For the past four hours, he had recounted the history of one of the nation's most notorious crime cartels. Some of it was true, some of it was false, all of it was theater. As the agent spoke, Qwess gauged the temperature in the room. He couldn't tell how things were going, but Shabazz didn't seem to be worried at all. He was even doodling on his yellow legal pad while the other members of his Dream Team were taking notes.

Judge Poston called a brief recess, and Qwess spun around to convene with his family in the front row. His father gave him a strong nod to insinuate that he was pleased with the way court was going. Qwess nodded his approval while he eyed the room. He saw the reporters salivating over his flesh, and countless nameless faces as well. He saw one woman whom he knew was related to Scar. It was weird for Qwess to see her after all these years. Was she still carrying animosity toward him? Qwess knew the impact his crimes had on certain people, but when he was in the life, whatever he had to do to win was justified. Once he was out of the game and he knew better, he attempted to right his wrongs by giving back to his community, and even paying for college tuition. He knew that certain things would be unforgettable; he just didn't expect it to be held on for this long.

Someone at the back of the courtroom caught Qwess's eye. He thought he saw her earlier, but now he was sure. Her little face resembled his, and her eyes followed his every move. Qwess quickly looked away to make sure no one else saw him looking at her. His heart thundered in his chest as so many questions rained down upon him at once: *Who was she here with? Why was she here? Where was her mother?* The little girl smiled and waved at Qwess. Qwess spun around in his chair and faced the front, standing as stiff as a statue.

Judge Poston recalled court into session and Agent Black continued his spiel, but Qwess was oblivious to what he was saying. Even though his life was on display right in front of him, and his future was on the line. Another part of his life—his past—was creeping up on him from behind him.

Chapter 31

Flame peeked at the crowd from backstage, and butterflies rumbled in his stomach. He couldn't believe this many people came out to show him support. He purposely remained out of the loop so there was no way for him to know social media was buzzing with his name. In fact, the top three things trending on Black Twitter were the Crescent Crew, Qwess, and Flame.

Flame closed the curtain and spun around in his wheelchair to face Kim.

"See, baby? I told you they still love you," Kim said. "Now let's go out there and remind them who you are. Same man, just a different message."

Flame took it in, but he was a ball of nerves. He had visualized this day for months, and now it was finally here. He bowed his head in prayer. That was the only thing he knew how to do to kill the nervousness. Kim grabbed his hand inside hers, and they prayed together. 8-Ball joined hands with them as well, and Flame led them in a prayer of gratitude and thanksgiving. He completed the prayer, then cracked the curtain to watch the opening act complete her performance.

She was originally from North Carolina as well and had a hit single called *Making My Way* that was tearing up the charts. Her song spoke to Flame's heart. He had been going through a lot, and sometimes he was just making his way. Now he had made his way through the storm and was now walking in the blessings.

The opening act completed her set, and it was time for Flame to perform. He reached out for Kim's hand and bowed his head in prayer. 8-Ball grabbed his other hand and Flame led them in the words. When he was done, he felt invigorated and ready to face the world.

"You ready?" Kim asked.

"Ready as I'll ever be."

Flame rolled to the edge of the curtain and waited for the lights to drop. When the arena became dark, Flame rolled to the middle of the stage with Kim beside him. He closed his eyes and sensed the crowd, felt them, allowed their energy to seep into his bones and power him up. He placed the mic in front of his lips and said, "I'm baaaaaaaaacccckkk!"

The arena went berserk! The lights flashed as Flame started singing:

> *"I've been through a lot, I've seen the pain/ And now I'm back, back to reign/ I'm the king of my life, my queen on my side/ With God as the head, I'll never die!"*

Flame pointed to Kim at his side, and the spotlight shined on her in her skintight bodysuit. Her new curves were popping out the sides of the outfit. She had also been in hibernation with Flame, so the world hadn't seen the results of her new Slim Thick body. Judging by the raucous applause, they approved.

Flame hyped the crowd, waving his arms in the air like an air traffic controller, then he rapped the next verse:

"Call me Lazarus, 'cause I rose from the dead now my life is lit/ He ain't died on the cross for this savage tip/ People loving Satan like his name Cupid/ Don't be stupid, kid/ Been there, done that, and got the plaques to prove it/ Now the tunes that I blast be the righteous music—now help me do it!"

Flame rocked in his chair, moving to the left and right as the crowd hyped him up. He scanned the crowd, seeing bodies as far as his vision would allow. The crowd seemed to be receptive to him. Why wouldn't they be? The beats were thumping, his flow was as smooth as ever, and his content was fresh.

Kim walked behind Flame in his wheelchair and began singing in his ear. Her voice seemed more powerful than it had ever been, and the crowd was loving it. Cellphones were held high in the air, capturing this moment on video. Kim slid her hands down Flame's chest and swung her close-cropped head in a circle. Flame reached above his head and pulled her head down to his face. He paused briefly, then kissed his fiancée in front of the crowd.

"Aye," Flame said. "I don't know if you heard it or not, but this is going to be my wife right here!" he announced.

Kim faced the crowd and smiled. She held her ring finger up, and the Johnny the Jeweler special blinged on the Jumbotron behind them.

"This woman saved my life," Flame testified. "She is the reason I'm here. I wrote a song about it. Wanna hear it, here it go."

Flame rolled away from Kim and stared at her in open admiration. He waited until the lights shined on her before he began singing:

"If love had a body it would look like youuuuuu/ If your name could be a poem, it would be Trueeee/ We're on

*the path of redemption, and I'm in it till the end/ You're
my wife, my lover, and my best friendddd/"*

Flame continued to serenade Kim from a distance while
the crowd looked on. He belted out his latest tune and ended
the song on a high note. As the crowd looked on, and as
Kim stared at him, Flame stopped singing.

"You want to see the power of love?" Flame asked. "The
power of the love of God?" he added. The crowd screamed
and chants of Amen lauded him on stage. "Watch this,"
Flame said.

While Kim watched him, and the crowd encouraged
him, and the world looked on via the internet, Flame placed
his hands on the arms of his wheelchair and pushed himself
to his feet. He stood proudly beneath the lights for a second,
then he shuffled one foot in front of the other on his own
volition. Once the foot was sturdy, he moved his other foot
in front of that one. He repeated the actions, each time getting faster and faster until he was walking upright. He took
several steps on his own toward Kim, who was in such disbelief that she dropped her microphone. His steps grew faster,
and his back more upright, until he made it to Kim. He
wrapped his arms around her and pulled her into his heaving
chest.

"I love you!" Flame said, and the whole world heard and
saw the power of love.

To Be Continued . . .

Visit our website at
KensingtonBooks.com
to sign up for our newsletters, read
more from your favorite authors, see
books by series, view reading group
guides, and more!

Become a Part of Our
Between the Chapters Book Club
Community and Join the Conversation

Submit your book review for a chance to win exclusive
Between the Chapters swag you can't get anywhere else!
https://www.kensingtonbooks.com/pages/review/